BLAZE OF GLORY

Tony wished he could see searchlights, flak, anything to show there was something down there beneath the thick cloud, that the world wasn't dead and gone.

'We still over the target?'

'By my DR, yes. But – ' Orders is orders, if you don't see the target, you drop on Dead Reckoning. 'Bombs fused, Bill? OK, leave it to me.'

Back safe, wonderful to be alive. 'Bombed target on DR?' said the rather twee Intelligence Officer at their table. 'Good show.' Tony caught Bill's worried eyes, where their bombs had fallen, who had a clue, but both of them were too shagged to argue.

Well, there it is, thought Tony, that's the secret.

BLAZE OF GLORY

Michael Carreck

A STAR BOOK
published by
the Paperback Division of
W. H. ALLEN & Co. Ltd

A Star Book
Published in 1984
by the Paperback Division of
W. H. Allen & Co. Ltd
A Howard and Wyndham Company
44 Hill Street, London W1X 8LB
Reprinted 1984

First published in Great Britain by
Robert Hale Limited 1983

Printed in Great Britain by
Cox & Wyman Ltd, Reading

ISBN 0 352 31471 0

For Sue, Simon
and Rosalind

"There's glory for you!"
"I don't know what you mean by 'glory'," Alice said.

Lewis Carroll, *Through the Looking-Glass*

"DAR-ling!" Heavenly blue eyes, shining halo of ash-blonde hair, smile of a randy angel, "Dar-LING! It's you!"

He gaped at her, astounded, who? Where? When? She was a corporal, about his age, nineteen, heart-wrenchingly pretty. No. More than pretty—beautiful. A gorgeous waif. Furious whisper: "Dance with me, clot."

Very bossy waif. Trombones, clarinet, the band of RAF Station Onley Market was deep into the new Glenn Miller, he took her in his arms, thistledown. In the stuffy, blacked-out Sergeants' Mess, stale with the pong of sloshed-over Watney's, stinging with the ghosts of Gold Flake and Players, she was a floating fragrance of fresh-cut clover.

"Music's stopped. Put me down."

She had a soft, low, husky voice, this small and scowling but curiously vulnerable urchin, yet it cut arrogantly through all the assorted chatter of Haileybury and Merchant Taylors', Old Kent Road and Wimbledon, Llangollen and Dundee, Saskatoon and Melbourne. "Know that long streak of misery over there by the bar, scratch, scratch, itchy vest?"

Bit much, this. He always enjoyed All Ranks Dances, rare democratic events in this war to save democracy, gave the officers a chance to get at the Waafs; tonight's was to celebrate the RAF's twenty-fourth birthday on the first of April, how apt some remarked, in this so far unvintage year of 'forty-two. Time now for him to assert his dignity.

Stiffly, "Know him? I do, rather. He's my wireless-operator, Pilot Officer Sills."

"Ask me," she said, "and I'll tell you. Sills is a pill."

Sills the Pill. Spot on. Couldn't stand the chap, only in his crew because Hickey and Tinker—

"Up he comes, wants to know, do I screw? Not on your nelly, says I, and off I pop." Yes, sounds like the charm and sensitivity of Sills, his heart began to warm towards her. "All for safety first, that's me," she said. "So I, um, introduced myself to you."

Oh, Christ.

Huge blue eyes read him loud and clear, she hooted with laughter. "Didn't mean that," she was gasping. "I don't feel safe with you. Not a bit." For a long moment there was no RAF Station, no Onley Market, no All Ranks Dance. Then she smiled, unexpectedly shy. He found he was holding her hand.

He squeezed. She squeezed back. He asked her, "Like a drink?"

"Not much." Music again, boom, clutch, clutch, boom, saxophones and a most insistent double-bass.

"Care to dance?"

"Can't stand waltzes," she said, "hurt my teeth. What I'd really like is some unbeery fresh air."

Wizard.

Durex optimistically dimpled his wallet, his car was parked craftily under the trees, come into my parlour. He unlocked the Morris Eight, thought of tilting the seat to usher her into the back, decided not. Wouldn't do to rush her, even if steering-wheel, gear lever and brake might soon be vexingly in the way.

He reached across her to pull the door shut, paused, held it open. She, too—"One of ours or one of theirs?"—had heard the drone coming nearer, low over the darkness of the Lincolnshire fens.

Louder. Not the where-are-you-where-are-you of Junkers Jumo diesels but a harsh faltering note, a single air-cooled Hercules.

"Wimpey. In trouble. On one engine."

A sixpenny moon tumbled from a cloud, silver light splashed the black Wimpey thundering over the treetops, glinted on the stark asterisk of the motionless starboard propeller, flickered along gaps in the shattered fuselage.

Sound dwindled from the sky. "Making for Hawksthorn. Emergency airfield, two whole miles of runway." He tried to pretend it was a piece of cake; but he kept his eyes from where she sat beside him, warm, near, scent of clover.

The cabin boy Agrippa, A filthy little nipper, He stuffed his arse with powdered glass, And circumcised the skipper, that's what they'd sung last night riding in the van, Hickey, Tinker, Geordie and Phil, when he'd gone to see them off in a Wimpey, sorry, Wellington bomber, The Good Ship Venus, bound for Cologne.

That crippled Wimpey was limping home so early that it must have been over a coastal target just after dark. He saw, beneath the winking flak, docks and factories and military installations sliding down the twin wires of the Mark IX bomb-sight, heard the navigator's voice in the pilot's earphones—"Steady. Steady."—and the industrial heart of the target neatly between the aiming pointers, what a charming picture he was to think later from time to time, what a load of old cobblers.

Nothing bossy about her now. "You really care, don't you, about the men in that bomber?"

Suddenly he wanted to tell her about Hickey and Tinker and Geordie and Phil, how they'd bought it on their first op, got the chop, gone for a burton. But what he said was, "We're all in it together."

"All doing the same job."

"Exactly!" He slapped the steering-wheel in unexplained emphasis, the horn beeped outrageously, their mood slipped on a banana skin, they both yelped with laughter.

Her eyes danced, God, she was beautiful. "Why toot? Didn't think I said anything particularly bright—"

"But that's precisely what I thought, oh, about a week ago. I was catching a train and on the platform there was this chap in an odd uniform, one of our comic allies, I thought. Then I saw the metal pilot's badge and the yellow patches on his collar and the Iron Cross ribbon—Luftwaffe, they'd been over the night before.

"There he was, hefty sort of chap, make a good second-row forward, standing between a couple of RAF Police with their beetlecrushers and dumb-ox faces, first German I'd ever seen. He looked up and saw the wings on my uniform and then, d'you know, he grinned and very, very slowly gave me the most enormous wink.

"I just had time to grin back before they hustled him into a carriage and I said to myself those very words—all doing the same job. All of us. On both sides. Except," he added, "we bomb factories and they bomb cathedrals."

Quietly, seriously, she said, "I think I'm going to be very fond of you." Then she spun in her seat, flung up her hands and harangued a crowd of unseen listeners. "Promises me a lovely ride and lots and lots of glorious fresh air and here we've been sitting hour after hour—"

He revved up with a roar, only way to silence her. He'd meant to stay cosy under the trees, why waste time driving, but now no choice, Plan B. He drove past the Mess and out of the Station gates and headed for a tactful lane off the road that arrowed through the eleven o'clockish black-out of Onley Market village. She spoke only twice on the short journey, once going in to the wide moonlit street, "Early English," once coming out, "Perpendicular."

She made no comment when he pulled up in the lane and backed on to the grass verge. He put an arm around her shoulders.

"Just posted in, are you?"

She chuckled. "Merciful heavens, small talk. Yes. This very day. New Map Corporal, that's me." She would be in charge of the squadron's plotting charts and the topographical maps and the target maps which showed places to be hit like, let's say, factories, and the places to be missed like, no doubt, cathedrals. "What use," she declaimed, "are Mercators, North Poles and Equators, Tropic Zones and Meridian Lines?"

He said, "So the Bellman would cry," and she looked at him as if he had just lifted a snow-white rabbit out of a Moss Bros. top-hat. He leant across and kissed her, she kissed him back, hardly mad with passion but yes, indeed, with relish.

She settled comfortably in his arms, fuck this gear lever.

"How come you know so much about churches?"

"My father's in the trade. She was only a parson's daughter but she knew her pews and Q's." A fingernail traced around his pilot's wings, moved lightly across his lips. His heart began to race, his palms were sandpaper. "I'm newish in the WAAF," she said and kissed the tip of his nose. "Is this what they call snogging?"

"No," thickly. He cleared his throat. "No. That was smooching. This is snogging." He deftly undid brass buttons and edged a palm beneath her tunic.

"Warm heart, cold hand." She lifted him out gently by his sleeve. "He's Vicar of Bexholt."

"Who is?"

"My father is."

"Oh, yes. Oh," surprised. "Bexholt? In Bucks? Friend of

mine comes from there, fellow called Allardyce, father's an Air Commodore—"

"Allardyce!" she whooped, "Dick Allardyce! I could eat him with a tiny silver spoon!"

Bugger it. He had trained with Dick, who was now flying Wimpeys over at Flaxfield, seven miles or so to the east of Onley Market. Oh, sod it. Dick Allardyce looked like an advertisement for Anglo-Saxon pilots, girls trailed after him, Pied Piper; he called them Irma the Squirmer, Tawdry Audrey, Mona the Groaner.

"Men!" She was laughing up at him, snuggling closer. You're super, too, like an untidy Cary Grant. Why do you think I picked you up? Pass the spoon."

Her lips were soft and cool and she made small contented sounds like a butterfly humming. He'd got her brass buttons undone again and had begun seriously on her shirt when much too soon she said, "Waafery! Back by twenty-three fifty-nine or I change into a pumpkin."

He twirled an imaginary black moustache. "The night is young, me proud beauty—"

"No, honestly, look, it's twenty to twelve by your watch—" hell, next time he'd take that off for a start and a lot more besides, "—and if I'm not back before midnight it's bread and water and dungeons and never seeing the light of day—"

A final inaudible curse at the gear lever and he reversed the Morris in the lane. On the drive back she asked him, casually, "How many ops have you flown?"

"Only been here a few days myself." Casually, "Still got my first to do."

He stopped outside the gate of the barbed-wire Waafery. Desperately he wanted to see her again, he began to rehearse an invitation, would she—

"Goodbye, Mr Chips," she said.

"What did you—"

"It's on at the Station Cinema tomorrow night."

"Oh, you'd like to see it?"

"My word," she said, "you do catch on fast."

"Twenty past eight? At the flea-pit?"

She studied him as though she'd just unwrapped him from a parcel labelled Harrods.

"Please." She kissed him, opened the car door, stepped out. "Oh, almost forgot. I'm Kate Elliot. How d'you do?"

"Tony Marlowe," he said.

"Goodnight, Pilot Officer Marlowe."

"Goodnight, Corporal Elliot."

He watched her go, clover scent of her lingering, warmth of her still on the seat beside him, he loved the hell-with-you way that she walked. Goodnight, Corporal Elliot. Till tomorrow night.

Unless, unspokenly understood, they wheeled out those little tractors that pulled long lines of trolleys carrying lumpish grey bombs chalked "Up you, Adolf," "All the best from Doug and Nobby," "Remember Coventry." Tomorrow night the RAF might want him to fly his first op, don't you know there's a war on?

* * *

Click, buzz. Tony shifted uneasily in his chair, beneath his shoe a piece of NAAFI rock-cake scrunched among the fag-ends as Chalkey tapped his finger three times on the big green table that stretched far down the Crew Room. Anticlimax. All the Tannoy squawked was, "LAC Higgins four-five-nine report to—"

Tony examined a ten and a seven. Expert tactic was to stick at seventeen but, what the hell, live dangerously. "Twist." A three, good show. "Stick."

Flight-Sergeant Chalkey White, hard-luck banker of the rainy morning's pontoon school, small and scrawny and a press-on pilot, blinked timid red-rimmed eyes, the kind you get when bullies kick sand in your face, and said, "Oh, dear, oh, dear." He laid down queen and deuce.

"Gotcha," said a statistical gunner. "Roll on the ten."

Chalkey flicked over a knave, bust. Three more pennies for Tony. Furtively, he twitched back the cuff of his battledress: eighteen minutes to twelve. No Tannoy announcement by noon, odds on no ops tonight.

"Check," murmured a navigator. Above his head a parade of dog-eared posters marched across the grimy wall. An oversized ear, "Careless Talk Costs Lives" and a railway guard, "Is Your Journey Really Necessary?" (odd question, considering his audience) and a prim official popsie, "Fly With Prudence," unofficially sexed up by a pencilled black triangle.

"Fuck," said his pilot, glaring at the board. "Oh. Aha. Take that."

"Stupid sod. You can't castle after you're in check."

"Lying bastard."

Goodbye Mr Chips, or hello Happy Valley? A film with Kate or a flight to the Ruhr, confidently tipped as the RAF's next customer, who knew what the night would bring? Certainly none of the Cream of the Empire's Youth, the flying crews, sprawling around in threadbare battledress, some in thick roll-top sweaters of dingy white, some wearing fur-lined Irvin jackets, some sporting suede flying-boots, a scruffy shower of frowsty layabouts gambling, nattering, writing letters, reading tatty paperbacks, idling the apparently unconcerned hours away.

Waiting, like the couple of thousand ground staff—fitters, instrument-bashers, wireless mechanics, armourers, admin wallahs, adjutants, cooks, electricians, firemen, van-drivers, accountants, dog-handlers, flying controllers, RAF police, tailors, from A/C 2s, aircraftmen second class, the erks who pushed brooms and peeled potatoes, all the way up through the ranks of tradesmen and tradeswomen to the Squadron-Leader Stores and the Wing-Commander Engineering to the Group Captain Officer Commanding—waiting in the enormous Wimpey garage that was RAF Station Onley Market, for the gen from the Tannoy; either the evening pint or two most had in mind at the NAAFI or the Grumble-and-Grunt with perhaps, later, a knee-trembler on a shared ground-sheet beneath the frost-bright moon . . . or ops, pressing on regardless.

Click, buzz, tap, tap, tap. "Warrant Officer Yarwood please report to Instrument Section, Number One Hangar." Corporal Elliot report to Pilot Officer Marlowe in nightie, one, wispy, transparent, black. God, he wanted to see her tonight, he'd fly tomorrow, OK? Happy Valley won't go away. Ten of diamonds, ace of clubs, smashing. Pontoon, pays double, pile of six pennies, wins the bank. Quarter to twelve, take the cards, shuffle, deal.

Click, tap, tap, tap. "Stand by for broadcast. Night flying tonight, repeat, night flying tonight. All personnel confined to camp." Amp-amp-amp-amp, the loudspeakers echoed their Chick's Own code for ops in hangars, workshops, armouries and offices, in messes, orderly rooms, aircraft dispersals and cookhouses, in the Flying Control Tower and in Station Headquarters, warning Kate among her maps in the Station Navigation Office that, maybe, Tony was in for a busy night.

Bit of a stomach-churner now, waiting for the Battle Order. Tony glanced swiftly at Chalkey, he knew the form, he'd flown twenty-seven ops and if tap, tap, tap meant he would finish his and his crew's first tour of thirty, tap away, Chalkey; he was ruminating over his cards; nonchalance, then, was the keynote.

Nonchalantly, Tony studied two tens. In bustled Twinkletoes, the big, burly Wing Commander; at the notice board he thumbed drawing-pins. Trying to show he couldn't care less, "Split," Tony announced, dealt a king to one ten, an ace to the other.

"Jammy bugger," snarled a wireless operator with overplayed fury. Pennies were pushed towards Tony.

Nonchalant. Done thing was to stroll up to the board, give an offhand glance to the Battle Order, check the list of crews to fly tonight. Just like School, seeing if you'd made the First XV.

He'd done it the day before yesterday, saw, typewritten, the names of Hickey, Tinker, Geordie and Phil; angrily, not his. He'd been proud of his crew, they had picked each other carefully in that strange courtship three months ago at Littledale Operations Training Unit, everybody pitchforked together and told to marry up into Wimpey crews.

There had been a stranger's name, MacSomething, typed in as pilot for Tony's crew, a lanky man from Inverness, with one more op to do to finish his thirty. Final op and first ops, to Cologne; turned out to be the last for them all.

But today Tony's name leapt from the list. Pilot: P/O Marlowe. Navigator: Sgt Wilberforce. W/Op: P/O Sills. Front Gunner: Sgt Ramsbottom. Rear Gunner: Sgt Eckersley. Aircraft: B Baker. NFT: 1245. Nav. Briefing: 1430. Main Briefing: 1545. Meal: 1915. Transport at Messes: 2015. Take-off: 2145.

"You're on, Tony?" A ruddy-cheeked Bob Cherry face—Tich Cattermole, who shared Tony's room in the Nissen hut on Site Four; an excellent co-tenant, always ready to offer toothpaste, lend ink, share a currant cake from home. Excitedly,

"Me, too!"

Tony nodded, wishing his own reaction were as simple, instead of a mixture: a dollop of pleasure that the time had come at last to justify his ten months of training, high time he broke his duck, hadn't liked telling Kate last night that he was a bombing virgin—mingled with an unconstipating dose of stage-fright, a tinge of terror and a taste of bitter disappointment. But then Tich hadn't been looking forward to Kate.

Everyone having demonstrated adequate nonchalance, the Crew Room became Piccadilly Underground in the rush hour, navigators yelled for wireless operators, pilots called piteously for gunners and where the devil were Tony's crew?

Something touched his shoulder. "Adsum," said good old Bill Wilberforce. He clamped his pipestem back between his teeth and his bald spot glistened as his head tilted back, making him look even older than his nine-and-twenty years. If only he'd had his thumbs hooked in a chalk-powdered gown instead of his battledress, he could have been back steering 3B through a dicey chunk of Pythagoras.

Navigator accounted for, thank God for old Bill, tower of strength, worth the other three put together, clueless nits all, in Tony's new here you are, take it or leave it crew. Over there, for example, was Sills the Pill, the dit-dah-dit duffer whose Morse was clumsy ("SWOF," listening operators would signal back, "Send With Other Foot") and slow ("UCP"—"Use Carrier Pigeon").

"Marlowe," the chronically unsuccessful wooer of Kate was calling imperiously, cigarette jumping in his lips, eyes screwed up against the smoke, thought he was Humphrey Bogart, only taller. "Marlowe!" All morning Tony had been pondering, kick him smartly in the crutch? Or thank him for last night's manifestation of Kate's sexy ectoplasm?

"Marlowe!" At Tony's elbow, anguished. "I don't see Eckersley and Ramsbottom, where are they?" When in danger, when in doubt, run in circles, scream and shout.

Trust Bill Wilberforce to have the pukka gen. "Eckersley's got a squeal in his earphones. Gone to have his electric hat fixed." For God's sake, he's had all week. "And Ramsbottom's been joed for Orderly Sergeant." Typical.

A powerful blast of Brylcreem, let the war continue, here was

Eckersley, oil-stained cap over one ear, uniform like an ill-made bed in a one-star dosshouse, tiny, canary-boned, sized by Nature to shoehorn into a Wimpey's tight-fitting rear turret. "I say, Marlowe, did you see we're on tonight?"

"I did happen to notice, Eck. Your earphones—are they unsquealed?"

" 'Fraid not, they couldn't put them right. Still u/s."

"Did you swop them for another pair?"

"Oh, I never thought of that. I'll go back to Electrical Section, shall I?"

Approvingly, Tony said, "What a good idea, Eck."

Hey, hey, the gang's all here, it's front gunner Ramsarse. He wasn't wearing the OS armband.

"Good show," said Tony. "Glad to see you got out of being Orderly Sergeant."

Ramsbottom blinked pale eyes in a long pale face and ruffled his tallow hair, a bleached Stan Laurel having a bad day with Ollie. "Gosh, Marlowe, was I really Orderly Sergeant? I didn't know."

Save us all.

Just time before Night Flying Test 1245 to try and phone Kate, no Mr Chips: they kept the names on the Battle Order secret, no way she'd know whether or not he was on ops tonight. He rang twice from the nearby Squadron Orderly Room but both times the Station Navigation Office was engaged. The sea-cook's name was Andy, He was a sod most randy, They squashed his cock on the Inchcape Rock, For coming in the brandy.

* * *

Laugh thy girlish laughter, weep thy girlish tears, some poetic halfwit had once told April and that second piece of advice she was taking right now, it was fair pissing down as Tony stared gloomily at B Baker and B Baker stared sullenly back, the knight of the air and his less than mettlesome steed loathing each other on sight.

B Baker, or B Bastard to those who knew its little ways, was a very tired and irritable Wimpey ("Clapped-out fucker," lilted the worried Welsh Leading Aircraftman) and if it had been a second-hand car with "Bargain" whitewashed on its windscreen, Tony wouldn't have touched it with a bargepole, kick a tyre, a wheel would roll away.

Nobody in his right mind would choose B Bastard to taxi across to the NAAFI van, let alone fly it over Germany. But the sprog, the beginner, always gets the ropey kite, that's the way it goes in the RAF, and if you can't take a joke you shouldn't have joined.

"Caught a bit of flak, she did, last time out," singsonged the anxious LAC from Maintenance Section. He'd copped the job of going up with Tony on this Night Flying Test, the pilot's check of take-off, circuit and landing, under the worldly-wise RAF rule of you service a kite, mate, you damn well fly in it, a prospect viewed with scant enthusiasm by the Welshman from Ubendem Wemendem.

Flak. Explained why the dull black canvas tight over the geodetic noughts-and-crosses skeleton of B Bastard was spattered with rust-red patches and why the rear turret was brand-new, must have taken the old one off after they hosed out the rear gunner, not a word to Eckersley.

In the pelting rain Tony gave the poor old relic the statutory walkaround, technically known as counting the engines. No idiot had left the locking pins in the elevators so you sat anxiously tugging at the immoveable control column till the final, fatal bounce. No stupid chancer had left the french letter on the pitot tube so your air speed indicator stuck at zero, up to you to guess your landing speed and quite likely make a nasty hole in the runway. Indeed, everything seemed at first glance to be in moderately reasonable order, though it would have been a whole lot kinder to pack B Bastard off to the knacker's yard.

Much wiser, too, there was always the chance that B Bastard would knacker you first. The last pilot to fly this sodding Wimpey couldn't have been more than two foot tall, Tony unlocked the seat, gave it a shove, odd how some aircraft seemed to be on your side, determined to make things easy for you, others, absolute swine, like B Bastard, fought you every inch of the way. Tony heaved again, the seat jerked violently back, a jutting, sharp-edged piece of metal slashed the shoulder of his battledress, bother.

The LAC, securely strapped in the right-hand seat, parachute within easy snatch, watched apprehensively while the corporal by the plugged-in battery trolley spun a finger above his head and Tony pressed first the port and then the starboard starter button. Each engine whined, spluttered and coughed a puff of black oily smoke, then roared as Tony thrust the throttles forward, faded as he yanked the twin levers back. The figures of the magneto readings tumbled down the vertical dials. The LAC drew in his breath in a reverse whistle.

"Just this side of u/s, whatever."

A whisker this side of unserviceability, that about summed up B Bastard. Tony checked revs and boost and airscrew pitch controls; tested elevators, rudder, flaps, bomb doors; made sure B Bastard was trimmed for take-off.

Through the open hatch the corporal from the battery trolley handed up a clipboard; Tony signed the Form 700, accepting B Bastard, thank you very much.

The hatch banged shut. Chocks away. Tony clicked the switch of the microphone in the oxygen mask hanging by one of its pairs of snaps from his flying helmet, what a glamorous cover for *Picture Post*, all ready for Kate to frame. Glamorous call-sign the squadron had, too: Starbright.

"Boomerang from Starbright B Bast—B Baker, request taxi clearance."

Crackle in his earphones, Boomerang, Onley Market Flying Control, "B Baker, clear to taxi." As if he were taking a very old dog for a very slow walk, Tony turned B Bastard carefully round on the hardstanding with fart of engine and hiss of brake and led it in a wheezing shuffle along the perimeter track on to the main runway.

From Boomerang, "B Baker clear for take-off."

Throttles forward, reluctant bellowing from the engines, gradually B Bastard began to roll, more throttle, trundle, speed building up, a gentle then less gentle pull on the control column, at last B Bastard was unsticking and lifting unwillingly off. Alarming length of runway it had used up. How much more Tony would have to use tonight with B Bastard weighed down by its operational load of petrol, ammunition, high explosive and incendiaries God alone knew and the best of Air Force luck to one and all.

Wallow, wallow, up to two thousand feet, sluggish to answer

rudder pedals and control column, but nothing actually fell off as Tony flew the circuit of the airfield, the LAC's eyes never leaving the ground below, more firma, less terra.

Turn in for the approach. Runway ahead. Throttles back. A blob of ice-cold rainwater from the leaking cockpit roof plopped down Tony's neck. Glamorous, eh, Kate? Undercarriage lever down, "We've got a red!" screeched the LAC over the beep of the alarm, Tony slammed the throttles forward with the heel of his hand, the engines howled indignantly and, protesting, B Bastard began to climb.

Out went the red undercarriage warning light, no more beep. Red glowed again, beep again. The warning light went out, the beep stopped. Flicker of red. No beep. The red light came on and stayed on.

"Dud wiring probably," said Tony, outwardly calm. Gamely the LAC nodded and a bead of sweat flipped away.

Shit, shit, shit, shit, *shit*. If the red light and the beeper alarm were both u/s, all well and good, the undercarriage was down and locked. If the light were doing its proper job and the alarm was u/s, Tony was in for a wheels-up landing to bring B Bastard skidding flat-bellied along the runway with a shriek of buckling steel, a shower of sparks and, who knows, petrol spurting from the tanks. Or for an unlocked undercart collapsing as he touched down like that Wimpey at Littledale OTU last month ploughing along the airfield, swinging, crumpling a wing, whoosh, red ball of fire.

"Boomerang from Starbright B Baker. Please check my undercarriage down and locked."

"Roger—" Crackle, crackle. "—check. Over."

Does nothing work in this bloody Air Force?

"Boomerang from B Baker, say again."

"Roger, B Baker. Fly past Tower for visual check. Over."

"Roger," said Tony, all calm and intrepid and splendid chap. "Wilco. Out."

He brought B Bastard as close to the windows of the Control Tower as he could without actually being court-martialled and saw the flash of binoculars. Ahead was Station Headquarters, Kate was down there in the Navigation Office busy with her maps, he roared over the roof in a bellowing climb, hello, Kate.

"B Baker, do you still have a red?"

On the instrument panel a malevolent ruby glare.

Ho-hum, airy-fairy, couldn't care less, "Boomerang, yes, I still have a red." Sweat soaked Tony's shirt.

"B Baker, your undercarriage looks fully down but it may not be fully locked." Very useful information, he could have asked the LAC to have a peer and tell him that. "Land with caution," instructed the Controller cheerfully, Bob's your uncle, that must have been the moment when he punched the siren button. The LAC pointed, horrified, as two fire engines and a red-crossed ambulance sped towards the runway. Scared rotten, Tony said, "At least it's stopped raining."

Should he climb, order the LAC to bale out? No, Tony decided immediately, he might panic, make a cock of his jump, pull the parachute ripcord too soon, wrap himself round B Bastard's tail. Or pull it too late, splat into the deck. Tony winked. "Devil of a lot of panic," he said, "about two wires getting crossed."

The concrete strip of the runway lifted up towards B Bastard, tiny black mannikins they'd taken out of the OTU Wimpey, gently, gently, back on the throttles, Jesus, sweet Jesus, at least Hickey and Tinker had flown on one op, gently, gently, beside Tony the LAC's lips were moving in a silent gabble, praying? Gently, gently, wait for the wheels to touch, here we go, Kate.

* * *

"Duisburg," murmured Bill Wilberforce. Tony took the chair beside him; went without saying, with too much care about touching down, B Bastard bounced heavily as the wheels met concrete but, of course, that meant the undercart was locked, piece of cake. Two more bounces, Tony had B Bastard down safe and sound, any landing you walked away from was a good one. Duisburg?

Main briefing 1545 at Station Headquarters. Tin-hatted sentry with fixed bayonet guarding the door, the room was hot and airless, with black-out shutters blanking the windows. A stage stretched along one wall, above it, a huge map covered by a brown blanket that hid the eastern half of Britain and most of Europe.

In the stalls, waiting for the curtain to go up, pilots,

navigators, wireless operators and gunners idly chatted at rows of long tables, each crew sitting together. Five to a crew, should have been six. The RAF had decided to replace second pilots with new-fangled bomb-aimers. So, no more second dickies—but the B/A's were still training in Canada, typical balls-up.

Twenty crews on tonight, a hundred aircrew. Sergeants, flight-sergeants, warrant officers, pilot officers, flying officers, flight-lieutenants. The youngest eighteen, hardly anyone over twenty-three. Ex-schoolboys, factory hands, shop assistants, bus conductors, bricklayers, undergraduates, apprentices, junior civil servants, junior bank clerks, junior shipping clerks, junior local government clerks (bloody marvellous to fly, beats sticking stamps and making tea).

Sons of solicitors, miners, chartered accountants, senior clerks, gardeners, factory foremen, managing directors, boot-makers, stockbrokers, shopkeepers, fishmongers, stone-masons. In good crews, dim crews, press-on crews, push-the-tit-and-let's-get-home crews, lucky crews who rarely caught a glimpse of flak, unlucky crews whose Wimpeys were regularly holed like colanders. Careful crews, feckless crews, hard-working crews, lazy crews. A fact some found disturbing, some reassuring, was that it wasn't always the good crews that came back.

Bill straightened his stack of neatly-folded maps and aligned them with schoolmasterly precision on his Mercator chart and logbook. He'd been here for over an hour (Nav. Briefing 1430) busy with dividers, protractor, straight-edge and the circular slide rule and perspex plotting panel of his Dalton Computer. What sort of a target was Duisburg? Easy? Dicey?

Sneak a peek at Chalkey. Looking bored. That's the cue, boredom. I'm like an actor, thought Tony, playing the part of Pilot Officer Marlowe, pilot on a Wellington squadron, calm and matter-of-fact, modestly heroic and magnificently unconcerned, ready and anxious to do battle in the skies of Germany. Errol Flynn. David Niven.

Biggles Flies Undone. Mastering an overpowering urge to yawn he took out the letter, hands shaking, hold still, damn you, that he'd collected from the Mess after the NFT and yet another attempt to phone Kate. "Official calls only," the operator had said ("This is an official call." "Balls.") and there was a sign, NO ADMITTANCE, on the door of the Station Navigation Office.

"Dear Tony, Quick scribble. There's a super little slice of crumpet on the way to you, seize her while she's up for grabs. Lives near Pa and me at Bexholt, the parson's daughter, name of Kate Elliot, awfully good value. Got any ops in yet? No such luck for me so far. Some night we're not busy, nip over to Flaxfield, why not, let's have a noggin. My local's the Wheatsheaf. Land Army girls. Huge bums. Whitbread's. Yrs, Dick."

Any night Tony wasn't busy and Kate was he'd be delighted to go on the Harpic with good old Dick Allardyce. Duisburg, the thought came and went, his throat was dry. Odd, Dick writing about Kate. He'd give you the shirt off his back but he regarded every girl as his own private property, keep off the grass, old chap, find your own popsies, chum. Who was this new Dick Allardyce?

"Station Commander, att-ten-shun!" Everyone on his feet, Wingco Twinkletoes and the squadron-leader flight commanders following in the Perambulating Prick, the strutting bantam of a Group Captain commanding RAF Station, Onley Market, who took off his gloves, flopped them into his gold-peaked cap, and held it out not bothering to look, for someone to guard with his life.

"Curtain!" The grubby brown blanket jerked along sagging string, on the vast map a strand of red wool zigged out to Duisburg, zagged back to Onley Market.

"Duisburg," Prick was saying. "Vital target. Impede the Hun's industrial production." Chalkey blinking away, he's bored, heard all this twenty-seven times before. Be bored, too. "Continuing air offensive." Bill's lighting his pipe, the whopper with the down-curving stem, a single fill must have lasted him all through navigation briefing. Puff. "Hun licking his wounds." Puff, puff.

Through wafting smoke Tony saw Eckersley and Ramsarse lounging dozily; but Sills, brown-noser Sills, was actually taking notes. Devilish warm in here. This chair's rickety, one leg splayed, table's old and dusty and covered with ancient ink stains, surely there should be, well, more spit and polish, more *ceremony* about sending a squadron of bombers to raid, Tony's mouth was dry again, Duisburg.

"Bring the war to a speedy conclusion." Puff, puff, puff. "Bring the Hun to his knees." Puff. ". . . final victory." The Group Captain sat down with the air of a job well done and the drowsiness went out of the muggy room as the Wingco took over. Not only was the real business of the briefing about to begin but Twinkletoes wore the fading ribbons of the DSO and the DFC while Prick only boasted a bright clean OBE, Other Buggers' Efforts. Twinkletoes said,

"Pilot Officer Marlowe, Pilot Officer Cattermole."

"Sir?" together, apprehensively.

"First op tonight for you and your crews, I believe?"

"Yes, sir."

"Do try not to get shot down." Laughter, Bill winking at him, Tony felt as if he'd been invited to join a rather good club.

"Navigation, please," ordered Twinkletoes.

The Station Navigation Officer was a plump squadron-leader appropriately named Tubbs. He spoke like Flying Officer Fix, P/O Prune's navigator in the funny bits in the RAF aircrew magazine, "Tee Em,", but there was the silver stud of a bar on his DFC. "Piece of cake. Full moon, so you'll pick up bags of pinpoints as you climb on course," his pinkie with the signet-ring moved along the map's red ribbon, "at the coast your turning-point is where else but dear old Lowestoft. Nip smartly over the North Sea, wind is two-two-five forty, cross the Dutch coast here, super pinpoint, can't miss the town of Westkapelle. Then off you scarper to where you pull the plug, Duisburg.

"You bods may have noticed that on the way in we're taking you north of the horrid guns at Eindhoven and clear of that bastard of an airfield at Venlo. But it's always liable to be a bit noisy over Happy Valley"—"Hear, hear" from the back—"so as soon as you've dropped your stuff at Duisburg, it's nose down and away like the clappers. Out across the Dutch coast here, near Leiden, on to this point in the North Sea, fifty-two twenty north, oh four hundred east and then back for your operational egg. Okay? Fair enough? Any questions?"

Sounded like a jaunt on a Green Line bus. "Intelligence," said Twinkletoes. Beside Tony, Bill unfolded his target map.

The only man in the room wearing glasses, the Squadron-Leader Intelligence Officer, before donning RAF blue, had been a schoolmaster; not the friendly kind, like Bill, but a martinet and proud of it; he glared around at the aircrew at their tables like pupils at their desks, obviously wishing he could keep the whole lot of them in for extra class.

"Duisburg," he began, in a weary patronising voice, not bright students, these, "at the junction of two rivers, the Rhine and the Ruhr, is one of the world's largest inland ports." His fingers ached for chalk. "Its main industries are," he paused, dictation speed, no heads were bent over splodgy exercise-books, everybody take a hundred lines, he remembered where he was, went on, "iron and steel, coal-mining, foodstuffs, textiles . . ."

Bill was pencilling marks on the irregular blob of the purple bull's-eye that was Duisburg on his target map, at the centre of concentric circles that marked distances to fly. Crosses showed Bill how to miss churches and hospitals. Hit me, said other symbols, docks, factories, military installations, slide me down the bombsight wires and press the tit when the industrial heart comes down between the pointers . . .

"Met, please," said Twinkletoes.

The Met king was a tweedy, leather-elbowed civilian old enough to be even Bill's father; with sparse confidence he hesitatingly spoke of an occluded front, cloud six-tenths here, three-tenths there, and sat down with relief to enthusiastic applause.

"Right, let's not play silly buggers," said Twinkletoes. "Bombing gen."

Tubbs again. Height to bomb, fourteen thousand. High explosive on these switches, incendiaries on those. Other squadron-leaders came and went. Gunnery. Keep your eyes peeled, get your squirt in first, shoot his goolies off before he can take a pot at yours. Wireless. Onley Market on this frequency, listen out on that, emergency airfields on these.

"Seems about it," said Twinkletoes at last. "And so—why are you jiggling up and down, Tubbs, you should have gone before you came. Oh, thanks for the reminder. Right, everybody, colours of the day: two-star reds. Anything else, Tubby? Good. Let's have your time check."

Five, four, three, two, one, precisely 1629 hours. Two and three-quarter hours to go before Meal 1915. Would have liked to look in on Kate, but No Admittance. Just as well, perhaps, suppose his hands shook. Hello, Kate, I'm just off to bomb Germany, oh, right-oh, Tony, have a nice trip. He had the memory of her in his arms last night, that was what he wanted to treasure. Must try again to ring her, though, tell her he was on ops tonight, not leave her waiting at the flea-pit.

"Sir?" said Twinkletoes. The Group Captain was on the eighteenth, carefully missing a putt, a delighted Air Vice-Marshal was holing out. "Sir?"

The Perambulating Prick came slowly back to this tiresome war, how he wished it was over, how he'd like to get back to real Service life, Dining-In Nights, Mess Dress, proper weekends, proper leave, proper seniority, no more of those jumped-up wartime promotions.

"Well," he was about to say "gentlemen" but the word stuck in his craw, I mean, since 'thirty-nine the Royal Air Force had taken on all sorts of wartime ragtail and bobtail, "Well," said the Perambulating Prick, "hit the Hun hard tonight. Knock Dusseldorf flat."

Twinkletoes' jaw dropped; instant recovery; stony glare swivelling round the grinning aircrew, just one ha-ha, you're for the high jump. "Att-ten-shun!" Prick was gone, gold-braided hat askew at what he thought was a jaunty angle, one glove to wear, one to carry.

They were coming round now with envelopes, you wrote your name on the front and put in any valuables together with any papers which might give information to Conrad Veidt or George Sanders or whoever was wearing Gestapo uniform when you were taken prisoner and invited downstairs for a chat. Bill took a photograph out of his wallet before he filled his envelope, a pleasant, harassed-looking woman with crimped hair, and two small children in shorts and Clark sandals squinting at the sun. "The family," he said fondly. Must get a picture of Kate.

At the door of the Briefing Room, like kids leaving a party, everyone was handed a little pile of goodies, Presents For A Good Boy. A small tin of orange juice, another of evaporated milk; a packet of Wrigley's PK gum; a little bag of barley sugar; a fold of banknotes, French, Dutch, Belgian and German; a silk scarf that turned out to be a map of northern Europe; a brass RAF button.

"Part of your escape kit," explained the Intelligence Officer testily, Tony obviously wasn't a favourite pupil. "Unscrew it and there's a compass inside." A little box with two tablets nestling in cotton-wool. "Wakey-wakey pills," said Chalkey, in front of Tony in the queue.

Anxious for any word of advice which might fall from the lips of a veteran campaigner, Tony followed Chalkey, tap, tap, tap on the doorknob, into the Other Ranks loo. Standing busy at his stall he watched as Chalkey twice jabbed a ferocious penknife to open holes in his tin of orange juice.

"Always a good idea—" Chalkey had to raise his voice, someone was noisily puking in one of the bogs "—always a good idea to scoff it soon as you can. Otherwise if they scrub the op they make you hand it back."

Aiming at nonchalance, Tony asked very quietly, Careless Talk Costs Lives, "What's Duisburg like—as a target, I mean?"

"Haven't a clue," said Chalkey. "I've looked for it three times already, never once caught sight of it. If you find it, do let me know."

Thoughtfully, Tony borrowed Chalkey's penknife and stabbed his orange juice.

* * *

The Meal 1915 wasn't ready. Aircrew sitting frustrated at the white-clothed Mess tables sang quietly, more in sorrow, "Why-y are we waiting, Always bloody well waiting." Aggrieved explanations were heard from the kitchen, it's not my fault if, well, Sergeant Someone said, and you can't blame me for.

Fried rubber and catshit gravy, liver floating in speckled goo, finally arrived at 1945, bit of a rush to gobble it and the stale cake in custard and lift a leg before the expected Transport at Messes 2015.

2015 came and no transport. At 2020 the Tannoy announced without so much as a by-your-leave, take-off postponed to 2345, transport at Messes 2230.

"Such a shame," drawled the languid voice of a wireless-operator called Winwood, was it? Woodham? "Do so hate to keep my clients waiting." Twenty-one minutes past eight,

Kate's outside the flea-pit, Mr Chips here I come.

The audience was streaming in when, out of breath, he reached the Station Cinema, no sign of Kate. He stood, miserably disappointed, as the blue uniforms pushed past, he felt his hand grabbed and he was sitting beside Kate as a moth-eaten lion gave a meagre growl, "Where have you been? Ssh!" she said.

Mr Chips, cute as a marshmallow chimpanzee, was late for Assembly, locked out with a squeaky little new boy. Was this supposed to be School?

Tony stole a look at Kate, she was gazing raptly at the screen, fiercely intent. In the dim light of the cinema he drank in the loveliness of her profile, the gleaming hair sweeping past the delicacy of her ears, her high forehead, the exquisite modelling of her cheekbones, the sweet curve of her lips. She felt his eyes upon her, she turned and her smile was the swoop of sun across a meadow and a bird singing high in the sky.

He realised then that he didn't just want to get the clothes off her although, by God, he would as soon as he got the chance, he wanted to walk with her through autumn woods, make buttered toast with her beside a roaring fire and talk, talk, talk.

He wanted to talk to her, for example, about his School, what it was really like, so different from what was going on up there, a line of meek, well-pressed scholars touching straw hats and politely giving names. School was Jowett ma., seventeen to Tony's thirteen, four inches taller, three stone heavier, at the bicycle shed, "Now I've got you, Marlowe."

School was old Blotto, hard-on tight against stretched corduroy, lashing away at Harrison's arse, round and white as a hunter's moon. Was Hyphen-Smith the prefect, discovered with a first-former in the long grass and told to pack by the Head, waiting for the bus at the school gates, stepping under the wheels.

School was real, School was earnest, he wanted to tell Kate, he had been a hell of a lot more frightened of Jowett ma. than he was tonight of the Germans. But then he knew what Jowett meant to do, to make him eat that dog turd—he'd have succeeded, too, if Tony hadn't stabbed hard and accurately with the bicycle pump and left a moaning Jowett writhing on his back, hands clutching, knees hunched to his chest.

Whereas what the Germans would get up to—those school buildings up there on the screen were strangely familiar, "Good God," said Tony out loud, lost in time and space between a bicycle pump, a cinema seat, a Wimpey's cockpit and Duisburg, "that's Sherborne!"

Absent-minded still, he was puzzled by the immediate storm of laughter. He turned to Kate, her hands were over her face, her shoulders shaking. "It is, you know, it really is," he insisted but all he got was a strangled hoot.

Mr Chips was mouthing noiselessly, drowned by catcalls.

"Fawt it was 'Arrer!"

"Get your tie on straight, Marlowe!" Chalkey White.

"Floreat Borstal!" Tich Cattermole.

"St Bee's!" "St Jim's!" "Greyfriars!" "Westmount High!" "Bedford!" "Dartford Grammar!" "Eton!" "Wot, Eton College?" "No, Eton Central!" It was minutes before the chatter and laughter died down only to start up again when a Waaf piped up, "Chislehurst County School for Girls!" trumped by a perfectly-timed bass croak laying claim to "Roedean!"

Half the squadron's here, Tony had recognised many a barracking voice, we're off to war tonight and it's not a bit like All Quiet or Journey's End or Dawn Patrol. He glanced at Kate, a tear was sliding down her cheek, Greer Garson had just hopped the twig.

Music, The End, lights up. 2215, have to hurry, Transport at Messes 2230. In the darkness outside the cinema she said, as the crowd dispersed, "Thank you. Loved it. Had a very happy sob."

"It *was* Sherborne, you know. Used to play cricket against them." Time for him to go, a Wimpey was waiting, so was Duisburg, but he didn't want to leave her. "I used to open," something to say, "for the First Eleven." How much that had mattered, once upon a time, less than a year ago.

"I'm sure you did." She was laughing up at him. "Yes. Indeed. Indubitably. Quite. Of course. If you say it's Sherborne, Sherborne it is, and I say it's chilly and why are we wasting your nice warm car—"

"Kate," he said, "I have to go now."

Quicksilver change, fear instantly in her eyes. "You're on ops tonight? When you came, I didn't think—" Her arms were tight round him, a half-heard whisper, "Oh, darling, I've only just found you—"

* * *

It wasn't next month's issue or next week's or tomorrow's, it was here and now and if life hadn't been real with Mr Chips, now it was real, extremely real. Across B Bastard's windscreen a dotted line of lights stitched a black nothingness. Yet another dim shape began a howling acceleration down the spangled runway until the red and green navigation lights at its wingtips soared into the sky as the murmur of its engines faded into the howl of the next waiting Wimpey.

The blur in front lurched elephantinely forward, Tony, follow-my-leader, gave a burst of throttle and, again in turn, squeezed the brakes on the handlebar of the control column. Dit dit dah dit, green flashes, letter F from the Tower, the black silhouette in front swung around to point in profile down the runway; hesitated; engines thundered and F for Freddie hurtled between the dots of light, up and off into the darkness, a disappearance of red and green specks.

Through Tony's opened side window the breeze stroked chill on his cheek, rich aroma of tyre-crushed grass, acrid taste of petrol, pear-drop tang of aircraft dope. A blazing green circle blinked dah dit dit dit, letter B, here we go, he snapped the window shut, the world became a Wellington cockpit fuggy with warmed second-hand air, a dimly-lit lonely cell with its windscreen window and its wall of dials with green glints of figures and luminous white live-or-die needles.

Crossed straps of the Sutton harness locked across his yellow Mae West and held him tight against his seat of parachute and the compact parcel of his square-packed dinghy. He was a piece of equipment as functional as the power of the twin engines, nerves and muscles integrated into the hydraulic systems to feed rudder and elevators into the airflow to track B Bastard along the zig and zag of the pencilled lines of Bill Wilberforce's chart.

He lifted his rubber mask, awkward with hanging wire and concertina oxygen tube and clicked the microphone switch.

"Stand by for take-off."

B Bastard heaved forward, slowly the windscreen slewed round to frame the glitter of beaded parallaxing lines, throttles wide open, engines bansheeing, beads moving past slowly, B Bastard reluctantly gathering speed, faster, you swine, faster, just ambling along, cold sweat between Tony's shoulder-blades.

Deafening roar of engines, on and on, still the tail stayed down, come on B Bastard, lift, sod you, lift. On, on, heavy with petrol, incendiaries, explosives, ammunition, at last the tail is coming up, pull back on the control column, no response, get unstuck, lousy B Bastard, get into the air.

Pull back, nothing, God Almighty. Try again. Never make it, never, boundary lights ahead, if B Bastard doesn't lift off now, right now, we've had it, absolutely had it, oh Jesus, up, up, just over, what maniac left a brick wall there, nurse B Bastard up, up, up.

Undercarriage retracted, they seemed to have fixed the warning red light, what else should they have fixed, on the dial of the artificial horizon the miniature aircraft luminous above the level line, throttles back to climbing speed. What the hell was that, something fell, rolling over the floor, quick, flying boot, reach down against the Sutton straps, an empty bottle of Woodpecker cider.

"Do us a favour, sir, drop this on the buggers, lots of crews do, puts the shits up them Germans, whistling down," the Welsh LAC had said when the WAAF driver dumped Tony and the crew at the banjo-shaped, oil-stained concrete hard-standing where B Bastard loomed against the darkness of a clouded sky. Tony stuffed the bottle back inside his Irvin jacket, pulled the zip, a flash, the sky dazzlingly bright, two Wimpeys climbing ahead, red as blood reflection on the wind-screen. "Cor! Look at that! Talk about Guy Fawkes ni—"

Bill Wilberforce's voice cut across Eckersley's. "Navigator to pilot. First course 137 Compass. Estimated Time of Arrival at Lowestoft 0019."

"Thank you, Bill, climbing on 137."

Unclamp the ring of the P4 compass, set 137, re-clamp. Bank into a left-hand turn, the line on the artificial horizon tilts, the turn-and-bank indicator registers Rate One, the numbers of the oblong gyro window slip slowly round from the 280 direction of the Onley Market main runway, through 270, 260, 250, round to 170, 160, 150, 140, 137.

Automatic actions, unthinking, and an emotion filling Tony with shame and disbelief: the primeval glee of the survivor, back beyond civilisation, it's him the sabre-tooth is eating, not me, a surge of hard-to-quell joy, it's another crew, not us, they hit the wall, they're the ones frying down there.

He scanned the dials, trying to dull his guilt, air speed indicator, altimeter, artificial horizon, engine revolutions, oil pressures, oil temperatures, on the circles of their dials the glowing needles flickering against the glinting numbers. Engine noise a murmur, he squeezed his nostrils, blew, ears popped, once again a roaring background.

Black and featureless ground below, already he hadn't a clue where they were but Bill would know what the scattered red airfield beacons signified, the double Morse letters they flashed were coded, changing every night, to nightly varied positions of latitude and longitude.

No red beacons in Germany. None here now, either. The long needle of the altimeter moved around the hundreds as B Bastard climbed into cloud, nothing but black, bags of pin-points be buggered, Tubbs. For as long as this cloud hid the ground they'd be flying on DR, Dead Reckoning, on the by-guess-and-by-God sums worked out by Bill with dividers and protractor and Dalton Computer, war by pencil.

Tony checked the course he was flying by the P4 compass needle steady between the grid of parallel lines. Gyro's wandered three degrees, he turned the knob to make the small correction, a touch of rudder, all Sir Garnet on 137. At least he was kept busy driving B Bastard, no time to brood on what lay ahead, no time to keep reminding himself that German radar was already plotting the track of the incoming bombers, shells up the spouts of guns, searchlight crews on stand-by, night-fighter pilots alert to sprint to their cockpits.

It was Eckersley and Ramsbottom in their turrets he was sorry for, they could brood themselves rotten if they dwelt too much on the hours ahead, all they had to do was stare at the night sky watching for the tiny shadow instantly an Me 110, cannons firing to roast a Wimpey into molten metal with a two-second burst, poor Hickey, poor Tinker, poor Good Ship Venus.

But if Eckersley and Ramsarse had it rough, it was rougher still for the wireless-operator, all Sills had to occupy his time and his mind was twiddling with his Marconi radio. Oh, well, hard luck, chances were that the three of them were half-asleep, at that.

Tony yawned. Very soporific, ops. Monotony. Engine noise. Solitude. You were shagged out, anyway, before you started, what with NFT's, briefings, unsuccessful telephone calls—

Touch on his arm. Bill handing over a slip of paper, going back to his seat in the cabin behind. Unfold it. Icy finger at his spine, Tony leaned forward, clicked down twin switches.

"NAV LIGHTS STILL ON." Get on with your job, you bloody fool, concentrate, stay awake, with the wingtip lights shining over Germany half the Luftwaffe would have been in the queue, thumbs on firing-buttons.

Gyro 134. He made the slight correction, hint of rudder, three degrees to starboard, back on 137. Felt bad about those nav lights, Bill's got enough to do without passing reminders; thoughtful of him to write a note and not tell him over the intercom, keep his boob secret from the other three. Good old Bill.

Tony forced his flagging energy into a set routine, whacked out already, hardly fifteen minutes into this first op, continuously searching the cloud below and above, scanning the array of dials, gyro, ASI, altimeter, artificial horizon, revs, oil pressures, oil temperatures, petrol gauges, gyro.

Gap in the cloud. Below, a white-edged line. Sea? Couldn't be, it's only 2357, ETA Lowestoft is not for another twenty-two minutes, all to cock already—Bill *taught* maths, for God's sake, couldn't, could he, have made such a balls-up?

Tony felt a stab of terror; no mistake, coastline; never mind the Germans, not yet, what was really putting the wind up him was the fear of making an almighty bloody fool of himself.

Think. Check the P4 compass, OK, 137. Gyro 137. All well, Watch stopped? No. Then what's the coast doing down there? Close to panic, his finger reached for the microphone switch.

"Good show," Bill's voice, "just got a pinpoint, ten miles south-east of Boston, we're crossing the coast of the Wash."

Moral: keep off the intercom when shaken rigid, don't give yourself away.

Cloud above and now unbroken cloud below, darkness all around, Tony felt isolated in his cell as if he were hanging motionless between the cloud above that shrouded Tubb's full moon and the cloud that now banished all sight of whatever was below. As if the rumbling engines were rolling an invisible world around to bring up Lowestoft, the North Sea, Westkapelle, Duisburg.

The long hundreds needle of the altimeter moved round to the glimmer of zero, the short thousands needle set itself on the glint of nine. Ready for more discomfort.

"Pilot to crew. 9,000 feet. Oxygen on, everyone." He clicked the snaps of his spit-smelling mask, turned the oxygen tap.

"Navigator to pilot. Oxygen on."

Go without oxygen long enough in a bomber at height and you laugh and sing, fall asleep, die. Drill was, you came on the intercom and acknowledged that you'd heard and obeyed the command. Unless you were Sills, Ramsbottom and Eckersley.

Not a sound.

"Pilot to wireless-operator, are you on oxygen?"

"Oh, yes, thanks, old chap."

Save us all from a debonair Sills. Probably too stupid to be scared. So am I, come to think of it, admitted Tony.

"Pilot to front gunner."

Ramsarse, irritably, "Oxygen? Yes, I'm on oxygen." Sorry if I woke you up.

"Pilot to rear gunner, is your oxygen on?" Not a word, probably bashing his bishop.

"Pilot to rear gunner—"

"Who, me? Sorry. My intercom plug came out." Jesus wept, our lives depend on Eckersley and his plug came out.

"Oxygen on, rear gunner."

"OK, just a minute. Tap's stuck. Oh, no, it isn't, I was turning it the wrong way."

No point in being irritable, you did what you could with what you'd got and what you'd got were Sills, Ramsarse and Eckersley, not forgetting clapped-out B Bastard, now showing marked disinclination to climb.

Why was it vibrating like a car bumping over a rutted track, what's wrong, Tony's eyes swept the dials, all well, he looked up, flickering little yellow flames, exhaust stubs, another Wimpey terrifyingly close, immediate right bank, right rudder, a diving turn, sky clear.

Heart thumping as he clicked the microphone switch, "Sorry, everyone, had to dodge a Wimpey." Ramsarse should have warned him, should never stop searching the sky, Tony longed to give him a good bollocking, better not, pretend we're all pals together, that's called keeping up morale. "Didn't you see it, front gunner?"

"Gosh, no, 'fraid not, just undoing a bit of chocolate."

Tomorrow Kate will want to hear a tale of heroes, what shall I tell her? What have we done to Bring The War To A Speedy Conclusion? I got a sore arse, Eckersley's plug came out, Ramsbottom ate a bit of chocolate, God knows what Sills did. Not that even Bill Wilberforce has all that much to do right now, not a break in the cloud. One thing, B Bastard's finally staggered up to operational height.

"Navigator, we're at 14,000. I'm changing to cruising speed."

"Roger, thank you. Remain on same course, 137. ETA Lowestoft still 0019. Five minutes to go. Hope we see it."

They didn't. 0019. "Navigator to crew. Can't see a thing down there but by my Dead Reckoning we're over Lowestoft, just crossing the coast. Tony, course for Westkapelle 156 Compass. ETA Westkapelle 0044."

Bill was having to use the wind that Met had calculated and as the cloud forecast was obviously to cock, not much chance that their wind was anything near right. 225/40 was that Met wind, supposedly from the southwest at 40 knots. If the real wind was from the northeast at the same speed it would put them 80 nautical miles southwest of their calculated, DR, position in one hour. Made you think.

Stooge on. Must try to stop checking the watch every minute or so. Won't look for fifteen minutes.

Fifteen minutes up now, surely. God, only six gone. Stop looking. Three more peeps at his watch, and:

"Navigator to pilot. Estimate fifty miles out from English coast."

"Thank you, Bill." Tony waited. Sills the Pill should have

reported that he'd switched off the Identification Friend or Foe, which showed British radar you were RAF, not to be shot at. But if you left the IFF on as you approached the enemy coast, German radar used its pulsing signals to aim flak at you, to home fighters on your tail.

"Wireless-operator, is the IFF off?"

Pause. "Yes." Sills, of course, had forgotten, dreamy sod.

Hell of a draught from somewhere, cold as a frog in an icebound pool, cold as the end of an Eskimo's tool, can't expect the windows to close properly, not called B Bastard for nothing and all the time the hot air pipe scalds your knee. Weird way to fight a war, this. Like to fly over Germany? Yes, after I've seen Mr Chips.

Weird war. Odd how none of the instructors ever talked about what it was like to fly on ops, as if there were some secret which could never be revealed.

They'd spent an evening in a pub, a couple of weeks ago, Tony and Hickey and Tinker, with one of the instructors at Littledale OTU, a Warrant Officer Whitehouse. He'd done a tour in Whitley IVs, the Flying Coffins. "You could read in its bog," he said. They bought him beer, he was a regular, an ex-Halton apprentice, had a regular's thirst.

Three remarks he made about operational flying. Cold sober, he said: "Damned inconvenient, ops. You have to stay up all night." Still fairly sober, "You just sit there on your aching arse, stooging along, and hoping to Christ nothing horrible is about to happen." Bit piddled: "It's like sitting on a lumpy cushion between tanks sloshing with petrol, waiting for some cunt to chuck in a lighted match."

He was pissed as a fart at "Time, gentlemen, please" but still the secret was unrevealed.

Gyro, ASI, altimeter, artificial horizon, inconvenient, aching arse, lumpy cushion, stooging along, something horrible happening, staccato hammering of machine-guns, sharp smell of cordite. Heart leaping, "Front gunner, where is he?"

"Where's who?"

Who? Out of your mind, Ramsarse? "The fighter!"

Eckersley: "Fighter? Fighter? Where?"

Oh, Jesus, the Marx Brothers.

"Front gunner, what were you shooting at?"

"Shooting at? Oh. Just testing my guns. Forgot to do it after we crossed the coast."

Thumping stammer, whiff of cordite, now that quim Eckersley has loosed off his guns, tracer lighting up the sky, come-and-get-us invitation for any wandering Me 110 or Ju 88 searching the North Sea.

You stupid bastards, he wanted to yell, he took a long deep breath, instead he said calmly, "Don't forget next time, gunners." Leadership. "And always warn me before you test your guns." No answer. Sulking, no doubt.

Heartbeat coming back to normal, stooging on, he was driving with Kate down the High Street, left at Christchurch Road, left again along the curve of trees heavy with pink blossom, into the gate and up the drive, his mother laughing and coming up from her knees by the flower-bed, his father hurrying out of the house with Trixie barking and bouncing beside him—"Navigator to pilot, ETA enemy coast in three minutes. Looks as if we won't see Westkapelle, have to turn on DR."

So Holland—or Belgium or France—was below the cloud. First time he'd been abroad, "Right you are, Bill." Cheerful. Not feeling cheerful; if you want to know where you're going, you have to know where you've been.

"New course 105 Compass. ETA Duisburg in 39 minutes."

"Thank you, Bill. Turning on to 150 Compass."

"Correction, Tony. 105 Compass."

Watch it, Marlowe. Fatigue caught up with you, mistakes got made that later seemed impossible to understand. If you lived to discuss them. "Sorry, Bill. 105 Compass." Concentrate.

Stooge on, fighting to stay awake, to scan the dials, to search the vacant blackness outside the windscreen for a glimpse of land or a shadow of a night fighter. So incredibly lonely.

Tony wished he could see searchlights, flak, anything to show there was something down there beneath the thick cloud, that the world wasn't dead and gone and all that was left was B Bastard. So damned tired. He put the two wakey-wakey pills on his tongue, bitter taste, he swallowed.

Touch on his arm, Bill holding out a Thermos cup. Tony nodded, thanked him with a wink, unsnapped his oxygen mask for a moment of not just hot, steaming, sugary coffee, but an event, a human happening in this desolate, empty night; aah, that's better, Tony felt reality surging back, this was his first op, a warrior bold was he. Nothing like a swig of hot coffee to stiffen the sinews, summon up the blood, once more unto the breach, dear friends. Good to be Doing One's Bit.

One of Dad's phrases from the Last Lot, his '14-'18 war. He did his bit, he'd say, of the clerk in his solicitor's office, who'd also done time for embezzlement. But the ex-convict had left a leg on the battlefield of Passchendaele, for doing his bit Dad gave him a not dared to be dreamt of second chance; just as any organ-grinder with the Pip, Squeak and Wilfred service medals was sure of half-a-crown and the shabbily neat out-of-work at the garden gate who spoke of Bullygrenade and the Somme found a crackling white fiver pressed into his hand.

To Tony's father there were two kinds of men. Do your bit, ask Dad what you like. The others, he didn't want to know, outer darkness. Good to feel even closer to him—

"Navigator to crew. If my Dead Reckoning is right, we're just crossing the frontier into Germany." Cloud looks exactly the same.

Stooge on, cushion lumpy, all those cunts waiting with matches, yet we could be over Wolverhampton for all the interest the Germans are showing. Stooge on, everlastingly on.

An eternity later: ETA Target. Duisburg might possibly be below.

Beside Tony, Bill, bulky in helmet, fur and leather; no moon, no stars, no flak, no fighters, no sign of Duisburg, miles and miles of sweet fuck-all.

Tony said, "Going down to look for the target."

Bill stuck up a thumb and went back to his own cell.

Precious stuff, height, lose it and it was devilish difficult to regain and the lower you went the easier meat you were for flak, couldn't be helped, down we go.

Throttles back, control column forward, on the dial the miniature aircraft dips below the horizon line, rate-of-descent needle steady on 500 feet a minute, altimeter unwinding, from darkness into a deeper darkness, B Bastard heaved skyward, dropped sickeningly, this is cumulus, dropping like a stone, maybe even cumulo-nimbus, thundercloud, hellish dangerous, lurching up, dropping again.

Still no sign of a gap, perhaps we'll come out of cloud right over Duisburg, what a tale that would be to tell, what a line to shoot, drop, lurch, B Bastard getting sluggish, more thrott— slam, something smashed into the fuselage, intercom loud with startled voices.

Surprised how calm, Tony said commandingly, "Mikes off, everyone." Realising, "That was ice." Ice flung off a propeller and along the wings a shine, clear ice building up, fast. Quick, the decision, down or up. Up. Take clapped-out B Bastard all it's got to climb out of this icing cloud even now, daren't risk taking it any lower, more ice building up, never be able to climb back.

Throttles wide open, full boost, B Bastard barely holding its own, tossed all over the sky. Nudge back on the control column, engines howling, an aged, aging aircraft staggering upward, thrown about by the angry air, lighter blackness, smothering darkness again, lighter once more, above cloud, thank God. "Pilot to crew, everybody OK?"

Four quick yeses, frightened men answer fast.

Bill again, they must have had liver in the Sergeants' Mess, too, speckled goo all down his Irvin jacket.

Weakly, "Going up front to bomb."

"I'll drop the stuff, Bill. We still over the target?"

"By my DR, yes. But—" Orders is orders, if you don't see the target, you drop on Dead Reckoning. "Bombs fused, Bill? OK, leave it to me." Lever down, red light, bomb doors open, jettison handle, pull, job done, lever up, bomb doors up, red light out, let's get the hell home, wasting our time here. "Bombs gone, Bill. Course out from target, please."

Oh, God, the LAC's contribution to the night's frolic. Tony unzipped his Irvin jacket, wriggled out the Woodpecker bottle and froze into sudden stillness. Unbelievable.

"Navigator to pilot, new course 290 compass. ETA enemy coast in 29 minutes."

"Thank you, Bill." Set 290 on the P4, bank, rudder, figures spinning round on the gyro. "Steady on 290."

Unbelievable. Can't drop this bottle, the thought had come, it might hurt somebody. Summed up the whole eldritch day, Mr Chips on the way to war, wandering all over Europe, ignored by flak and fighters, bombs gone, don't drop this bottle, it might hurt somebody, for Christ's sake what was he being paid for?

"Pilot to wireless-operator, come up front, please."

Sills looking decidedly groggy, smell of spew.

"Heave this down the flare chute, there's a good chap."

Stooge on, bugger-all happening, rather boring really, gyro, ASI, altimeter, artificial horizon, revs, pressures, temperatures, stooging on. Not a sausage to be seen at the DR time of crossing the enemy coast, no change in the cloud above or below as they stooged on, altering course at Bill's Dead Reckoning 5220N 0400E, God knows where we actually are, where we've been, where we're going, hopelessly lost ever since that long-ago glimpse of the Wash.

It was Tony who first saw the white light blinking, should have been Ramsarse but he, no doubt, was having a quiet kip. It was a pundit, one of the coastal and inland aerial lighthouses that spelt out a single Morse letter.

"Pilot to navigator. Pundit up ahead. K King."

"Jesus Christ Almighty," strange that, Bill never swore. "Are you sure, Tony?"

"Yes, Bill. Dah dit dah. There it goes again, dah dit dah."

"God, that's Orfordness, we're forty miles south of track—"

"Oh, jolly good show."

"Shut up, Ramsbottom. Not to worry, Bill, just get us home." Forty miles south, God alone knew where those bombs had fallen. "Clouds breaking up," said Tony. "Should be a piece of cake from now on," and right then was when the cunts started chucking in the lighted matches, Tony saw the gun flashes below on the sea, flak all around, sparkling, crackling close, closer, louder, all hell breaking loose, see flak, Chalkey White had said, bugger all, hear it, dicey, smell it, you're up shit creek. "Sills," Tony yelled into his microphone, "is the IFF on?" The control column was alive, leaping and bucking, blast of the bursting shells flinging B Bastard about the night sky.

Something Tony had to remember, couldn't think, couldn't think, noise battering, blinding flashes—Verey pistol, he grabbed at the butt above his head, Bill's hand there already, phut, two red stars eye-hurtingly bright, drifting slowly down smoking in the sky, don't shoot us, we're on your side, abruptly the flak stopped, two late loud cracks, cordite smell strong and sharp.

"IFF is on now," said Sills, pathetically jaunty, lackadaisical idiot nearly got us shot down by our own Navy.

The clouds above and below had cleared when they crossed the coast at Orfordness pundit, losing height as Bill's new course took them northeast towards Onley Market, Tubb's moon visible at last, low in the sky, lighting their way over the red flashing beacons marking their track, Woodbridge, Mildenhall, Feltwell, Methwold . . .

"Navigator to pilot, should we call Onley Market in case we have to land away?"

What was on Bill's mind, why should they land somewhere else, oh, Jesus, yes, he'd forgotten, so bloody tired, that Wimpey that hit the wall might have scattered bits all over the runway—

"Wireless-op, give Base a buzz, see if we've been diverted."

Predictably, Sills couldn't raise Onley Market. So on they stooged until they saw Onley Market's red beacon flashing IR, home at last, the flarepath beading the short auxiliary runway, no sweat, B Bastard was a lot lighter now than when it took off.

But, dead tired, Tony brought B Bastard crunching down with a bounce that tilted a wing close to the ground for one horrifying second, B Bastard bumped, bumped again, settled, speed was spilling off, Tony was squeezing the brakes, just a touch, then more and more firmly, slowing, stop. The red undercarriage warning light came on. "Get stuffed," said Tony.

Led in by a Flying Control van, he taxied to B Bastard's hardstanding and switched off the engines at the dipping cross-over signal of two torches. The hatch opening, someone coming up the steps outside, smell of grass wafting crisply in. A torch shone, behind it the shadowed Mephistophelean face of the Welsh LAC from Unbendem Wemendem. "Everything go all right, did it, sir?"

B Bastard had as near a toucher killed them on take-off, climbed at a crawl and taken its own sweet time lumbering up out of the icing cloud but here they were back at Onley Market.

And truth to tell, Tony felt absolutely bloody marvellous. Back safe, wonderful to be alive. "Well, the kite brought us home," said Tony. "Can't ask more than that." He grinned. "Dropped your bottle over the target. Diarrhoea in Duisburg tonight." The LAC beamed. Scraps of paper twirled in the breeze, shreds of Bill's target map.

The crew sat at the same table at which they'd been briefed, Tony with his hair itching abominably from the tight leather helmet, his cheeks stiff and black-lined by the sticky rubber of his oxygen mask, Bill with his eyes troubled, Sills, Ramsbottom and Eckersley groggy with fatigue.

Tony sipped scalding hot cocoa laced with rum, soon there'll be the operational egg to look forward to in the Mess, then off to pit for a good long kip. Probably be seeing Kate tomorrow—this—evening. Wizard.

No egg for those chess players, theirs had been the Wimpey that pranged the wall. Chalkey was back, so was Twinkletoes, the room was crowded with crews struggling to stay awake. Three of the squadron's Wimpeys weren't back yet, one of them Cattermole's; Tich had landed at a Beaufighter airfield in Yorkshire. Not too much anxiety about the others so far, still time and petrol for them to get back.

"Bombed target on DR?" said the rather twee Intelligence Officer at their table. "Good show." He wrote neatly on the form before him, carefully shaping his Greek "e"s, gold-plated pen moving in time with his words. "Bombed Duisburg, primary target. Good show," he said again, as he collected Bill's chart and log. Tony caught Bill's worried eyes, where their bombs had fallen, who had a clue, but both of them were too utterly shagged to argue.

Well, there it is, thought Tony, that's the secret.

The secret that Warrant Officer Whitehouse and all the other instructors never revealed, drunk or sober. That Bomber Command was one bloody great enormous confidence trick. Nobody finds the target, let alone bombs it. In spite of the crews dead and missing, in spite of Hickey and Tinker and crisp black chess players, Bomber Command was a conspiracy, a hell of a lot of fuss for fuck-all, Was Your Journey Really Necessary?

A conspiracy you automatically, unthinkingly joined. The LAC had been delighted when Tony told him his bottle had whistled down on Duisburg. Duisburg? If you find it, do let me know.

* * *

The six pips of the BBC time signal squealed through the Mess and Tubbs and the other navigators set their issue watches to the second of one o'clock. "This is the BBC Home Service. Here is the news, read by Alvar Liddell." In green leather armchairs beneath Peter Scott paintings of birds in flight—someone had chalked in climbing streams of tracer—*Daily Telegraph* crosswords were laid aside and many a *Daily Mirror* put down, open at the undressed Jane cartoon.

"Last night a large number of aircraft of Royal Air Force Bomber Command attacked military installations, rail and river transport centres and war production plants in Duisburg." Derisive cheers. "Fires were started and extensive damage was done to war material factories and enemy lines of communication. From these operations, sixteen—"

Immediate chatter drowning Alvar Liddell's "of our aircraft have failed to return." The chess players' crew and those of bags of other kites weren't even a statistic; they never announced you as a casualty if you hit a wall on the way up or Hawksthorn runway on the way down.

Confidence trick, mused a weary Tony later in the Crew Room, where you had to report at two o'clock after a previous night's op, conspiracy. How many people knew of the way that Bomber Command was pulling the wool over everyone's eyes? A few thousand aircrew? And Dick Allardyce's father and the other officers at Bomber Command's headquarters at High Wycombe?

The rest of the world, it seemed, took it for gospel that Germany was reeling under the deadly accurate bombing of a mighty attacking force. Well, somebody, some beringed Air Marshal, was doubtless in charge and, one hoped, knew what he was up to; Tony's not to reason why.

Meanwhile they were putting Tich Cattermole in the Line Book. His bed had been empty last night across the room at Site Four as Tony lay awake and dawn gave way to bright daylight; the wakey-wakey pills hadn't taken effect until he slipped between the sheets, not that he minded, he was exhilarated by the knowledge that he'd flown his first op, done his bit.

The laughing Tich, sunburnt in April like the farmer's boy he was, had just flown in from that Beaufighter airfield in Yorkshire, Ashley Down. Hadn't a clue, apparently, where he was when he got back to England. Saw a lighted airfield and lobbed in; the runway, he maintained, was one foot eight inches long. Into the Line Book:

"Date: 3.4.42. Place: Crew Room, Onley Market. Name: P/O Tich Cattermole. Line: Such a teeny-weeny airfield, Ashley Down, I had to flip my Wimpey in like a tiddly-wink."

Tony had hardly met the other two crews unaccounted for last night, not to be wondered at; a hundred and twenty-five aircrew on the squadron changing, if you wanted to brood about it, rather often. One of the crews had phoned in from Hawksthorn; bit of a dicey do, they'd had to land on one engine on the grass beside the concrete runway where bods were filling the hole an exploding Wimpey had made the night before, sadly Tony remembered moonlight through a shattered fuselage.

The crew were all OK except that the front gunner had ricked his ankle climbing out of the Wimpey. "Probably bucking for a wound stripe," said Chalkey. The other Wimpey was now posted missing. "People come, people go. You get used to it."

A yell, "NAAFI up!" Torrent of aircrew through the Crew Room door. Beside the van, Tony ("Tails") tossed Chalkey who to pay for char and sticky buns. "Heads." "Bugger."

"Widga jee wadgemund?" Chalkey asked.

"Eh?"

Swallow of bun. "Did you see Duisburg?"

"Not a sign. You?"

"No. Fourth try. Don't believe it's there at all."

What a waste, Tony thought but didn't say, this stupid sodding Bomber Command conspiracy was. Waste of lives. Waste of petrol. Waste, even, of money; he could have qualified as a doctor for what it cost to train him to fly; the price of B Bastard would have built a cottage hospital.

"You've got the first one over, Tony." Chalkey was looking at him very seriously over the brim of his mug. "That's the diciest." Hickey, Tinker, Geordie and Phil. "Big chop on number one. That's when you make the real bloody fool mistakes." Nav lights on. 150. No, 105. IFF.

"Then, the next few"—Chalkey was fiercely willing him to listen—"the next few seem almost like a piece of cake, a worry or two, maybe, but the danger is, Tony, that you start thinking ops aren't dangerous." Listen, the tone of his voice was urging, listen. Unnecessary: Tony knew this was the real pukka gen, rare enough in Bomber Command. "Until something happens, Tony, that really puts the shits up you."

Chalkey paused, looked embarrassed. "Toss you," he said, gruffly, "for another bun."

To Bill Wilberforce and anyone else who might be fascinated by the news, Tony called that he was off to the Station Navigation Office, "Going to change a map," he alibied.

A red needle-sharp pencil pierced her gleaming hair like a near miss from an over-excited Iroquois, she was balanced comfortably, leaning back on one chair, feet up on another, idly sipping tea. Her mug had K-K-K-Katie painted all around, she raised it in greeting as Tony came into her storeroom-cum-office, shelves to the ceiling stacked high with maps.

"Heard you were back. How was the Third Reich?"

"Boring. Not nearly as exciting as Mr Chips. I suppose you know the Station Navigation Officer is out there counting maps. How do you manage to get him to do your job?"

"One is a witch. One casts spells."

"One will get one's pretty little bottom spanked if one doesn't move one's feet so one can sit down."

"Ooh, goody." She swung glorious legs clear, her chair clattered forward on the concrete floor. "I had a letter about you today."

"Who from?"

"From whom, Dick Allardyce, how I swooned. He tells me you're awfully good value." Dick wasn't a man to use a new phrase where an old one would do, what can you expect from a chap who, Tony had actually seen him do it, sent off letters to his assorted crumpet in carbon copies.

"Anything we can do for you, Tony?" Squadron-Leader Tubbs in the doorway. Sounded friendly enough but obviously Tubby considered that the sooner Tony left the better he'd be pleased, already he was Kate's abject slave.

"Came to change a worn-out map." Tony held up the perfectly good topographical he'd crumpled on the way over.

"Local half-million?" Kate plucked one from its shelf without looking, an efficient witch. "Just in, hot from the oven."

She rolled the map briskly, a suspicious Tubbs went back to his own office. Tony murmured, "See you tonight?"

"Oh, lollipop, nothing I'd like better, but tonight's Domestic Night." Once a week the Waafs were confined to camp to sew on buttons, mend their issue passion-killer underwear and shine up the windows of their Nissen huts.

"Sneak out," cajoled Tony.

Kate did something with her lower lip, miming despair, a blue-eyed poodle who'd mislaid a bone. "Do that and it's jankers, shan't see you for a never-ending week."

Tubbs or no Tubbs, Tony kissed her right eyebrow and got back to the Crew Room just in time to hear Twinkletoes tell his intrepid birdmen that they need no longer stand by in case duty called them to fly their aerial juggernauts against the warlike hordes of Germany.

"Piss off," said Twinkletoes.

Tony, disappointed, no Kate, went in search of a telephone to ring Dick Allardyce before rolling up in his downy for two or three hours of catch-up kip.

* * *

Against the noisy rhubarb, rhubarb of the Saloon Bar, "Quite a girl, Kate Elliot," said Dick Allardyce. "Known her since she was in pigtails." He dipped his MGM profile into a glass of Whitbread's and gulped down a good quarter-pint. "Used to lie in wait for me behind the Vicarage gate, I'd pedal past on my bike, whoosh, whoosh, she'd pelt me with apple cores."

"Grown up since then. And cut off her pigtails."

"No doubt, no doubt. But when you see her eating apples, duck. Must say, didn't take you long to meet her, you horny bastard." Swig.

Dick Allardyce really did belong on a recruiting poster. Six-one to Tony's six foot, about a year older, chiselled features, strong white teeth like Joel McCrea, fair hair, grey eyes, long artistic fingers from a story about a sensitive, misunderstood surgeon redeemed by the love of a nurse who's beautiful without her glasses.

Fingers now prodding Tony with an empty glass. "Sex, sex, sex, all that's on your mind, never a thought of standing a chum a Whitbread's."

NO MUSIC NO SINGING NO GAMBLING WE HAVE AGREED WITH THE BANK NOT TO CASH CHEQUES THEY HAVE AGREED NOT TO SELL DRINKS. Lousy pub, this Wheatsheaf. The bald, surly barman banged two slopping pints on the beer-swilled counter.

"To our jovial host," toasted Dick. "Ever heard of a girl called Judy Gale?"

"Can't say I have—"

"I met her at a party on that forty-eight after OTU. She's mildly terrific. Actress, no less. Well, dancer. At the Windmill."

We Never Closed, said the posters, the theatre had stayed open throughout the air raids of the Blitz. We Never Clothed, said the wags. On its stage, Everyman discovered his dream girl. Everymen stood in queues that stretched all the way down London's Great Windmill Street and when they got in out of the cold and rain they stayed for hours, moving up from seat to seat as other patrons finally and regretfully left until, at last, they reached the Mecca of a goggle-eyed front-row view of striptease, erotic dances and glorious girl-flesh.

"Arse like a jelly on springs," said Dick.

Mildly terrific. For Dick, someone special; this explained the new here's-a-popsie-for-you Allardyce, Lonely Hearts Allardyce, all-for-one-and-one-for-all Musketeer Allardyce. "Nudey Judy?" suggested Tony.

Severely, "You are talking of the woman I love." Urgently, "Two targets. Starboard." Light of Dick's life this Judy may be, didn't mean he was going to pass up a chance to practise.

They were two well-uddered Land Army girls in brown whipcord breeches standing alone at the bar, both with big brown bovine eyes, both masticating placidly from rustling bags of Smith's Crisps. One had light-brown hair and a tawny skin, the other was dark-haired and freckly-pale. "You take the Jersey," Dick's big shoulders were cleaving a path through blue

RAF uniforms, "and I'll have a bash at the Hereford."
"Hello," said Dick.
"Hello," said Tony.
The two girls looked at each other and giggled. "Hello," said Jersey. "Hello," said Hereford. The twentieth century came to a grinding halt. Chamberlain snivelled, "This Country Is Consequently At War With Germany." Germany invaded France. France chucked in the towel. The British Expeditionary Force sailed home from Dunkirk on Little Ships. The Few fewed. Germany invaded Russia and the Japanese bombed Pearl Harbour.
Jersey it was who broke the everlasting silence. "We're sisters."
"Wouldn't have thought so," said Tony. Both girls looked pleased.
Just above hearing level Dick said to Hereford, "I'd like to tickle your tits."
She looked up in slow amazement, saw fair-haired, grey-eyed innocence and, as time went by, decided she'd misheard. Fighting to keep a straight face, Tony asked, "How about a drink?"
"Well, we're with a friend, see," said Jersey.
"He's just gone to the Gents'," said Hereford.
He was, truth to tell, just coming back, not having quite finished adjusting his dress before leaving, short and hairline-moustached, in a sports coat like the fur of a small orange gorilla.
"You're back, then?" observed Hereford, after some thought.
"S'right."
"These two boys was going to buy us a drink."
"Ah." Lack of enthusiasm. Suspicion in curranty eyes in a polished roly-poly face.
"They're in the Air Force." Few facts escaped Jersey.
"Well," best of a bad job, "I'll have to buy them a drink, then, won't I?" People often went away after he'd stood a round. "Hey, Gerald."
Gerald was the bald barman. "Yes, Mr Tate?"
"Whisky for us all." Especially if it was an expensive drink.
Baldy jerked a thumb at yet another sign, NO SPIRITS.

"Come off it, Gerald, old man, I'm a regular. Five whiskies."
"Cherry brandy for me," protested Hereford.
"No, no, no, whisky, puts hair on your chest." Mr Tate laughed heartily, winking a currant at Tony and Dick in turn, pity to miss a joke, specially a good 'un. "Hair on their chests," again he laughed, like the creak of a rusty hinge.
Whiskies were grudgingly slammed on the bar. Mr Tate took a long noisy gulp and raised his glass. "Lead in your pencils." Wink, curranty wink. "Fliers, eh? Pilots," he confided to Jersey and Hereford, "can tell by their wings. Envy you boys. Be a flier meself if they'd let me. No good volunteering, though. Reserved occupation."
"Hard luck," said Tony, all sympathy.
"Always fancied the Raff. Like to fly a Willingdon."
"Wellington, actually," said Dick, courteously. Over the crunch of chips he said to the girls, "We call them Wimpeys. After J. Wellington Wimpey in the Popeye cartoons—"
Hastily interrupting, "Yes, s'right, them big bombers. Over Berlin, eh? Bombs gone, whoomph, whoomph, whoomph."
"Whoomph," added Tony. "Sticks of four," he explained.
Jersey said, "Spinach."
"Yerss, reely do envy you boys. Be up there with you if they didn't need me on the road. I'm a rep," he proudly informed Jersey and Hereford. "In biscuits. Travel a lot."
Dick bought two whiskies, a cherry brandy and two Whitbreads. "Yerss, travel a lot," said Mr Tate with an emphatic suck of his teeth, conjuring up blackened faces, rubber boats, a midnight beach, cold steel.
Beer glasses emptied rapidly. "Oh, must you go reely?" Relieved. "Well, carry on with the good job, blast them Huns good and proper. Finish the job this time, I say, teach 'em a reel lesson, no letting 'em off like we did in the last lot."
"Got some samples up in my room," they heard him say as they left, Hereford gazing after Dick as if he were pawing his hoofs on a distant hilltop. Jersey said, "You told us your name was Hotchkiss."
"Pity about that," said Dick. "Fancied a bit of horizontal dual." They were sitting in Dick's red Alvis Speed 20, the moonlit night unseasonably warm for the start of April, the hood was down and so was the windscreen, you turned knobs

and it became a shelf for Whitbreads.

The open Alvis was parked beside Tony's Morris Eight behind the Wheatsheaf on rough grass that fringed a quiet wood; so that's why this ghastly pub was Dick's local, Hereford might well have been getting up now, exhausted but gratefully content, brushing off twigs and moss.

"I thought you'd found your one true love, never again would you look at another girl."

"So I have, Tony, so I have, but you know as well as I do that if you don't keep using it, it withers away and finally drops off and then what use would I be to Judy, what indeed? Seriously, though, getting it in is always wizard but it's what she's like between fucks that really matters, don't you agree?"

Walks through autumn woods, buttered toast by a roaring fire. "Lot in what you say, Dick."

Swift, shrewd glance. "Kate?" Hoot of glee, slap on Tony's shoulder. "Couldn't do better, either of you."

Contented swallows of Whitbread's. "Used to hit me, often as not."

"With those apple cores?"

"Damn good shot, Kate."

Tony said, out here no Careless Talk Costs Lives: "Hell of a lot more accurate than Bomber Command."

Dick carefully put his half-empty glass on the flat windscreen. "I was going to ask you about that, you being the man with all the pukka gen about ops.

"What puzzles me, Tony, is how one finds the target. I mean, I can more or less guess what it's like over Germany, you just bumble along petrified with fear that some sod's going to poop off shells or cannon at you when you least expect it. But how to find what you're looking for, that's what foxes me. Can't help remembering what it was like when we were training, all those times everyone got completely lost. Like Cross—Brown—Naughton—and Ogilvy—"

They had all trained at Littledale OTU on the same course of twenty. Cross had flown his Wimpey into a slope of Snowdon one cloudy morning; Brown into Boulsworth Hill, not far from Burnley one moonless night when, apparently, he'd been looking for Flamborough Head. Naughton had radioed he was out of fuel, was ditching in the sea, should have been standing his round an hour ago. Ogilvy just didn't come back from a night cross-country, they found what was left of his kite in a wood a fortnight later, a hundred and ten miles from where he should have been.

"And all the time you and I spent, wandering about the sky wondering where we were—" Dick was laughing—"if that's Stow-on-the-Wold, why has it got a cathedral?"

"Is Salisbury on the coast?" reminisced Tony.

"But, Tony," Dick was serious again, "it is an absolute mystery to me, we kept getting lost over Britain, for God's sake—tell me, you're the man who's flown all the ops. Over Germany, how do you find the target, the factory or the marshalling yard or whatever it is we're supposed to bomb?"

You don't. But no point in telling Dick his newly-discovered knowledge, that ops were a fucking waste of time, no point in sapping his morale before he'd even done his first op—so that's why, to keep up morale, Tony understood now why Warrant Officer Whitehouse and the other OTU instructors had been so evasive.

Evasively, Tony said, "One's navigator slaves away, does his best to muddle through." Awkward pause. "You'll soon find out, Dick."

"But how—" Dick began, then he sensed Tony's continuing reluctance. "Well, anyway," he said, "my father says bombing will win the war. Very keen on Bomber Command, is Pa." Dick put down his glass, stole Tony's, swigged it dry. "Yes, he maintains bombing will win the war sort of convincingly, so the Germans will get out of the habit of starting a new one every twenty years or so."

"Hope he's right."

"Well, he's an Air Commodore and I'm only a Pilot Officer, so who am I not to agree? He's up there at Bomber Command Headquarters at High Wycombe with all those chaps covered in scrambled egg, they must know what they're up to, surely. 'Stand by your beds,' " he sang, " 'Here comes the Air Vice-Marshal, He's got lots of rings, But he's only got one arsehole." ' He picked up both glasses, lifted long legs out of the Alvis, "Quick slash and I'll be back with a noggin."

It was quiet alone in the Alvis except for a prolonged hissing which turned into splash, Good to sit here on a warm night—be better, much better, mind, with Kate—not listening to engines, not smelling stale spit in your oxygen mask, not waiting for the lighted match as you flew that murderous B Bastard on, on and on, towards the unfindable target.

Whitbreads on the windscreen. "Biscuits is still in there, drunk as a skunk, on his tod. Jersey and Hereford are grazing with a couple of sergeants from the King's Own Yorkshire Light Infantry."

"Does Biscuits mind?"

"Too sloshed to care, I'd say. But he's still terribly keen for us to go on bombing Germany. 'Give 'em hell,' were his words, 'for me. The only good German,' he mentioned several times, 'is a dead German.' "

"Reely very warlike, isn't he? But haven't you noticed how belligerent some civvies are? Remember that newsreel we saw, chaps climbing aboard a Wimpey and, what was that commentator's name, Leslie Mitchell, saying, 'Giving the Nazis a taste of their own medicine?' "

"Yes," said Dick, "and a kind of growl went round the audience, sounded like a lot of poor lions that hadn't got a Christian. But the fiercest movie I ever saw was a short last year, a Wimpey climbed away, all bombed up, 'Off to pay back the Nazis,' the commentator said, music played, believe me, believe me not, the Hallelujah Chorus, pom-tee pom-pom, everybody clapped."

"Can't blame them, I suppose, Dick, been through the Blitz, bombs showering down on them night after night—"

"This was in the flea-pit at home in Bexholt in beechy Bucks, not much of a blitz there, never a bang."

They savoured Whitbreads. After a while, "I'll be glad to get my first op in," said Dick, "get some idea of what it's all about. Can't believe that the RAF go out night after night and never find, let alone hit, their targets. Look what you read in the papers and hear on the BBC—all that news about factories being plastered and military installations clobbered. They can't possibly be making it all up."

Can't they just, thought Tony, sadly. Soon you'll find out, Dick. You'll become a member of the club. You'll join the conspiracy.

There were regular red flashes in the sky, on, off, on, off;

Tony wondered for a moment, then realised, reflections, clouds had drifted over the beacon at Flaxfield, Dick's nearby airfield. "After all," Dick was saying sombrely, "if we're not finding military targets and just chucking our bombs overboard, we're killing men and women and kids in their own homes. No, that's not on."

More cheerfully, Dick added, "Obviously it's not. The God-botherers, the bishes and archbishes and, damn it all, the squadron-leader padres on every bomber station, they wouldn't stand it for a moment, they'd put up one hell of a bleat."

Red sky at night, flashing on, flashing off, bombers' delight. We bomb factories and they bomb cathedrals, bullshit; we can't find cities, let alone military installations and rail and river transport centres and war production plants.

Two Wimpey crews out of twenty lost last night, for what?

* * *

Twelve minutes before the DR position of Mannheim the gleaming needle on the port engine temperature gauge was still climbing up towards the danger line. "This bloody kite," Tony found himself thinking, "will be the death of me," and in spite of himself he laughed aloud. All the same, B Bastard put the shits up him a sight more than the apparently unlikely prospect of flak and fighters.

For this second op was like seeing a boring movie round again, another waste of time, flying above cloud, killing icing cloud that hid the ground, below cloud that hid the moon, but essentially a Green Line bus trip to Wolverhampton, a repeat of the quiet times of the night before last's trip to, do let me know if you see it, Duisburg. Empty darkness, soporific rumble of engines. Gyro, air speed indicator, altimeter, artificial horizon, engine revs, fuel, oil temperatures—the port needle was steady, hadn't risen any higher.

Tony had landed from the afternoon's Night Flying Test with a u/s port oil temperature gauge, the needle stuck on zero. Whereupon an instrument basher had put in a brand new gauge and if this had been any other kite but B Bastard the only possible thing to do would be to drop the bombs somewhere over Germany and high-tail it for home, forget about

Mannheim and hope it won't be a single-engined landing with a feathered port prop.

But B Bastard notoriously crawled with gremlins, those mythical creatures that busied themselves around aircraft, doing mischief that defied all logic, gremlins that would, say, wreak havoc with a just-installed engine straight from the factory bench where it had been painstakingly tested and found perfect. A blasphemous pilot would land with it, dicey do, Ubendem Wemendem would take the recalcitrant engine to bits, find nothing whatever wrong with it, put it back on the kite and another white-faced pilot would lob in with a similar hell of a moan. Gremlins.

The luminous needle jerked up another fraction nearer the danger line. Hard-to-resist temptation to pull the plug and turn for home. For all Tony knew, the bombs might do a better job if they went down here and now, it it was only going through the motions of this bloody nonsensical raid to fly on to the Dead Reckoning position that a hundred to one was nowhere near Mannheim.

Flak and fighters and the chance, however, remote, of an overheated port engine catching fire were tiresome enough but Tony was as cold as charity and that's fucking chilly, the freezing draught was fair howling through the ill-fitting windows, his knee, far from being scalded, wasn't even warm, the hot air pipe just puffed from time to time, and Tony desperately wanted to pee but was too utterly shagged to go through all the performance of unstrapping and undoing, and fiddling with that absurdly ill-designed funnel that immediately filled up and slopped the stuff everywhere.

Hot cocoa, rum, safety and one's downy beckoned seductively. The needle edged up a trifle, oh, my, I don't want to die, I want to go home.

"Navigator to pilot, six minutes to DR Mannheim."

Gremlins in the temperature gauge or an overheating engine—on to Mannheim or turn for home? Stooge on, Marlowe, he chided. "Roger, Bill. Thank you."

On time but it felt like a whole hour later Bill was up front at his bombsight, going through the comedy of setting the timing switch and thumbing the button to drop the bombs, one, two, three, four, and the hundreds of tumbling incendiaries across the mathematical abstraction, the symbol Bill drew on his chart, the pencilled square with the dot in the middle that was DR Mannheim. Bombs gone, bomb doors closed, farce over, duty done, turn for home, henfruit and downy.

Stooging on, Tony found himself recalling the beaten-up old radio in his room at home, Dad had passed it on to him when they got their posh new Murphy. Trouble with the set was that programmes were always liable to shift off frequency, no great worry, you gave it a clout and Saturday Night Theatre was back, strength ten. He reached forward and gave the lagging temperature gauge a whack that hurt his knuckles. The needle sagged down, all Sir Garnet, back on normal.

Yet as they stooged interminably on, crossing the mathematical Dutch coast, turning on DR over the North Sea, crossing the English coast, pundits flashing as the cloud cleared, thirty-two miles south of track, once again only God knew where the bombs had fallen, picking up the red beacons, RJ, BL, FW, the worry nagged at Tony, something was wrong, was it just the worry of overwhelming fatigue, was it B Bastard's port engine—almost he decided to ask Bill for a change of course to Hawksthorn, now minutes away to the west of their track, to get down as soon and as safely as possible in case that damn engine started to play games. In spite of the needle sitting firmly at normal.

So strong was his worry that Hawksthorn was touch and go. But tiredness, he told himself, led to strange fancies. Onley Market next stop, he decided, can't be influenced by vague dreads. Besides, Tony was honest enough to admit, lob in at Hawksthorn and he might be stuck there for a day or more while they checked out the port engine and Hawksthorn was the last place he wanted to be, with Kate at Onley Market.

He was unbelievably tired but the wakey-wakey pills he'd taken, this time correctly at take-off, were doing their stuff, and he touched down, light as a feather, on the Onley Market runway. The port engine coughed three times and died. Christ.

If it had cut seconds earlier they'd have gone in like a ton of bricks. He sat, heart thumping. Took a deep breath, 'Pilot to crew, I'm taxying on one engine, no panic." Once again he rapped a knuckle on the temperature gauge and the needle swooped up far, far past the danger line. Gremlins.

"Lucky to get back with this bleeder, sir," said Chiefy Woods, the flight-sergeant of the ground crew, as Tony blissfully peed gallons. Chiefy spat on the engine cowling, a globule hissed. What the hell, B Bastard was down on the deck.

"Bombed Mannheim, primary target," wrote the Greek "e" specialist, the egg tasted scrumptious, the wakey-wakey pills had worn off. Number two done. Tony's face cracked with a yawn. Exhausted. Twenty-eight to go.

Everybody was back, Cattermole, Twinkletoes, Chalkey—only one more to finish his tour—no aircraft missing tonight. Tony's last thought at night and first next morning was, be seeing Kate tonight. Mistakenly, as next afternoon's Battle Order was to show.

* * *

"Tony! Tony!" Tich Cattermole urgently shaking him awake, Tony's eyes opening slowly, he came lurching up from the depths of sleep, the glare of the ceiling light a white explosion, slowly coming awake, remembering, angry, so unfair, so bloody unfair.

"Tony! Take-off in an hour!"

The room clearing around him, two metal beds, brown blankets, a window with a black-out screen, white walls, the pin-up of the luscious brunette rompily smiling in camiknicks, Cattermole's scribble, "More, Tich, more! Again! Again! Your adoring Rita." So bloody unfair.

Ten hours ago Tony had gone down to the Crew Room a walking zombie after last night's op to DR Mannheim. He'd seen the toy tractors pulling the lines of bomb-laden trolleys but known for sure he wouldn't be flying tonight. Amp-amp-amp-amp, couldn't believe his eyes, P/O Marlowe, Sgt. Wilberforce, Sills, Ramsbottom, Eckersley up on the Battle Order. They were one of only three crews to be operating. Chalkey wouldn't be flying that worrying thirtieth and, as for lucky Tich, he'd have his swede bashed to his pillow all night long.

Tony's afternoon had crept by in a daze of fatigue, concentration was a second-to-second effort, on the NFT he'd bounced B Bastard twice on the runway before it settled. "Essen," Bill had murmured before Main Briefing began, in which Eckersley wasn't alone in falling fast asleep.

Bit of a shambles anyway, chaps chucking facts at you, hurry, hurry, hurry. They rushed through the meal in the Mess, speckled liver again, cake in custard—and then, sure enough, take-off was postponed two hours, chance to snatch a small allowance of kip before Tich's rise-and-shine call.

"I've signed for you," Tich was saying. Signed? Oh, yes, they sent round an orderly to wake you, you wrote your name on a list to show you were conscious. Tony grunted his thanks, filled the canvas washbasin from the water-jug, stuck his head under, came up blowing and gasping. "Tea. Scrounged it from the Mess." Good old Tich was unscrewing the cup from a Thermos.

Hot and sugary. I'll live, thought Tony, as he pulled on his battledress. He'd brought his flying-kit into the room, helmet, parachute, Mae West, dinghy, the lot, after they'd changed take-off time; as a pyjamaed Tich held them out he climbed into Irvin jacket, heaved on flying-boots.

All ready now to be picked up by the van at the Mess; he thanked Tich for the tea, was wished all the best, was called back—forgotten his escape maps. Tich could now curl up and sleep the rest of the night away, Tony would be, cross fingers, back from Essen long before he woke. Lucky sod. Damn decent of him, though, to go to all that trouble about the tea. Good type, old Tich.

The van with its hooded headlights was waiting outside the Mess but Sills wasn't, it was almost ten minutes before he came dashing up, the damn fool had signed himself awake and then zonked back to sleep. The Waaf drove the van like the clappers to B Bastard's hardstanding, needn't have bothered. Ramsarse had picked up his parachute by the release handle, pop, nylon all over the grass, a billowing white lake in the darkness.

Nothing to do but wait and Tony slept in his seat in B Bastard till the van scurried back with a panicking Ramsarse clutching a fresh parachute. Everybody aboard, Tony taxied faster than he liked round the perimeter track and reached the end of the runway just as the second of the other two Wimpeys climbed away, dah dit dit dit, and B Bastard was airborne.

Nothing to remember about that op, moment to moment no more than a struggle to stay awake. Just a third run of the same movie, routine, flying in that same sandwich of cloud, routine to change course over Bill's dots in squares that marked the hope-we're-here DR positions, not a clue where they really were.

Routine for Bill to press the tit that dropped the bombs over one more dot-in-a-square that was supposed to be, where? Tony, not actually giving a damn, had to search his memory—Essen. Routine to stooge on and on, fighting not to doze and die, finally to pick out the white-flashing pundit on the English coast, Southwold, thirty-five miles south of where they should be, where the bombs had fallen only God, as usual, knew.

It wasn't until the final approach to the flare-path at Onley Market that Tony yielded to the temptation to put B Bastard to the test. The clapped-out fucker had droned on and on like an ancient family saloon due to be pensioned off but nothing, really, to complain about.

They had worked wonders on the port engine before that afternoon's NFT. The oil temperature gauge read a reassuring normal, goodbye gremlins, Tony rapped the dial, the needle shot above the danger line.

He was instantly wide awake, he was sure, absolutely certain the dial was u/s, but it was sick that he swallowed as he touched B Bastard safely down.

"Really behaved itself this time," said Chiefy Woods. B Bastard's having fun with us, it means to kill us, it'll be the death of us, but Tony just nodded.

Death of us, in his mind as the Intelligence Office wrote, "Bombed Essen, primary target." Bill said angrily, "But it's not—" and then was silent. Maybe he, too, thought ops a dangerous waste of time.

Death of us. But waste of time and energy to be afraid when you're out of danger, Tich Cattermole snoring in the next bed. Tomorrow—no, today—for sure Tony would be seeing Kate; Twinkletoes, up before dawn to welcome home his handful of crews had given them all the day off. Three ops done, twenty-seven to do.

* * *

"Early English," said Tony, revived by an eleven-hour kip, as he drove Kate into the rain-drenched early evening of Onley Market, "Perpendicular," as he drove out but still she sat silently staring ahead, she hadn't spoken, not even when he had picked her up at the Waafery. He was scared stiff he'd upset her in some unknown way and, troubled, he backed up on to the familiar verge.

She sat tense, rigid, her lovely face a marble sculpture. To destroy the silence he said, "There's a restaurant called the Magpie five miles on, sometimes they serve black-market—" her arms savagely round his neck, her lips twisting hard against his; she pulled her head back, wildness in her huge blue eyes, her face a mask of misery.

"In the office," between sobs, "in the office I had to pretend—that I was just pleased to see you and the night before, when I saw that plane blow up I thought, if that's you, I want to die."

God, he thought, things aren't real when they happen, a Wimpey crashing on take-off, B Bastard trying to kill you, it's afterwards that they start to have meaning. If you let them. His hands were trembling, he took her in his arms. She laid her head on his shoulder; gently, he stroked her tear-stained cheek.

"I'm sorry," not looking at him, "may I borrow your hanky?" She blew her nose loudly and they sat warm in each other's arms, too close for the need of words.

When she spoke again, he could hear her happiness. "Lucky you've got such a big handkerchief. Who's A.H.T.M.?"

"Me. My initials. My mother embroidered them."

"I feel as if I've known you the whole of my life," she said, "and I don't even know all your names."

"Anthony Hartley Tregellis Marlowe. Hartley's my father's Christian name. My mother was Tregellis before she married Dad, she's from the West Country." Then, "Sorry, did you say something?"

"No," she lied. She'd experimented: Catherine Marlowe.

The windows inside the car had misted up, Tony began to draw the outline of a Wimpey, then hurriedly scribbled a porthole. "Someone's coming down the lane."

"Tell him to cover us with leaves."

Of all people, Bill Wilberforce, trudging through the downpour in mackintosh cape. Sod. If there was one thing Tony didn't want it was extra companionship. "It's my navigator."

Couldn't possibly leave him out in the rain. "Better ask him in, I suppose?"

"Suppose so." Kate was cheerfully vexed.

Tony wound down the side window, yelled "Bill," opened the door, got out, pulled back the front seat, was soaked. Bill climbed in, rivers flooding down his shiny cape, introductions, fancy seeing you.

"You fly with Tony? Goodness, how brave."

"Where are you off to, Bill?"

Embarrassed, "I'm on my way home, Tony." Home? "I've rented a cottage about a mile further on for me and Beryl. My wife," he explained. "I'm living out."

Aircrew on ops, strictly speaking, were forbidden to live away from the airfield but one or two of the very few married ones did, perfectly possible, nobody ever asked you where you'd been so long as you were in the Crew Room by oh-eight-hundred. Funny, though, how Bill spoke with the guilt of a schoolmaster to whom all rules were sacred. Put up a fourteen-thousand-foot No Trespassers sign on the German border, Tony thought fondly, and Bill would obediently turn right back.

"We'll give you a lift," offered Tony. A protest, no, really, I'll walk. "Nonsense," said Kate.

The sodden lane led into a narrow waterlogged road where two rows of cottages stared amiably into each other's windows. "Potterhampton," said Bill, lengthy name for a tiny hamlet. "Here we are, third on the left. Come on in."

Squeak of gate, three strides of rain-pelted front garden, jingle of keys, another squeak, of a plain wooden door. "Ber-yl! I'm home! Brought company."

A black-out curtain rattled on wooden rings and they stepped directly into a little room crammed with furniture. Kitchen chairs, a table with a white cloth laid for two, with a massive EPNS gedinkus holding salt, pepper, oil and vinegar.

Shabby reddish sofa hung with bobbles, two antimacassared armchairs, one showing a glimpse of oatmeal guts beneath a discouraged cushion. A too-big sideboard. Small china ornaments everywhere on the mantelpiece and brackets and spindly tables, anxious to crash into tinkling pieces at the first unrestrained gesture. A large heavily-framed photograph, a patriarch with a white, tobacco-stained W. G. Grace beard and ventriloquist eyes.

The undersized windows were covered with cardboard black-out screens and shielded by cabbage-rose curtains. Beneath that laden mantelpiece a wood fire burned in a polished black grate beside a big-knobbed oven. Above, a bland round-faced loud-ticking clock, "Jno. Lowell, Sons & Coy., Spalding. 1907."

"Not grand, but it's homely," said Bill's wife, coming in from the door beyond, behind her a glimpse of hanging shiny sauce-pans and a probably 1907 cooker.

"Tony, meet the wife. Mother, this is Tony Marlowe, my pilot"—glance of surprise at Tony's age, look of reassurance at his officer's uniform—"and his good lady friend, Kate, er—"

"Kate Elliot." Firelight danced in her eyes. "How d'you do, Mrs Wilberforce?"

"Pleased to meet you, Kate, dearie, and you, Tony. Call me Beryl, do." She smiled, her teeth were noticeably false, her brown hair wiry sausages, she was wearing something brownish and woolly, a pink apron, red slippers. "Bill usually has his tea about now, you'll stay for a bite, won't you? Yes, yes, you must, I won't take no for an answer. Come on, Kate, luv, give me a hand in the kitchen, we'll leave the men to have their talk."

Bill said, "Look at that. Always does it, soon as I come in." He lifted a very plump tabby cat off the unoatmealed and obviously privileged chair. "Mother, Stripey's done it again!"

Giggle from the kitchen. "Pinched your throne again, has he, hubby?" Then Kate's voice and a shriek of laughter from Beryl. The cat was put down carefully, sparing his dignity, on the patchwork rug by the fire. "We've left both the kiddies with Gran," Bill was thumbing the tabby's ear, "But we couldn't leave you, could we? Not our old Stripey."

Puff, puff, Bill was lighting the pipe he'd filled from the tobacco-jar with the London University arms. Stupefied by domesticity, Tony said, "You've certainly made it very com-fortable."

"It's home," said Bill, simply. "Oh," shyly, "the arrange-ments. Outside, I'm afraid. Opposite the back door. Excuse me, Tony, I'll just go and change."

So much for the Magpie, the restaurant Tony knew that sometimes served black-market steak and where you could always rely on legal jugged hare or pigeon pie. They had stew and strong dark tea and, special treat, pineapple chunks with the evaporated milk Bill saved from briefings.

Photographs were passed round as Stripey stretched luxuriously by the blazing logs of the fire, Kate making all the right noises, Tony helping with admiring hmmmms. "This is Shirley, she's only four, wouldn't think so, would you, and here's Norm, not very good of him, he moved. He's two now, this was taken last year in his pram. Sturdy little nipper, isn't he?" Does he stuff his arse with powdered glass?

Close to Cinderella's midnight a dazed Tony was driving Kate back to the Waafery. Difficult to get a grip, he was staggered, in fact, awestruck at how deeply Kate felt for him—and he for Kate. Enough and to spare, this discovery.

But on top of that was this new knowledge of a Bill Wilberforce so unlike the Bill he knew in the Crew Room and aboard B Bastard. Kate said, "Nice people."

"Yes." Being with them was like soaking in a warm bath of affection. "You can't believe how different Bill is at home to what he's like in a Wimpey."

"I can imagine," said Kate. "Two kinds of Bill."

This other Bill had been a stranger, likeable, but older than Tony by a whole generation, not just a matter of ten years; schoolmaster, husband, father, breadwinner. He'd worn grey flannels, a cardigan like a very old retired Airedale and felt slippers. His bald patch had been very pink in the firelight.

This hubby, this proud displayer of kiddies' photos, this contented family man seemed to have no connection whatsoever with the Bill Wilberforce in leather helmet and fur-lined Irvin who spoke so calmly in Tony's earphones, who had flown with him in meccano and canvas in the cumulo-nimbus that had switchbacked B Bastard—chill at Tony's heart, the aircraft that wanted them to die—the Bill Wilberforce who grabbed and fired the Verey pistol as the flak flung them about the darkened sky. Perhaps, Tony thought, there are two kinds of me. One Tony in love with Kate; the other Tony a machine that sat in a Wimpey's cockpit, nerves reacting to luminous needles and numbers, obeying the demands of Bill's pencilled lines and symbols.

2357, here was the Waafery. He and Kate kissed goodnight,

mustn't take too long, she was through the gate seconds before they began taking names.

It hadn't by any means been the evening Tony had planned but it hadn't been wasted, oh, no. Just before they left an embarrassed Bill had taken Tony on one side, fumbled with his pipe, and told him quietly, guiltily breaking rules, that he and Beryl always went to see the kiddies and Gran whenever there was a forty-eight and would Tony and Kate like to, er, use the cottage while they were away?

* * *

On ops you could usually rely on a stand-down, a day off, once a week and your seven days' leave came round about every six weeks and now and again you got a forty-eight if you were lucky and Tony couldn't believe his luck when the very next morning Twinkletoes told him and the crew in his normal courteous way, bog off for the next couple of days and try not to get a dose.

So Tony bogged, immediately. The first day he joined the squadron he saw what happened if you didn't, that single neat perfectly circular hole in the centre of the perspex of that Wimpey's rear turret; the crew's regular Arse-End Charley had gone sick and if the chap who replaced him had gone on leave right away and not stayed for a second cup of tea he wouldn't have been sitting behind that hole. "Silly bastard," said Chalkey.

No pausing for a cup of tea by either Tony or Bill, the Morris shot out of RAF Station, Onley Market, like a jack-in-the-box and now here they were at the cottage with Beryl giving a whoop of glee. Half-hour drive to Lincoln station, Stripey in a wicker basket muttering to himself, a train was caught with three minutes to spare—long enough for Beryl to say, "I've changed the sheets, Tony," and then to hug him tightly, camphor and lavender.

Tony went to two chemists in Lincoln, that packet in his wallet was getting a bit rumpled. You couldn't be sure that the shop in Onley Market village would be stocked and both times a girl assistant came to serve him and both times, shyly, he bought aspirins. Third shop, he decided he'd got enough aspirins.

"Yes, how many?"

"Er, six packets, please."

When the middle-aged woman in the white smock smiled, a dimple came. "If you find yourself running short," she said, "we're open till ten tonight."

On the road back there was a Good Pull-Up for Lorries where, rumour went, you could fiddle the odd gallon or two at black-market prices. A rubber tube was dipped into the lorry's tank, petrol was sucked up and siphoned into Tony's Morris. The walrus-moustached lorry driver wouldn't take a penny over the petrol-pump price. "Least we can do for you boys in blue," he said irritably.

One more chore remained, once back in Potterhampton. There was a public telephone in the post-office-cum-sweet-shop, the hamlet's sole commercial enterprise. Tony pressed Button A, heart pounding, ops tonight and his call wouldn't be answered, no Kate, she'd be confined to camp-amp-amp-amp.

"Royal Air Force Station, Onley Market"—thank God for that. Then Kate's husky voice, "Station Navigation Office."

All he told her was, he'd got a forty-eight, would pick her up at the Waafery at six-fifteen. "Yes," she said formally, "I've made a note," Tubbs in the next office, probably, "thank you."

Jno. Lowell, Sons & Coy., Spalding, bonged half-past two. Tony had lunched nutritiously if undeliciously on cod and chips in Lincoln, he hadn't wanted to ring Kate till well after the noonish deadline for ops and now he'd got absolutely nothing to do and had begun to feel that same mixture of emotions, dash of terror, attack of stage-fright, that he'd experienced before his first op—was that really less than a week ago?

Only seven nights, after all, since he'd met Kate at the All Ranks Dance, wasn't he taking a hell of a lot for granted, loading himself up with purple packets? Her father's a vicar, she's probably been very strictly brought up, apple cores or no apple cores, tonight may start and end with a furious blue glare, she'd be affronted, insulted, he'd never know the nearness of her ever again.

And even suppose she wasn't angry, didn't say no, suppose he made a balls, oh, hell, a cock-up, oh, damn it all, suppose things didn't work? Not, mind you, that at nineteen he was totally inexperienced, what with elementary explorations on many a sofa, which, by the time he reached the Lower Sixth, constantly resulted in his and Janet's or Betty's or Jennifer's or whoever's mutual pleasure and relief.

He didn't use it to stir his tea, in fact he'd actually Got It In (just): last summer a friend's sister had got married and the sister's sister, eight years older, had been a bridesmaid. He'd given her a lift home to her flat and she asked him in for a cup of tea. You could have knocked him down with a feather when she came out of the bathroom, starkers.

No sense in standing here idly worrying, getting cold feet, or cold whatever. He began to mooch about, exploring the cottage. Didn't take long.

A tiny kitchen where you washed as well as cooked, for anything more ambitious you had a tin bath by the fire, he pictured Kate soapy in a rosy glow, cheered up enormously. Two bedrooms upstairs, one crowded with a couple of belted trunks, a pile of suitcases, some without handles, a treadle sewing-machine and a dressmaker's dummy like an executed dowager, bric-à-brac left behind by the owners of the cottage.

The other bedroom had a massive mahogany wardrobe, two wooden chairs, a couple of bedside tables, on one a book on conic sections, on the other a pile of *Woman's Own*. The bed was, wizard, a big double. He prodded it experimentally and a spring loudly twanged.

Back in the kitchen three-quarters of a loaf and a saucer of margarine camped under a muslin wigwam with two precious tins left for them by Beryl in the kindness of her heart, corned beef, sliced peaches, treasured, saved-up rations. Not forgetting a large jar of home-made pickled onions, the size and apparently the hardness of golf balls, Tony longed for one, just managed to stop himself in time.

To keep busy he went out into the tiny garden and found a rusty lawnmower in a tumbledown shed next to the arrangements. He cut the grass in his shirtsleeves, after which he got down to some therapeutic weeding; devil of a job later, scrubbing the earth out of his fingernails.

He stopped the Morris outside the gate, found he couldn't look at her. Ashamed, he mumbled, "Bill said we could have the cottage," felt himself blushing, not just his cheeks, flushing all over. Kate didn't speak, he waited, apprehensive, heard her opening her WAAF issue handbag.

"Tony," she said, he still couldn't look at her. Again, "Tony. Beryl told me." He turned towards her, she was holding up a bright red toothbrush.

She went upstairs first while he waited below in the cramped front room, his nervousness returning; almost, when the time came, he was too scared to go up to her.

Shining hair strewn on a pillow, huge blue serious eyes. He kept his back to her as he undressed, quickly pulled back the covers, put his weight on the bed, PLOI-ING!

Kate started to giggle, they both burst out laughing but they didn't laugh for long, he was smoothly, warmly, gently, then urgently inside her, they were thrusting together, she winced, clutched him even closer, thrusting, thrusting, thrusting and then, oh, Jesus, Jesus, B Bastard could kill him any time it wanted, this was the life he'd lived.

* * *

The telephone was burr-burring the engaged signal in the stillness of the early Potterhampton afternoon. "If you're calling that there airydrome," said the tiny postmistress, in her big brown spectacles peering like a friendly owl between jars of Pascall's fruit drops and Mackintosh's toffee, "You won't get no answer, them airyplanes is going out tonight."

Nothing for it, then, but a solitary evening drive without Kate for company to meet Bill, Beryl and Stripey from the eight-twelve, pity; but better by far ops tonight than last night. Five hours Tony and Kate had been together before he had to drive her back near midnight to Onley Market. Five hours, five days, five weeks, five lifetimes.

Back at the cottage he put clean sheets on the bed, tidied up, ate six pickled onions, read an entire serial in *Woman's Own* and got in some more weeding. Off to Lincoln—train was twenty minutes late, what did you expect? Bill and Beryl were quiet on the way home, tired out probably. Bit of a wrench, too, leaving the children.

So when they invited Tony to stay the night, he accepted, sensing they'd be lonely, just the two of them in the cottage after the noise and fuss of Shirley and Norm and Gran at somewhere called Little Harbury, change at Peterborough.

"You never touched the corned beef! Or the peaches!" tut-tutted Beryl, as she went straight into the kitchen to peel potatoes. They shared a late supper, scrunching onions, the wireless a quietly burbling background, a nice talk on the rather charming habits of the otter, as the squadron airyplanes climbed noisily over the roof, ignored by common consent.

Not long before dawn they came droning back, waking Tony as he lay curled up on the bobbled sofa beside the last embers of the fire, Stripey comfortable behind his knees, how many coming back?

The white-haired squadron-leader with the God-bothering collar held out his hand. "It's always better," he said, "if I read them first, before we send them on, I'm sure you understand." Tony passed over Tich's bundle of letters, fastened with an elastic band.

There were cardboard boxes strewn on the floor and on the bed where the Station Padre sat; beside the wardrobe the Squadron Adjutant was going through uniform pockets. The Committee of Adjustment always got there in a hurry. It was odd how often a father or a wife would make all kinds of fuss if something quite inconsequential wasn't sent back, a cigarette-lighter, a fountain pen, a paperback book. The Adjutant held up a tortoiseshell hairbrush, lifted an eyebrow, Tony nodded yes, it was put carefully in a Carnation Milk box.

Tony unpinned Rita Hayworth, ripped the picture across, dropped it beside two torn-up letters in the wastepaper-basket. The Padre was skimming through Tich's diary; the Adjutant counted a few pennies out of his pocket and put them in an envelope. Awkwardly, "Makes it look as if we've really been careful."

"Anything else?" asked the Padre with great politeness. "Anything he lent you, I mean?" Tony considered a moment, he and Tich had shared soap, books, writing-paper, what's yours is mine. He went through his chest of drawers, found nothing, at the last moment saw the Thermos flask on top of the wardrobe.

"That's it, then," said the Adjutant. Hadn't taken long, wasn't much more than half an hour since the Tannoy had called Tony to the room on Site Four as he and Bill waited in the empty Crew Room well before the statutory oh-eight-hundred. He helped carry the carefully-marked boxes out to the Padre's car and stacked them among the others already on the seats, five Committees of Adjustment every time a Wimpey went down. Poor bloody Tich.

The thrash, and what a thrash it turned out to be, started in the Mess well before lunchtime, no ops tonight. When they started taking the trousers off Flight-Lieutenant Watson, Chalkey White's navigator, the Queen Bee eyebrowed up the other WAAF officers and shushed them away, grinning, into their own hidey-hole.

"Sorry to hear about poor old Tich," Doc Watson was saying to Tony, by now they were drinking the Harpic straight out of the white enamel jugs. His eyes shone with happiness, he was wearing a kind of emergency kilt made out of *The Times*. That was just before they all went over to the Sergeants' Mess, Twinkletoes leading the way, everyone singing, "All of a sudden came into my head, A thought concerning O'Reilly's daughter, Up those stairs and into bed . . ."

Under the stony, contemptuous glares of the Station Warrant Officer and his admin cronies, how they loathed the NCO aircrew—jumped-up sergeants, numbers like the population of China, in the Service less than a year, up go their three stripes, hard to swallow that, when you've waited twenty for yours—Twinkletoes led his squadron in songs, leapfrog and such other games as The Muffin Man. "Does Eckersley know the Muffin Man, the Muffin Man—"

"Hard luck, Eck," said Tony, all charm, as the pint mug on his gunner's head slipped, staggered and drenched him with mild ale. "How are you feeling now?" soon after Ramsarse threw up. "Good time, Sills?" White-faced stare, dash for the ablutions.

Away from the general riot, Bill was sitting quietly in an armchair, looks as if even he'd had enough beer to glaze him over. But Bill's probably welcoming a bit of a coma, must be hell to leave Gran and the kids and return to ops.

Come to think of it, Tony was feeling just a bit hazy himself. Here was Chalkey, back from the op that had claimed Tich, thirty-trip Chalkey, tour-over-and-done-with Chalkey, six months to go before he need ever fly another op. Fly another tour, Chalkey, and you'll be finished with ops altogether. A second tour? When they make so much fuss over a crew finishing one?

"Christ," said Chalkey, he wasn't sober. "We made it, we fucking made it. Last time we had this kind of bash was the middle of February." He screwed up his eyes, smaller and redder than ever. "Oh, it's you, Tony. Bloody good show, wasn't it, Tich Cattermole pranging B Bastard?"

B Bastard? He'd been flying B Bastard? Super. Wizard. B Bastard had killed its victims. Not Tony. Not Bill. Oh, Kate, Kate, woozily said the voice in Tony's mind, I'm two people, I really am, your Tony and operational Tony. Squadron life is like no other life, Kate; Tich was my friend, the chum of a week. I liked him, but not as much as I hated B Bastard. B Bastard wanted to kill a crew. It killed Tich's. It's life and death, see, Kate, my life, Tich's death. He was drunker than he thought, chessmen frying, Cattermole dying, I'm a poet and don't know it, oh, Kate, what's happening?

* * *

They'd got a new kite now that Tich had pranged B Bastard. It was G George, count the bombs stencilled on its nose, it had done eleven ops. After the Bastard it felt as reliable, if far less comfortable, as Tony's father's Rover. And now that Tony had three ops under his belt, a sprog was he no longer, for those were the worst killers of all, those first three ops, when crews dropped the real clangers, didn't know whether you were on your arse or your elbow.

Now Tony was settled down, he imagined, to the sheer routine of ops. Another to be flown? Same old movie, he'd seen it before, three times, Duisburg, Mannheim, Essen, Errors and Omissions Excepted. This afternoon it was running again.

"Hanover," Bill had whispered before the Perambulating Prick scowled from the stage at the aircrews and prattled testily on about It Not Being In The Tradition Of The Service for officers to address non-commissioned officers by their Christian names (odd way to run an Air Force: in the air Flight-Lieutenant Doc Watson had to jump to it every time Flight-Sergeant Chalkey White issued an order. On the ground Chalkey was supposed to spring to attention and salute Doc) as Twinkletoes sat with his face unreadable, everyone knew about the rocket he'd got from the Prick over yesterday's thrash in the Sergeants' Mess.

Not to reason why, treat everything as routine, that was the only way to handle life in Bomber Command. Routine that Hickey and Tinker and Geordie and Phil hadn't come back. Routine that Tich and his crew were dead—a stutter of Morse had told Onley Market they were ditching, Tich's wireless-operator screwed down his key for a fix to be taken on their position, the steady tone stopped abruptly; at dawn Twinkletoes and Tubby in a squadron Wimpey had gone out with the Air Sea Rescue Walrus amphibians to fly a search. Nothing.

Routine, too, that Chalkey and his crew had finished their thirty and gone off to instruct at an OTU for a statutory six months before their next tour and presumably do their part in keeping the Bomber Command conspiracy going. Also routine not to ponder too long that no other crew had completed a tour since five weeks before Tony had joined the squadron.

Flak winking in the sky a dozen miles to starboard, first they'd seen over Europe. "Seven minutes to Dead Reckoning Hanover," said Bill.

Bill, as always, was his quiet, efficient self—too quiet, perhaps, he'd hardly spoken a word since yesterday's thrash, maybe that glaze had been more than beer. Gaps in the cloud.

"Going down, Bill, to look for Hanover."

Further gaps opening up, out of the cloud altogether, that was Germany down there, seeing it for the first time, featureless, just a darker black than the night.

ETA Hanover. Still nothing.

Bill up front at the bombsight, there should be the hell of a great river, the Leine, curving in front of G George, not a glint of it, they were over the dot in the square that should have been the target—

"Airfield!" shouted Tony. Tiny lines of dotted lights had suddenly switched on, moving red and green specks far below, a runway, a Luftwaffe night-fighter on the approach to land, "Airfield! Plaster the bloody thing!" At last, some return for all this useless stooging—

Bill, urgently, "Open bomb doors!"

Christ, he'd forgotten, down with the lever, "Bombs fused, Bill?"

"Bombs fused." No chance of Bill's not remembering. "Left, left. Right." Calm as you please. "Right. Steady. Ste-a-dy. Ste-a-dy." Excitedly, "Bombs gone. Bomb doors up."

"Bomb doors closed, Bill." Wait. Watch. Four winking bomb bursts across the flarepath, flarepath goes out. "Bloody good sh—" Curving up, pretty splinters of light, climbing slowly, gathering wicked speed, tracer, dead men's fingers, blobs of orange, yellow, bright red, exploding far below, fired uselessly in anger.

Nose down, dive for speed, from the ground three blazing shafts of light, ruler straight, tumbling up towards G George, throttles wide open, full boost, dive steeper, speed, speed, dazzling light, brilliance in the cockpit, darkness again, a searchlight had snapped over G George, fewer blobs, fewer still, none. Don't just sit there, a nightfighter's climbing towards us, he's in a snit, wants another RAF roundel on his nose, another line to shoot in the Mess, up, up, up, hide in the cloud, come on, G George, thank God we're not in clapped-out B bastard, thank you, Tich.

"Keep your eyes peeled, gunners," up and up towards the cloud, "if you see him, shoot his goolies off," up, up, first wisps of cloud coming and going, cloud closing in, darker darkness, wisps again, stammer of guns from the front turret, tang of cordite, "Stop firing, Ramsbottom, that's a Wimpey," fancy meeting you, cloud deepening, safe.

"Course for enemy coast, please, Bill."

"Tony, steer 326 Compass." Sounds on top of the world.

"326, roger."

Safe? Don't be a quim, flak to dodge at Bremen, Wilhelmshaven, Emden and all stations to Onley Market. But stooge on, exhilarated, at last something worth while, our Trip Really Was Necessary, not to mention flak dodged and two fingers to a fighter.

Stooge on.

White fringe of sea, enemy coast. An island.

"Pinpoint, Tony. Nordeney. Somehow we're where we ought to be." Where Hanover moved to, we'll never know.

Onley Market, the circuit full of Wimpeys. K King calling

the Control Tower, "Boomerang, we have a wounded wireless-operator." Pleading, "Request priority, repeat, request priority."

"Roger, K King. All aircraft from Boomerang, all aircraft from Boomerang, do not land, do not land. Clear to land, K King."

K King landing, streak of dimmed headlights, ambulance.

Round and round the circuit, a long time later, "Boomerang to G George, clear to land."

A van swung out of the darkness on to the perimeter track beside G George's hardstanding. "Died," said the big WAAF driver they called My Brother Sylvest. "Johnny Woodham. Dead," she said flatly. Tony felt a surge of delight, loathing himself, there it was again, we left the cannon shells and flak behind, it's Johnny Woodham who's dead, not us. He'll never do that trick again, walking upside down, bottles in his hands, saw him do it at Chalkey's party, Johnny's dead and we're alive, alive-oh.

They were piling their equipment in the back of My Brother Sylvest's van and Tony was heaving his harness of parachute and dinghy aboard when they heard the Wimpey coming in, engines grinding like berserk ironmongery. A shape darker than the blackness behind skimmed low over the runway lights, lower, lower, hit the ground with a ripping, squealing crash, bounced high, ripped and squealed again, an engine rather informally detached itself and lazily climbed away, up and over in a parabola, streaming flame, as the Wimpey bounced yet again, rather gently, and swerved off the runway to come to a sudden stop, apologising for all the fuss, nose pointing towards G George's hardstanding a couple of hundred yards away.

Splashes of petrol burning in bright pools lit the ruin of the Wimpey, Dick's in there, Tony knew it with unsurprised, absolute certainty, "Out!" he yelled at My Brother Sylvest, shoving her from behind the wheel.

He kicked down the clutch, slammed in the gear, lurched away, bumping, gathering speed across the grass. Was Dick, of course it was Dick, slumped over the control column, nobody else in the Wimpey, Tony could see through the flak-ripped canvas, the twisted aluminium struts, to reach Dick he only had to step into the cockpit. A fringe of fire laced the Wimpey's wing, come on, Dick, don't loll about, Tony was swamped with a shuddering wave of terror, not at the pretty blue flame flooding the wing above the petrol tanks but at the whisper in his mind, leave him, leave him, the kite's going to explode, run, run, leave him.

Without undue haste, Tony undid the strap beneath Dick's chin and lifted off the helmet, quicker than disconnecting oxygen tube and intercom lead. He reached for and pulled the pin of the Sutton harness and hit the metal circle of the parachute release, a loud click, Dick was free. Christ, he was so heavy, he pulled with all his strength at the deadweight, Dick's dangling feet were scraping channels in the grass, blood pounding in Tony's ears, can't pull him much further.

Dick mumbling, coming round, he said, fuzzily, "What the fuck?" Tony wheezed, "Move! Move!" they were running, Tony felt his legs lifted from under him, the shock of the explosion flung him down on his face, Dick beside him. Out of nowhere, inches close, a fire-engine roared past.

They sat together, panting, the sky red with the bonfire of Dick's Wimpey, the air heavy with the choke of burning oil. After a while Dick said, with extraordinary politeness, "Thank you, Tony. Thank you very much indeed."

Tremendous fuss made of Tony at debriefing by Twinkletoes, the other crews, the Waafs with the cocoa and rum, after a protesting Dick had been whisked off in an ambulance. Now the crew sat alone, everyone else except Johnny Woodham gone for the operational egg.

Gold-plated pen, "Bombed unidentified enemy airfield, target of opportunity," lovely Greek "e"s. The Intelligence Officer sounded dissatisfied, he and Bomber Command would very much have preferred bombs on a dot in a square, primary target.

* * *

Twinkletoes leaned back in his chair and put a size-12 foot on the paper-strewn desk in his untidy office next to the Crew Room. "Tony, I hate to do this to you, but—"

Brr-brr. "Excuse me. Yes? Yes, Tubby, he's here. Put her on, who can say no to her." He held the phone out to Tony.

"For you."

"Tony?" Clear, husky voice. "My Brother Sylvest told me all about last night. She thinks you're marvellous. So do I. And, Tony—I love you." Click.

"Something important? asked Twinkletoes.

Tony grinned through an ache of fatigue. "Very."

"Well, as I was saying, I'm sorry to do this to you, but I've got to put you on ops again tonight. Christ, if anyone deserves a rest you do, after last night's bloody wonderful show. But I had a direct order—" only the Perambulating Prick gave orders to Twinkletoes at Onley Market "—and no matter what, we've got to put up a maximum effort."

Unsaid, but they both knew: the higher the number of Wimpeys that took off on ops from Onley Market, the nearer Prick's hat got to an extra helping of scrambled egg. Awkward pause, then Twinkletoes going on, "I liked that chap Allardyce, saw him in Station Sick Quarters when they were making sure he was still in working order. You heard he was fine, went straight back to Flaxfield, they sent a car over?"

Twinkletoes seemed fascinated by his foot, the one that had cannonballed in a cup-winning goal eight seconds before the final whistle, RAF 1, Army 0. Staring at it, "He said he was looking for Flaxfield, saw our runway first, and what with one thing and another he thought it a good idea, once his crew had baled out, to lob in here and save time, understatement of the year." Still engrossed in his foot, "Said he was a friend of yours. Is his father Air Commodore Allardyce?"

"Yes, he's at Bomber Command."

"Used to know him. Man who likes his glass of whisky. Same as the rest of 'em up at the Hole."

"The Hole?"

"That's what they call the underground HQ at High Wycombe. Well, Tony, can't stay here nattering all day. All the best to you—and once again, that was a tremendous show of yours last night."

Back in the Crew Room, Bill just nodded when Tony told him they were on again tonight. No reaction. These days, Bill's thoughts always seemed elsewhere, the only spark of life he'd shown for ages was last night when they hit that Luftwaffe airfield.

Tony was about to ask Bill, what's wrong, but the moment came and went as the other squadron aircrew started coming up to Tony and patting him on the back, super job, pulling that chap out of the Wimpey. Unusual, when you came to think of it. Except for your crew, the other fliers on the squadron were little more than shadows.

Everybody was chummy enough, mind you, stand you a glass of gnat's piss, but unless you were going strong with a popsie you went out on the Harpic around the pubs and crumpet-hunting only with members of your own crew—make another friend, lose him, was it worth it? Eckersley and Ramsarse, for example, prowled the boozers together. Not with Sills, however, never find officer Sills mixing with NCO's; anyway, his idea of a good time was doing a Bogart, down these mean streets a man must go and make propositions to unwilling, if gorgeous, girls.

Twenty-five crews on the squadron, hundred and twenty-five bods, you did have a lot of acquaintanceships, not necessarily long-lasting. When you first came, it was a lot like School, nobody took any notice of you till you'd been around for a while, you had to find the lavatories for yourself, then slowly you got to know everyone's name. Tony hadn't known who from whom not so many days ago and now it was thank you to congratulations from Blake, McCall, Wilder, Rowe, Crichton, Green, Proctor, Griffin . . .

New acquaintances; but he'd made one friend, that's for sure. He smiled at the recollection of Bill last night, he'd come panting up as he and Dick still sat on the grass, he'd hunched down, put an arm around Tony, hugged him, then dropped his arm, scandalised, silly chump, starkly obvious there was nothing queer about old Bill. The Battle Order was going up, P/O Marlowe, Sgt. Wilberforce, same old movie.

Chiefy Woods welcomed Tony at the hardstanding where G George stood waiting for its NFT; out on the burnt grass of the airfield a tractor was hauling away the last few charred and twisted bits and pieces of Dick's Wimpey.

"Gallant thing you did last night, young 'un—" he went bright red, he'd been in the RAF almost since the time it was called the Royal Flying Corps, unheard of to address even a nineteen-year-old officer as anything but "Sir". Tony burst out laughing, a moment later so did Chiefy.

For while it was true that the administrative and disciplinary NCO's detested the wartime NCO aircrew, the Chiefies who supervised the ground crews that serviced the Wimpeys couldn't do enough for the young men who flew; they missed meals to polish perspex, missed sleep to listen at the dark dispersals for returning Wimpeys, sometimes they wept in the silent dawns.

Tony counted G George's engines, climbed aboard, was squirming into his Sutton harness, God, he was shagged, when Chiefy stuck his head through the hatch. "Sir—there's a sergeant to see you. Says your op's been scrubbed."

Ramrod-straight, no young 'un from this NCO, salute like the Brigade of Guards. He spent his time among scrambled egg, an Air Officer's pennant was curled tightly round the staff on the bonnet of the big camouflaged Humber with the BC/HQ stencilled on its mudguards.

"Sir! Compliments of Air Commodore Allardyce and I've been ordered to drive you to his home. The Station Commander has authorised you to leave the airfield, sir—" catch Prick saying no to an Air Commodore— "and we'll go off, sir, as soon as you're ready."

* * *

Tony jerked awake terror-struck, hammer-blow heart-beats, asleep at the controls, the wing tilting, we'll topple out of the sky, spin down faster, faster, spiral down, tighter, tighter, Kate, Kate, we'll never get out, "We're here, sir," the sergeant driver was saying; louder, "we're here," Tony coming to, kipped all the way from Lincs to Bucks stretched out on the back seat. Uniform a bit creased, perhaps, for meeting an Air Commodore, 'strewth, look at those gateposts, carved stone.

No gates, though. "They went off to Beaverbrook, sir, when he asked for iron to build Spitfires. But the Air Commodore told him to use 'em for Wimpeys."

The drive was lined with beech trees, wide and tall, lavish foliage shining in the soft mellow sunlight of late afternoon, here was a forecourt with a fountain, dolphins, mermaids, the lot, everything but the splash, off presumably for wartime austerity.

Long, low house, gables, bags of chimneys, Elizabethan, reds of bricks, black stripes of wood against white plaster. Wide oak doors opening into a big square hall with a tiled chessboard floor. Behind Dick's father a wood fire burned spicily, flames mirrored in shining brass bowls spraying blue and pink lilac.

Not a bit like Dick to look at, shorter; red-faced where Dick was fair-skinned, stocky instead of slim, a powerfully-built man; to Tony's surprise he was reminded, in spite of the kiss-my-arse authority of the thick Air Commodore's stripe on the blue uniform sleeve, the line of gongs, DSO, MC, DFC, AFC, of a village bobby—Police Constable Allardyce, collar off, digging his cottage garden of a summer's evening.

Firm hand grasping Tony's, whiff of whisky, the other hand clasping his shoulder, Tony feeling the picture they posed was held too long, where's the photographer to focus and flash; no word yet to Tony, but a theatrically barked command: "Cutts!"

From around a corner, "Sir!" In an alpaca jacket, Cutts, jockey-sized, hurrying in, neat, quick, deft, for all his dot-and-carry limp.

"The sergeant's waiting outside, tell him to run the Humber back to HQ. Then bring Mrs Cutts."

"Sir!"

"And Cutts—!"

"Sir?"

"Whisky and glasses, for four."

"SIR!"

Mrs Cutts was a plumper jockey and the whisky Glenfiddich. Allardyce lifted his glass.

"To Pilot Officer Anthony Marlowe. The man who saved my son's life at the hazard of his own."

Theatrical again. Act I, Scene 2. Embarrassed, Tony made some sort of mumble, drowned by the noise of a car coming up the drive. "That'll be Dick," said Allardyce. "With his chorus-girl."

Mild surprise seeing Dick in check shirt and dark grey Daks instead of blue uniform, surprise eclipsed instantly by the sheer delight at Dick's luck.

"I'm Judy. Judy Gale."

Red hair tumbling over the shoulders of a sweater of Kelly green. Calm, serene, so utterly still. She held Tony in a steady, direct gaze; she knew, how he didn't understand, but she knew about that voice as the flames nibbled at Dick's Wimpey, leave him, leave him, run, run, run.

Judy Gale. Not pretty, at first glance. At second, who cares pretty? Laughter seemed to have tip-tilted her nose, over-generoused her mouth; and behind the chartreuse green of her eyes was somebody shrewd making wise remarks while some-one else giggled in a corner. Lucky Dick.

God knows why Dick's father disapproved of Judy but you'd have to be an insensitive clot not to feel the echoes of an almighty row hanging in the air. Had got worse when Tony came back from lifting a leg. Hardly hidden displeasure because Dick and Judy weren't staying to dinner. Dick due back at Flaxfield tomorrow morning, Pa; only one day off after the crash, Judy due at the Windmill, matinée tomorrow, et cetera, et cetera.

"Smasher," Tony said quietly and inadequately as he and Dick finished goodbyes, see you soon. Peck of politeness from Judy, but she laid her cheek against his for a long moment.

"So," said Allardyce, "to-night we dine alone."

"Be a great pleasure." Sounded a shade unctuous.

Candlelight at a table which had never graced a shop window, china whose lime and daffodil had never gleamed from a shiny catalogue, in a panelled room that glowed with the care of generations.

"Yes," said Allardyce, more loudly then you might expect, Glenfiddich sinking lower in the bottle. At first, Allardyce had insisted that Tony keep pace. Luckily, an understanding Cutts had dribbled into Tony's crystal glass, sloshed into Allardyce's. "Yes," again, quieter, "Grateful to you for saving my son." Scene 3. Heart-to-heart talk. "Damn brave of you. Sure Rick-Walker would have put you in for a medal if you'd been a regular." Rick-Walker was the Perambulating Prick.

"Might have picked up another for myself back in 'eighteen, eh, Cutts?" From beside Tony, Cutts was pouring a glass of white wine, "Might well have done, sir." Stand by, the atten-tive ear might have sensed, for an oft-told tale.

"Bomb slipped out of the rack of a V-Fifteen-Hundred, fell

on Cutts's foot, crushed it. Managed to roll it off, pull him clear, damn thing didn't go off, might have done, blown us both to kingdom come. No medal, though. Like you, I was only a temporary gentleman then." No gong for Tony either, but what the hell, Dick was still alive; My Brother Sylvest thinks you're marvellous, so do I; a cheek soft against his own.

The rich, mused Tony, sitting on the embroidered seat of a slender mahogany chair, Chippendale? don't have to buy anything much. Silver, crystal, mahogany, linen, all bills must have been settled long before Tony or Dick or his Air Commodore father had been born.

Allardyce, moreover, didn't have to dig too deeply into his pocket for grub or bother that much about rationing. "Delicious trout, sir. Catch them yourself?"

"No." Pompously. "Present from Sandy and his Wickham's Fancy."

Tony's family weren't country-house rich, nowhere near, but no need to try and put them down, Dad was suburban, professional, bit of money of his own, big garden, two-car garage. Nor was Tony all that awed by Allardyce's liquorice-allsort stripe, his equivalent army rank would be brigadier and there were a couple of rather boring retired brigadiers in Dad's golf club. Nice enough old boys, mind you.

"My father often ties a Wickham's Fancy." Sucks to you, Allardyce. God, he'd almost said that aloud, must have soaked up more alk than he thought.

The hard little round specks in the jugged hare were from Allardyce's Holland and Holland; the red currants in the jelly had been picked from the bushes that patched Allardyce's rough shooting. From out of a long silence, interrupted only by the gurgle of Glenfiddich, came an outburst of anger, "Chorus-girl! Contradicts me in my own house! Having a dis-discussion with my son, nobody asked her to join in. I was telling Dick about the Prof."

Who?

"Marvellous character, the Prof," Glug, glug, more Glenfiddich, go on like this he'll be well and truly pickled, well, Twinkletoes was right and no wonder Dick and Judy had bogged off. "Saved Bomber Command, that's what the Prof did.

"Bloody admirals rubbing their hands, all ready to grab our aircraft, want to fly them over their ridiculous convoys, peering about for U-boats. All set to call our airfields HMS Spalding, HMS Wyton, crews *boarding* their Wellingtons, *liberty boats* driving off to Lincoln and Huntingdon—"

Christ, thought Tony, it's the Germans we're fighting, not the Merry Andrew, even if they did take a pot at B Bastard, but Allardyce sought no comment, all he wanted was an ear for his seven-whisky monologue, not even that, the room could have been empty, Allardyce was all the audience Allardyce wanted.

"Brown jobs, just the same," glug, glug, "want our crews in khaki, boss us around, we go in first, do all the fighting for them, then lef'ri'lef'ri, in they march, present arms to General Lord Quim and Field Marshal Earl Arsehole.

"Yes, here's to the Prof. Professor Lindemann. Loathed him at first, mind. Doesn't touch a drop, y'know. Lives on beaten white of egg, nice cup of snot. Never had his hand up a woman's skirt, so they say. But big man on stachtistics. Got together the Command's strike photographs, ones that show where the bombs fell. Starts to make one hell of a fuss, says they show that only about one in every four crews ever got within five miles of the target."

Faint buzz in Tony's head, finding it hard to concentrate, must listen, Dick's father has swallowed easily three times as much whisky, got him chattering. Hearing what's what about Bomber Command at long, long last.

"And that's only on nights with a full moon, says Lindemann. On moonless nights, it was one crew in every twenty." Allardyce's laugh was half a sneer. "That was his stachtistic for all Bomber Command. We had him by the short and curlies, and he never knew it. We kept our mouths shut, never told him that we only gave cameras and photoflashes to our best crews, never to the rabbits.

"Shook us, though. Big panic. Thought we were scuppered, off to Gieves for us, fittings for navy or khaki. No more Bomber Command, yes, sir, no, sir, brown jobs, blue jobs promoted over our heads." Glug, glug, last of the bottle. "But then stronery thing happened. Prof gets hold of Churchill, grabs him by the ear, says, here you are, Winnie, here's how to win the war. More stachtistics, see. Proves Bomber Command can beat the Germans all by itself. Know how?" he demanded, suddenly noticing Tony.

Cutts had pulled away the cloth, before leaving he put a decanter beside Allardyce, glug, glug, port now, man must have a head of teak. Decanter pushed toward Tony, he wetted the bottom of his glass, pushed it back. "No,' he said. Lot more he wanted to say. Questions to shout, why had Hickey and Tinker and Geordie and Phil and Tich and all those squadron crews died for fuck-all? Why were he and Bill risking their lives to drop bombs on dots in little squares? But much better to stay silent, to listen.

Brave man, Dick's father, DSO, MC, DFC, have to respect him for that, must be a better man than this ranting drunk at the other end of the table. "No," said Tony again, "I don't know how."

"Knock down German working-class houses," said Allardyce in tipsy triumph. "Fifty-five cities in Germany with p-populations of more than a hundred thousand. Set fire to working-class homes in those cities, nobody to work in the factories, Huns can't make planes and tanks. War's won," he said, sitting back, nodding; Tony, in spite of himself, in spite of the moment, remembered School, about a year ago. Somebody asked that twit Blotto: Sir, what's the purpose of Latin?

"Well, you need it if you're going to be a doctor (Not me, sir!) or a lawyer (Never!) and you can read the masterpieces of Roman literature (What, for fun?) and—" Blotto leaning back in his chair, nod, same stupid nod as Allardyce's "—you'll be able to understand Latin mottoes." Nod, nod; listen to me, trust me, how fortunate you are to have the benefit, nod.

Allardyce, nodding finished, was busy with the decanter. "Chorus-girl! Contradicts me at my own table, front of my own son. Know what she says? Why working-class homes? See—Up The Workers, probably belongs to the Chorus-Girls' Union. I tell her, workers live close together, cooped, cramped, dirty little streets. One bomb knocks down lots of little houses, kills lots of little workers.

"Why kill workers, she says. Hear that? Seems to think it's wrong, killing people—in the middle of a war, can you believe that? Says, why not bomb factories, railways, docks? Can't tell her, of course, one in twenty, five miles. But I do tell her and

Dick, too—Bomber Command's in business to kill people. Know what Butch calls those quims who want him to bomb factories, railways, docks, oil installations, radar sites?"

Butch? Who the hell's Butch?

Spit at the corner of Allardyce's mouth, voice very loud. "Butch calls them *panacea-mongers*!"

Panacea? That's a pill, isn't it, does you no good, just encourages you. No, that a placebo. Panacea? That's it—something that cures everything.

Allardyce leant across the table, his breath a whisky-laden breeze. "Here, I'll tell you something. Should have told it to that chorus-girl. Arguing with me. Me! I was in the Royal Flying Corps before she was born. Something about Butch. He was driving his Bentley, he doesn't bother about speed limits, not Butch. Policeman has the imp-impertinence to stop him. Says to Butch, drive like that, you'll kill somebody. Know what Butch said?" Fiercely, "Know what Butch said? Butch said, 'I'm *paid* to kill people.' Put that policeman in his place eh?" Nod, nod. Pity this drunk is Dick's father, can't call him stupid bloody twit to his face. Again, who's Butch?

"Time someone put that chorus-girl in her place."

Tony could stand it no longer. "No, I don't agree, she's—"

Not listening, Allardyce was in full flight. "Bares her tits, bares her arse, she the kind of bint you'd like *your* son to bring home?"

"Frankly," said Tony, "yes," but unheard, Allardyce was nodding again, confident of victory.

In the study—heavy masculine furniture, black leather sofa and chairs—they had coffee, Allardyce a cigar and, from a newly-opened bottle, Glenfiddich. On one panelled wall was an oil painting, a young woman, fair-haired, fair-skinned, so that's where Dick got his looks.

"My wife. Died in India when Dick was born."

On another wall, cartoons sketched in chalks. One of a man in a white pudding hat, trousers rolled, arms full of an impossible load of fishing-rods and butterfly-nets. "Sandy?"

"Yes, Sandy Saundby." Yawn from Allardyce, he was fading rapidly, becoming genial, a drunk's swiftly contrasting moods. "I'll be giving him a hand with his layout tomorrow."

"Layout?" Tony hid a yawn, exhausting evening.

"Yes, trains."

"*Model* trains?"

"Hornby. O Gauge. Nothing Sandy likes better than a good pile-up. We'll be working out some really spectacular crashes." Allardyce yawned again. "Well," he said, "up the wooden hill to Bedfordshire." A chuckle. "Haven't said that since Dick was seven years old." Very mellow now. "Hope I haven't talked too much tonight. But one thing I'd like to say again—thank you for pulling Dick out of that Wellington." Yawn.

This bedroom was four times the size of Tony's on Site Four, the mattress five times as soft. Lonely, though; lucky Dick with Judy.

"The purpose of Latin," Harrison, a fifteen-year-old sophisticate had suggested to Blotto from the back of the class, "is to provide employment for Latin masters." That had been when Blotto lost his temper. Did Allardyce believe that the purpose of Bomber Command was to give jobs to Air Commodores?

Sandy? Butch? Figures of fun, no doubt, like Blotto. With, like Blotto, a proper headmaster to keep them in order most of the time. Well, after all, Dick's father was nothing more than a brigadier, like those old boys at Dad's golf club.

Nice enough, the brigadier who'd married, rather late in life, a Maisie, her laugh squealingly punctuated mid-day gins at the bar, she was in and out of Members' beds, as one of them said, like a well-banged drive bouncing down the fairway. Nice enough, the other brigadier, except, "Jews, old boy? Give Hitler his due—"

Got to allow for bats in bonnets, God, he was tired, not all that sober, bees in belfries. Somewhere someone must be headmastering Bomber Command; Tony put his arms around a pillow, ready to pretend it was Kate.

* * *

Apple blossom foamed white each side of the gate—good cover there for sniping cores at a passing bicycle—he rang the bell of the Vicarage, Kate's mother said, no hesitation, "My gracious! It's Tony!" Kate's father said, "Oh. good, we meet you at last—hoped you might look in, Dick and Judy told us you were here." Kate's mother said, "Such a *lovely* girl, Judy. Actress, isn't she?" Behind her shoulder Kate's father flicked a parsonical take-the-mickey wink.

Had breakfast? Sure? Wouldn't like a quick bite? *Must* have at least a cup of tea. Driver in a hurry? Sitting out there grumbling? We'll take him a cup in the car, he'll need it if he's taking you all the way back.

Her eyes had the same blue blaze as Kate's, she had the same cheekbones and beneath the grey hair the same beauty as Kate but she'd had it a great deal longer. There were lines on her face written there by parishioners' worries—wayward sons and daughters, terrors of old age, fears of poverty, poverty itself—and the claims of bazaars, coconut-shies and Women's Institute. Her face was no longer a glorious gift, like Kate's; was what she deserved; in middle age she was as striking as her daughter.

They had their cups of tea in thick white china mugs at the oilcloth-covered kitchen table, among piles of papers and envelopes and a puppy-expecting dachshund with her paws in the air. Kate's father's ancient Harris tweed coat had been the target for countless squadrons of moths, leather patches held it together. Shiny black parson's bib, wrong-way-round glossy collar; until he smiled, he had the look of a melancholy labrador.

Everybody talked all at once, yes, well, indeed, but, gracious, Kate says in her letters, did you really, until at the car door Kate's mother said thoughtfully, "Next time we'll have Bovril."

"Bovril!" Kate laughing, "you *have* made a hit. *Nobody* gets Bovril, ever. The original sinful treat." They'd found this pub with the riverside garden, there was still warmth in the slanting rays of the evening sun; Kate sat neat as a small blue-and-alabaster idol, Tony sprawled on the grass beside her.

Twenty yards away a shirtsleeved angler in braces slowly and very solemnly rowed a boat along the poplar-lined river, fishing-rod high in the air. Water gurgled. Birds sang. From inside the pub came the leisured burr of Lincolnshire voices. The war? A hundred years ago. A thousand miles away.

The squirrel came in little criss-cross rushes towards the piece of biscuit, ginger nut, in Kate's slim fingers; always, her uniform pocket held some offering in a screw of paper for any creature met by the way. Tiny leathery paw on Kate's hand, a hoist on to back legs, both paws now holding the bit of ginger nut, whiskers busy, munch, munch.

Ops tomorrow night, probably, but that was tomorrow's issue. Think about today, that had been engrossing enough, what with meeting Kate's mother and father. Bovril. Shocker, though, that chat with Twinkletoes in the Mess after the six o'clock news (Bremen, war material factories, marshalling yards, docks, twelve of our aircraft).

"As I said, I knew Allardyce when I was at Bomber Command headquarters, not a posting to be enjoyed, I can tell you. Did he stay sober? Thought not. Have an interesting evening?"

"Did, rather." Twinkletoes nodded, enough said. But Tony did ask:

"Who's Sandy?"

"Sandy? Air Vice-Marshal Saundby. We called him the Head Prefect," said Twinkletoes and then obviously wished he hadn't.

Air Vice-Marshal. Very big nob indeed. Plays with trains. Called the Head Prefect.

Tony persisted, "Who's Butch?"

"Come on now, you ignorant airman, you should know. Air Marshal Harris, Commander-in-Chief, Bomber Command."

I'm paid to kill people. So much for factories, marshalling yards, docks, communications . . . Not only did the conspiracy pretend that Bomber Command hit military targets, it also pretended that it aimed at them.

A twin-engined bomber, tails like big cufflinks, lumbered overhead; one moment the squirrel was contentedly nibbling biscuit between its paws, the next it was gone. "Manchester," said Tony, automatically. Kate wrinkled her nose, nuisance. Tony was trying to keep his thoughts, aircrew die so people can lie, under control.

He turned for relief to a story he'd been saving up to tell Kate. "Odd thing happened before I met you this evening. I'd got back and gone to my room in the hut. I went over to the washbasin for a quick swill and d'you know, on it was a bar of soap I hadn't seen before, hardly used. Camay, it was called, pink, delicious whiff, scented, not like English wartime stuff.

Foxed me, I can tell you.

"Couldn't imagine where it had come from. Then I saw the wastepaper-basket, there were a couple of torn-up letters in it, the envelopes had Canadian stamps—"

He saw Kate's face crumple. She'd guessed. He'd been away from Onley Market between early yesterday afternoon and five-thirty this evening. A new crew had arrived after he left, had been put straight on ops, maximum effort, maybe taking the place of Tony's crew. While he was away, they were come and gone. Missing.

A Canadian navigator from Winnipeg, Tony might never have known about him, how he'd been meant to share Tony's room, sleep on Tich's bed, unless he'd seen that Camay soap. Hadn't even finished unpacking, the Committee of Adjustment were only there fifteen minutes, the Station Padre had told Tony in the Mess. "People come, people go," as Chalkey had observed. "You soon get used to it."

You get so used to it; thank God he'd seen how the story had affected Kate, oh, Jesus, he was going to tell it for laughs.

* * *

Routine, mixture as before, cloud above, cloud below, same old boring movie, seeing it for the fifth time, after DR Duisburg, DR Mannheim, DR Essen, DR Hanover. In the same old weather system that kept sending fronts across the Atlantic with cloud scudding over Europe in sandwich slices between which flew the bombers from Dishforth, Middleton-St-George, Linton-on-Ouse, Driffield, Scampton, Onley Market, Swinderby, Flaxfield, Waddington, Woodhall Spa, from all the huge flat roaring fields by the quiet little villages with the Beatrix Potter names.

Routine: round dials like eyes of night creatures, soporific rumble of engines, loneliness in the moonless dark, Bill's voice with the figures for compass and gyro, along the pencilled lines we track to the dot in the square, bombs gone, where was that supposed to be? Ah, yes, Münster.

More figures: the course from the target coming up on the gyro as the numbers spin slowly round, level up G George, needles all Sir Garnet, operational egg here we come, a blazing whiplash arches over the cockpit roof, tracer, kick the rudder, wrench around into a diving splitarse turn, throttles, boost, engines screaming, G George can't take it, G George bloody well will.

Tracer again, the fighter's changed his mind, not firing at us. Found someone else. Falling out of the sky, fiery cross, a plunging Wimpey, a single sheet of flame, fire filling G George's windscreen, another crew dies for lies, don't watch it, you bloody fool, get into the cloud, bags more tracer where that came from, hide, hide.

Amazingly, the fiery cross levelling out ahead and below, there's the rear gunner revolving his turret, he's out, falling clear, like a cigarette-lighter's flame his parachute snaps alight, somehow the pilot's got out on to the top of the fuselage, he's a tiny burning doll, there he goes, turning over, a Catherine-wheel, slowly over and over, blinding red flash, the Wimpey's gone, shapeless black blur of smoke against darker black. Could have been us.

Cloud, in wisps. Cloud building up.

He braked hard and skidded the Morris on to the same grass verge where they'd first parked, and was immediately out and pulling open the door on her side. He held out his hand, she took it as if it were a gesture to help her out, looked startled as he jerked her towards him.

They were behind a bush but the leaves were sparse, they could easily be seen from the road, it wasn't really dark yet; he was fumbling frantically with her skirt, something tore, she was helping his frenzied hands.

God, almost forgot, rolling the skin-thin rubber, fingers trembling, now, now, now, now, NOW.

He said, "I'm sorry."

Eyes serious, she eased off the zeppelin-shaped balloon, tied a knot in the open end, swung it round and let it go. "Wheee," she said. With a plop it landed in a circle of primroses.

She smiled as if they'd been friends mending a chair. "Why sorry? Why so hangdog?"

Wretchedly, "Did I hurt you?"

"Well, I'm not made of Dresden china, you know. Must confess, bit of a shock at first but I quite enjoyed it, especially towards the end. Very flattering to a coy young girl, let me tell you."

He asked her, really wondering, "Do you laugh at everything?" and was surprised at how sharply she said, "No."

More softly, "No, I don't." She was doing some complicated tidying-up with an emergency safety-pin. "What happened on last night's op?"

Caught unawares, he almost told her: the tiny flame-fringed doll cartwheeling in the sky. "Nothing," he said. She started to speak, checked herself.

He was squirming back into his uniform slacks; she pushed him gently to the grass in the gradually darkening twilight, her palms against his shoulders. Arms round each other, they lay silently together. In the quiet of the evening, the noise of a car murmured, muttered, passed by, the dim wartime headlights oozing over them, come and gone.

Slowly Kate moved apart from Tony and sat up. "Mind you, if you wanted to send me off into hysterical giggles, just say what you nearly said."

"What did you think that was?" again really wanting to know.

"That you were sorry you *used* me." As Tony began, "But—" Kate rested a finger on his lips. "Because," she said, "that's what I'm here for, Anthony Hartley Tregellis Marlowe. For you to use."

He reached across her, undid the brass buttons of her tunic, "Rape!" she cried in a cheerful whisper but as Tony buried his head in the soft warmth of her breasts, her eyes were troubled as the last light of the evening faded.

The same time a day later Tony sat huddled on Tich's bed, the Canadian navigator's bed, the unlucky bed; somebody superstitious was leaving it empty, not assigning it to any newcomer, wanting no part in the guilt, however fanciful, of killing the next man to die.

Tony drew himself up into an even tighter bundle. His stomach was sore from puking, what little he'd been able to swallow at the Meal 2015 was flushed down the bog. Four out of eighteen Wimpeys the squadron had lost on the Münster op. Might so easily have been five. He curled up on the bed like a rabbit hypnotised by a weasel, staring at the death to come.

Wilhelmshaven. At Bill's whisper at the briefing, he had made up his mind. He'd go to Twinkletoes, tell him it wasn't fair to Bill, to his wife and children, to Sills and Ramsbottom and Eckersley, wasn't fair for them to fly with a pilot with a yellow streak, too frightened to do his job, too scared to give them a fighting chance when the searchlights came grasping up, when the flak began hunting, when the sudden fighter came firing tracer.

After he left Kate last night, he tried not to sleep, every time he dropped off he lurched awake, he was standing on top of that fuselage, once he'd spread his hands open in front of him, his fingers were fireworks, Roman candles shooting stars. Everybody gets dreams, he told himself as the daylight came but he walked all day like a ghost until the Battle Order went up, P/O Marlowe.

He rolled off the bed. Going to Twinkletoes now. Right now.

Gaps in the clouds. Quarter moon. That's the sea—islands below. "Land coming up, Bill. I can see the Frisians. Looks like Wangerooge. Islands to starboard, none to port, yes, it's Wangerooge, we're right on track, good show, Bill."

"Thanks, Tony. Target in five minutes, coming up to bomb."

Coastline clear in the shimmer of moon. Bill's voice, "That's Wilhelmshaven, sure enough. Going to aim at the docks—"

Aim at what you fucking well like, Bill, never mind the industrial heart coming up between the aiming-pointers, let's drop the stuff and get the hell out—

"Bombs gone. Close bomb doors. New course 278 Compass."

"Roger, Bill. 278 Compass, turning now. Right, everyone, eyes peeled, you know what happens if you don't see a fighter."

"Bombed Wilhelmshaven, primary target—" Gold fountain-pen, Greek "e"s, six ops done.

Twenty-four to do.

* * *

One of the really tricky things about ops was the contrasts that happened so violently, in half a dozen hours you could go from an airfield deep in the night-time peace and calm of the English countryside into a bloody awful shambles of death and destruction and then be part of a Beautiful Britain illustration soon after the cockerels started crowing.

Pretty tough to take that, played hell with your emotions, you kept being reminded of all there was to lose; the only answer was, on ops think only of ops, off ops take all the peace and quiet that was going.

Plenty of it about at the moment, Tony and Dick were sitting on side-by-side swings in the children's playground of Onley Market village, beside the (Early English) church, whose spire pointed to a Constable sky, blue-washed, with cauliflowers of cumulus.

"Keep you busy, ops—" Dick waited politely while the church clock, half clonks, half bongs, indicated seven of a mid-April evening. "Lots of things keep happening so fast. I mean, chap pulls you out of a burning aircraft, saves your life, when do you have a moment to say a proper thank-you?"

"Well, you have just bought me a fourpenn'orth and a tuppennyworth." Fingers were busy with fish and chips, strong pongs of coarse salt and pepper and vinegar.

"True, and I did think it was a bit fulsome of me at the time. Hey, look at this." Dick held up a greasy headline from the *Daily Express*. "Bomber Command Hammers Wilhelmshaven. So that's where our brave boys have been."

"I Hammered Wilhelmshaven, ta-ra, with my Wimpeyful of heroes," said Tony. No need to mention how touch-and-go that had been. "Did you Hammer Wilhelmshaven?"

"We did, as a matter of fact, Adolf turned quite pale. First time we'd ever seen a target, let alone bombed it. And I," Dick thumped his chest, "am a veteran of no fewer than three furious onslaughts against the dastardly Hun, from two of which I have actually brought back a complete aircraft." Dick held up a limp, drooping chip. "Hope I never get like this. Awppp," a baritone belch. "Glad to hear you hit it off with Kate's people. How did you get on with my father?"

"Well," hesitantly, "reasonably, I think. Likes his glass, doesn't he?"

"Pa drinks like a fish," said Dick. "Lots of them do, up at High Wycombe. Comes of not having any adventures to be brave about, I suppose, no chance of putting up any more gongs. Pa was a big hero in the last war, did you know? Flew fighters most of the time, shot down seventeen Germans."

"Seventeen! He must have a tale or two to tell."

"One, especially. How he got in a squirt at Fatty."

"Fatty?"

"Fatty Goering, our old chum Hermann. Back in nineteen-eighteen." Dick began to swing gently to and fro. "Near as a toucher clobbered him. Knew it was Goering, flying his white Albatros DV, ribbons on his helmet—he was leading Richthofen's mob after someone shot that bastard down. Stitched a neat little row of holes all along Fatty's fuselage. 'If I'd had my sights an eighth of an inch to the left,' Pa says, 'I'd have changed the history of the world.' "

"And maybe you and I," said Tony, "wouldn't have had to hammer Wilhelmshaven." And maybe Tinker and Hickey and Geordie and Phil wouldn't have died for fuck-all and nor would Tich and Johnny Woodham and that Canadian navigator and all those other squadron crews, there might have been no burning parachute, no blazing, spinning doll. "Highly intrepid, your Pa."

"Yes." Dick scrunched the *Daily Express* into a tight shiny ball, dropped it on his toe, expertly kicked it over an imaginary crossbar. "They won't let him fly on ops, you know, much as he'd like to, too senior, Air Commodores know too much. Dangerous, they say, if they're taken prisoner."

Mistake to think of Dick's father as no more than a drunk, but "So nobody at Bomber Command HQ, none of the top scrambled egg, has ever flown on ops in this war, none of them have ever seen for themselves—"

"No," said Dick, savagery in his voice, "and none of them want to listen. If I tell Pa what it's really like, what a balls-up it all is, he shouts me down, shouts Judy down, too, if she so much as opens her mouth and gives any clue of what she and I have talked about. About the things we have to do—oh, Christ, that's enough of talking shop, let's shut the hangar door. What do you say to a Whitbread?"

* * *

Surprising how often you could tell when someone was marked

for the chop.

"Compass all to cock," Griffin was nattering away in the Crew Room, the squadron (Tony included: routine) had gone, some thought, to Osnabruck the night before.

"There we were, wandering about all over bloody Germany, by the time we got any sort of a fix the sun was coming up. So we came home across Happy Valley all on our tod in broad daylight, every fucking gun in the Ruhr banging away at us, one batch of the bastards would have a go and then they'd hand us over to the next batch.

"Honestly, there was so much flak all around us, we could have stepped out of the kite and walked home on it. Went on and on and on, never stopping, and I thought, if they want me so much they can have me."

They put the bit about walking home on the flak in the Line Book but Tony knew, and judging by the sudden changes of expression so did many others, that Griffin wouldn't last. Sure enough, three nights later, he didn't come back from Homberg.

You could tell by the whiff of surrender or by the way someone would start acting oddly or go broody. Nobody knew that Blake could play Three Blind Mice, let alone that he was studying to become a concert pianist. Until Rowe, who'd been having it off with a market-gardener's daughter, got back to the Mess at half-past five one morning, and "There was Blake at the joanna, banging the living daylights out of Ludwig van."

Then there was that poor sod Proctor. Got compassionate leave to get married, came back, trailed around like a tit in a trance, chop written all over him. Went for a burton same op as Blake. Oberhausen.

Start to brood and you'd had it. Only thing to do was lock everything, abso-bloody-lutely everything, out of your mind. Shame about Proctor's wife, especially with the sprog on the way, but lock that out, too.

Lock everything out and you'd lock the tiger inside its cage, the tiger of fear that was always trying to escape its bars, the fear that could devour you and send you to Twinkletoes: "I can't take it any more," flame of a parachute; a pilot, alight, twirling like a Catherine-wheel.

Ask to be taken off ops and they stamped your documents LMF, Lack of Moral Fibre, and sent you somewhere where they stripped the wings off you and rubbed you in all the shit in creation. But that wasn't why Tony had stopped at his bedroom door when his tiger was loose, clawing and ripping at his nerves. Go LMF and he couldn't face his father who'd seen the Last Lot through; and, deep down, Tony knew he couldn't face himself.

So he slammed shut the tiger's cage. When he flew, he flew. When he wasn't flying, he kept all thoughts of ops out of his mind, rigid discipline.

Mornings, though, were bad in the Crew Room, dread at every click of the Tannoy. Chill fear, the rattle of the cage on the four mornings when Twinkletoes thumbed up the Battle Order; three times their names were on it, P/O Marlowe, Sgt. Wilberforce—not to mention Sills, Ramsbottom and Eckersley, all three of them unchanging, dim as ever, Tony sometimes wondered if they knew there was a war on.

Worst of all, worse than the actual stooging along over Germany, was the moment of pulling up the chair next to Bill in the Briefing Room, waiting for his whisper: Osnabruck. Homberg. ("Hamburg?" "No, Homberg. In the Happy Valley.") Oberhausen.

Admittedly, Bill was broody, but only on the ground, in the air he was his normal cool calm self as they took G George through the now cloudless skies; you could pick up a pinpoint on the shape of the coastline, on the glinting bend of a river, sometimes even see an irregular blur on the ground below which could perhaps be the city you hoped it was.

Osnabruck? Homberg? Oberhausen? Certainly there was something down there, as searchlights nearby coned a tiny silver toy of a Wimpey, don't stare at it, spoil your night vision; foolish, too, to watch for the red puff as the flak finally hits, lock the thought away, hope it wasn't Dick. Glad it wasn't us.

Plenty of flak about on all three nights, none near G George, bombs gone, there's an enormous blob beneath waiting for them, somebody else's stick marching soundlessly across it, the blinks of four flashes: the Ruhr.

Gold pen, Greek "e"s, bombed primary target. Osnabruck, Homburg, Oberhausen. One hopes.

Nothing wrong with Bill in the air. All the same, away from G George, he was quiet, withdrawn; could be, of course, that he was fully occupied with locking away his own tiger. "Bill and

Beryl," said Kate, "are leaving the cottage."

Tony was driving her back to the Waafery, they'd spent the evening at Potterhampton. Soon after her whispered cry of "Rape!" a few days ago, it had been, as she elegantly put it, "That time of moon with me," and, except for Osnabruck, Homberg and Oberhausen, life had been, one might say, uneventful.

Tonight had been much as usual, Bill, friendly but, must confess, withdrawn, reading a book on spherical trigonometry, sitting comfy in cardigan, meerschaum and carpet slippers, Beryl serving Spam and chips and suet pud (precious Golden Syrup on points), Kate gazing into the fire, Stripey snoozing on Tony's lap. "Ker-ist!" he said.

The wheel met a hole in the road, they were doing fifty, the steering-wheel bucked in his hands, something black, tall and solid dead in front, he jerked at the wheel, slowed, braked, stopped. Duisburg, Mannheim, Essen, Hanover, Munster, Wilhelmshaven, Osnabruck, Homberg, Oberhausen, nine ops survived, nearly shot down by a telegraph pole.

"Leaving the cottage?" What about our forty-eights, he wanted to bleat, that was what he was staying alive for, living from op to op, he loathed himself in mid self-pity. "I thought there was something on Bill's mind, he's been so quiet and inside himself lately."

"So," said Kate, "has Beryl," almost a reproof. "Oh, darling, didn't want to snap at you. But it has been so very, um, rough for her, waiting all day to see if Bill comes home on time, knowing if he's not, he's flying on ops and, darling, please kiss me, kiss me properly."

"Did Kate tell you?" Bill asked next morning in the natter and clink of pennies of the Crew Room. "About the—" Tony began, the Tannoy clicked, he waited, heart beating fast, "Corporal Harris six-five-nine report to."

"About the cottage? Yes, she did, Bill. Sorry to hear it. But it must have been a strain for Beryl."

"Strain on both of us, Tony." Bill woke a little from his now-accustomed lethargy. "I was thinking of her all the time and she was thinking of me." He smiled ruefully. "And there's plenty to occupy one's mind these days." Keeping a tiger in a cage. "We thought it best for her to go back to the kiddies. So she won't have to be on the spot all the time, if you see what I mean."

Like Kate.

"Be a lot easier for Beryl down at Little Harbury. So much better for the kiddies, too. And a lot easier for me, I must admit." Perhaps this means the end of Bill's broodiness off ops.

"How soon—" trying not to show disappointment "—is Beryl leaving?"

"Tomorrow." Lots of things keep happening so fast, as Dick had said. "But the new people don't move in till Sunday. So the cottage is yours from tomorrow night until then." Stammered thanks. What was today? Thursday.

Tomorrow, sod it, was Domestic Night. Left only Saturday, so long as there wasn't an op.

Be nice and tidy if there was an op tonight. Could then very likely drive Beryl to Lincoln railway station tomorrow evening. With luck, be with Kate at the cottage day after tomorrow, marvellous. Ops tonight? Too much to hope for—

"Stand by for broadcast. Night flying tonight, repeat, night flying tonight. All personnel confined to camp-amp-amp . . ."

* * *

The rest of that morning Tony was competent, in charge, getting things done. Only one flying-boot in Eckersley's locker, in the next-door locker there were three, he cleverly helped Eck solve that particular conundrum. Ramsarse had an appointment with the Dental Officer that afternoon, what should he do? Ring up and cancel. "Gosh, right-ho, Marlowe." Looked pleased. Did he realise that an op could be more painful than a drilled bicuspid? When the Battle Order was pinned up, no sign of Sills; Tony knew he was doing a Bogart with a bored Waaf in the Parachute Section; acting with remorseless efficiency, he asked Eck to fetch him.

He flew a highly expert NFT, never before had he felt so ready for his night's work. And then all at once as he came past the sentry and into the Briefing Room he knew that tonight's op would kill him. Just like that. No emotion. Just the certainty as he stood there, blocking the door, aircrew pushing past.

Somehow he was at the rickety ink-stained table, out of a

reddish mist Bill Wilberforce was coming into focus before his neat pile of meticulously-folded maps and charts. "Gelsen-kirchen. In the Ruhr."

"Happy Valley, here we come," Tony heard someone—him-self—say.

Most ordinary thing in the world that tonight's op would kill him, just as ordinary as taking up a Wimpey full of bombs and dumping them into the darkness, somewhere, God knows where, on someone, God knows who.

Going to die, odd how easy it was to face. Nothing to do, though, but to face it, what else? Tell the Perambulating Prick, now standing up there on the stage and glancing irritably at his watch, important engagement for tea, no doubt. Sir, I don't want to fly on this op, the Germans are going to kill me. What would Prick say? Twinkletoes? Same stale jest—if you can't take a joke . . .

Stop this bloody nonsense, only a sudden dose of shits-up, stupid to be frightened by a trick of nerves, plenty that's real to be scared of. But the deep conviction remained, inside Tony a voice clamoured, say you're ill, say you can't fly, hide, hide. But he had to fly. That was that.

That was that, Kate. That was that, Mum and Dad. That was that, Bill Wilberforce and I hope you get out, Sills, Rams-bottom, Eckersley, too, I hope you all get out before G George catches fire.

Time now to lock all thought away during this briefing that was part of the machinery that processed Bomber Command through its nightly farce. For Tony was part of the machine as were all the aircrews that sat at the tables in their stained and rumpled battledress, raggle-taggle gypsies, oh, as was the hesitant Met Officer droning away up there, lost his audience. No stopping the machine, that was that, Meal: 2100. Transport at Messes: 2215. Take-Off: 2345. Death: some time later.

Black spots scattered on its red wing-case, eyes black and white, legs slender and almost invisible, the work of a master craftsman, in the dim light of the cockpit lamps Tony stared, transfixed, at the ladybird on the handlebar of the control column, so much time and effort spent on something so insigni-ficant. With very great care, he edged the tiny creature on to his thumbnail.

A head came through the open hatch, the corporal armourer with the four steel prongs that flaunted gaudy ribbons, the security pins that kept the bombs from becoming live, to be handed to Bill as proof that they would be ready to explode as soon as he tripped his fusing switches when they crossed the English coast.

"Corporal—"

"Sir?"

Tony carefully eased the ladybird on to the hairs on the back of the armourer's bushy hand. "Look after her for me."

"Right you are, sir." Wasn't the first time something like this had happened, often behaved oddly the aircrews did before an op, suppose you can't blame 'em.

Thump, the hatch door shut, five men alone in an openwork lattice of steel and aluminium struts covered tight with canvas, below them firebombs and high-explosive, beside them wings full of petrol, how would the lighted match come tonight, flak or fighter? Bill tapping Tony's shoulder, pointing to his watch, holding up two fingers, indicating the throttles. Two minutes to the time of start engines. How many hours to live, two, three?

This is the op I die on but let it happen after the target, let's get the bombs down and the job done, however useless. Two minutes up. Press the port starter button, the propeller jerks, slews slowly round, vanishes in a shining disc to the roar of engine.

Press the starboard starter, both throttles forward, against the brakes G George starts to shake as the glinting needles swoop up and around the glowing specks of the figures on the rev counter dials. Healthy bellow from the engines. Throttle back. No worry about the mag drop, all well and good. Never thought much about dying, not at nineteen, not before that pilot twirled away like a firework, not before something, as Chalkey had said, really put the shits up you.

Strange how easy death was to accept now it was inevitable. Brakes off. Hand on port throttle ready to swing G George slowly round, a car with shaded headlights speeding along the perimeter track, slowing, turning on to the airfield grass. Someone was signalling, a pair of torches crossing over, beams pointing down.

Scrub.

Tony flipped the throttles forward for a final full-throated roar, yanked them back to a murmur. Engine switches off.

Ramsarse and Sills had shot through the hatch before the corporal's face reappeared, split by an enormous grin.

"Hope you didn't want your ladybird back, sir. I found a daisy and gave her her freedom."

Tony leaned forward against his Sutton harness, sweat streaming down the small of his back, he began to laugh, good, oh, so good to be alive again.

* * *

Tony was the sort of chap who carried an extra fan-belt in his Morris Eight, always kept his battery terminals covered in grease and frequently checked the pressure in his spare tyre. Efficient fellow, you might say, and as such he thoroughly approved the way Kate went about the business of everyday living.

Just watch her peeling spuds on this eagerly-awaited Saturday evening; he'd been laboriously doing the job holding the potato in one hand and slicing that slit-bladed what's-it towards him.

"Nit!" She took the peeler from him and used it as if she were rapidly sharpening pencils, plop, plop, plop went the shining white spuds into the saucepan on the ancient stove.

He watched as she sliced onions under water. "Idle! We'll be needing a lot more wood for that fire." Obediently he collected the torch from the Morris, shut the door of the woodshed next door to the arrangements and got down to some sawing.

Why does she want more wood, there's a big enough pile beside the hearth, this was a warmish evening—all of a sudden came into his head a thought concerning a Vicar's daughter, could she possibly have in mind, he saw blazing logs, a naked Kate, ivory skin lit by a rosy glow, and found himself sawing like a maniac.

The steak (black-market, cost him a packet after a call at the back door of the Magpie) was exactly how he liked it, charred outside, pink inside; they ate like a couple of starving young animals, piles of fried onions, masses of boiled potatoes, not forgetting two each baked in their skins.

That was the first thing they'd done when they got to the cottage, as soon as Tony had got the fire going, stuffing the spuds in yesterday's ash. After which, of course, they'd gone straight upstairs.

"Let's not waste too much time eating," Tony said later, gloating goatishly. "No need for pud." They were sitting at the table, empty plates, Beaujolais at the bottom of their tumblers. Yesterday evening had seen some busy shopping by Tony after he'd driven a silent Bill and Beryl through the rain to Lincoln station, the boot and part of the back seat of the Morris crammed with suitcases.

On the way back with Bill, besides that call at the Magpie and a successful visit to the Good Pull-Up, he'd also popped in at an off-licence. It had been pissing down but he had left off his uniform raincoat, dead crafty. The doddery old boy behind the counter took a shufti at his wings.

"For something special, is it?"

"For someone special."

From under the counter, a couple of worthwhile bottles.

"Drink up," said Tony. "Other one's waiting."

No answer from Kate, he looked at her over the top of that extraordinary EPNS gedinkus. Dismayed, he saw two lines of tears grooving her cheeks like those that had stained Beryl's as she sat in the Morris, Stripey's basket on her lap.

He went quickly round the table to stand behind her, holding her in his arms, sweet clean girl-scent of her hair. "I've known for days," tears in Kate's voice, "I've been dreading telling you."

"Come on, now. Can't be as bad as all that."

It was. "I've been posted."

"From Onley Market?" he said, not taking it in, not too bright.

"Worcester," a sob. "I'm posted to Worcester. For twelve weeks."

Christ, Worcester, bloody miles, hopeless train service. Twelve weeks. His tour of ops could be over by then, one way or another. They moved, arms around each other, to the bobbled sofa. "I'm going on an Intelligence course."

"They can't do that to you," but as Tony said it he knew they could, they could do anything they liked to you in the RAF except put you in the family way and they'd have a damn good try at that.

Comfortlessly comforting her, he said, "We'll still be able to meet. Now and then."

She said, very sadly, "I'm going to miss you so much."

They stayed, quiet, on the sofa, the only sound wood crackling in the fire. Until Kate said:

"Wasting time."

Rosy glow, shadows on ivory.

* * *

Squadron-Leader Tubby Tubbs gazed around at the spick-and-span Navigation Office and the neatly-stacked shelves in what had been, until three days ago, Kate's cubbyhole. "How I miss those capable hands, those gorgeous legs." Sigh. "You going to marry Corporal Elliot? If not, may I have her?"

Tony smiled what he hoped was an enigmatic smile. A month ago nodody married at nineteen but then nobody died at nineteen, either. Nor then had he known that poor sod Proctor, married, tit in a trance, Oberhausen. Ludicrously, "Keep your mind on your work, Marlowe," popped into his mind, old Chicken Hennessey chalking away last year at his blackboard. Nice chap. Hated Oliver Cromwell.

Well, with Kate away it was a lot easier to keep his mind on his work, just as well considering what work it was. He missed her, Christ, how he missed her. But he realised now what torture it had been for him, for her, in a pub, in the Morris, or at Bill's cottage, to know that this evening might be he last they'd ever spend together, in tomorrow's moonlight a firework spinning. Slam the tiger's cage.

Tony was bored with his enigmatic smile, so was Tubby, who said, "I didn't really ask you here to talk about la belle Elliot. I'm worried about Sergeant Wilberforce."

"So am I," said Tony.

"Not about his navigation, he's hell's-own good at it, all his calculations spot-on, should bloody well think so, maths master, wasn't he? Neatest charts I ever saw, except for one chap's, who used to be an architect, poor bugger. What bothers me, Wilberforce is like NAAFI, No Aims, Ambition or

Flaming Interest. Just mopes around all day, not a word for anyone. Even his pipe's empty most of the time, have you noticed?"

Tony had.

"I've found on ops," Tubby was saying, "that it's bad for a chap to get turned in on himself. Doesn't do to spend too much time aimlessly thinking. You've got to go out on the piss, chase crumpet—"

"Bill's a family man."

"Worries me, that. You can't think of anybody or anything but yourself, not on a squadron. Brood and you go round the bend. Well, there it is, Tony. Just try to get him out of himself. Believe me, it's the cunt-happy pissy-arsed fuckers who get through ops. That dreadful disease, lackanookey, has done for many an honest airman."

Get Bill out of himself. Well, he'd try.

Lackanookey, mused Tony, walking back to the Crew Room, wonder how many aircrew suffered from it. How many of them died virgins? The Station Warrant Officer turned the corner in front of him, tried to avoid his eyes, Tony stared him into a salute. Had Hickey, had Tinker, had it off? Had Tich? Bet your bottom dollar Ramsarse hasn't, nor Eck. Sills the Pill? Doubt.

Obviously, Bill Wilberforce had something on his mind. What? He'd find out, sooner or later. On ops, you had to take everything as it came.

Best of all, you just accepted the fact that you were on a production line, processed from arsehole to breakfast. Although most of the time Bomber Command didn't have a clue what to do with you. In the mornings they dumped you in the Crew Room like a lot of bothersome children, left you, bored, to amuse yourself as best you could.

So, each day was a mixture of fear and boredom, pontoon for pennies, every click of the Tannoy a cold clutch at your heart, almost a relief when "confined to camp-amp-amp" echoes over the buildings and the huge concrete-striped green-grass airfield. Taste of spew, mind, as the Battle Order went up, even so, again something strangely like relief, P/O Marlowe, Sgt Wilberforce, P/O Sills, Sgt Ramsbottom, Sgt Eckersley.

Night Flying Test: at least that kept you busy, made you

concentrate, no thinking to spare for the tiger in the cage, lift off G George, thank Christ it wasn't B Bastard, poor bloody Tich, now nothing else in your mind but the landing, concentrate, concentrate, G George sinking slowly, hold off, craftsman's pride at a feather-touch landing.

Briefing: always the tiger rattling the bars as Tony slipped into the chair beside Bill.

"Bochum." Wherever in hell that was.

It was in Happy Valley beneath a moon that was sodding well full and it might even be that black blob fourteen thousand feet below. For they'd crossed from Holland into Germany over what might well have been the River Maas where its northerly flow changed to northwest and five miles to port some poor bastard was coned over what might be the guns of the town of Geldern, a Wimpey crew dying, there they go, red flash, to give a hundred and eighty-odd bombers a probable pinpoint.

"Left, left. Steady. Steady. Left, left. Lot more left, Tony. Lot more. Ri-ight. Left, left. Lot more left, Tony." Pause. "Sorry, Tony, have to go round again."

Jesus! You don't go round again over Happy Valley, there's plenty of it down there, pull the plug, you're bound to hit something.

"Oh, God, no—"

"Shut up, Ramsbottom. OK, Bill."

Port wing down, splitarse one-eighty-degree turn, back the way we came, level up, flak all around, nothing near at the moment, but any second now—

"Right. Right. Left, left," again quickly, "Left, left." A moment's never-ending silence. "Sorry again, Tony." Splitarse, absolute quiet on the intercom, nobody breathing, go round for the third time, suicide: the black sky outside full of clusters of winking white flak, hundreds of guns keeping up a carpet of flashing stars, each one an exploding shell, just one jagged smoking-hot splinter was enough to slice through a Wimpey, cutting you in half on the way, what in hell was Bill playing at?

"Left, left. Left, left. Left, just a bit. Bombs gone."

Immediately G George standing on a wingtip, throttles rammed right forward, nose far, far down, diving, bomb-doors lever up, maybe they've torn off, who gives a shit, no, OK, indicator light's off, up in the patch of sky, exactly where they'd just left, white explosions like the opening petals of an enormous obscene flower.

Nobody spoke in the van as it left G George, Bill sitting there, staring straight ahead.

Some days it was just pontoon, nattering, reading (the tired-out copy of *No Orchids for Miss Blandish* going round the Crew Room nearly went missing one morning but luckily someone spotted it in the wastepaper-basket after the Committee of Adjustment had finished filling their boxes when Crichton got the chop), writing letters—"Kate darling, How much I miss you—"

Some days, no Tannoy amp-amp-amp; yet another day gone, too, without a chance of getting through to Bill, Tony wanted to talk to him, get close again, but Bill wasn't Bill any more, speak to him, all you'd get were yes-or-no answers, no chance of taking him out on the piss.

Which was one reason why his arms were around this Waaf, in the front seat of the Morris. Yet another mumbled "No, thanks" from Bill and so he'd been sitting in the Mess with the *Daily Telegraph*—"RAF Bombers Hit Ruhr"—on his knees, stuck with the anagram of fourteen across—"carthorse"—and bored to sobs. Outside was a lovely late April evening, as if summer were getting in a bit of practice. Waste sitting there, he'd muttered to himself, so he'd driven to Onley Market and the White Horse.

She'd been perched quietly, like a cat, a Siamese cat, on a chair in the corner of the Saloon Bar, a neat tawny-haired Waaf, a pretty girl with far-apart almond eyes. Tony watched a New Zealand sergeant air-gunner come up to her, speak, shake of her head, no drink thanks, with a smile. Nothing dramatic, the gunner had grinned at her, gone off; bags of talent in the White Horse, wasn't known as the Grumble-and-Grunt for nothing.

Before Tony looked away, their eyes met. He raised his glass in invitation, she came across to where he stood at the bar.

"Why are you laughing?" Kensington-ish.

"That New Zealander. He just drew a ring around his sleeve, insinuating that you only talk to officers. Shall I bark my knuckles on the cad?"

"Don't think they go in for cads much Down Under." She

turned and mock-saluted the Kiwi, already busy with an armful of plumpish blonde. "I ought to know. I was engaged to a New Zealand sergeant. Once. That's why—"

Tony asked, "Aircrew?"

"Navigator. Hanover."

They were very much at ease together in the cheerfulness of the pub—bad attack of Ye Olde Worlde black beams, picture of steeplechasers in nightshirts—as if old friends were meeting after a time apart. Her name was Helen, she hated hockey at school, adored Westerns ("Stagecoach!"), her father a bank manager.

Seemed only good manners after "Time, gentlemen, please" to drive a short way up the farm track behind the White Horse and take her in his arms, only common courtesy, after all, to kiss her. What shook him rigid was her tongue forcing its way between his teeth, her body twisting and squirming against his, her arms squeezing him breathless.

He felt his excitement rising, that wasn't all, he thrust his hand down the top of her skirt; locked and writhing, they were on the back seat, he was fumbling for his wallet.

He was hard inside the moist warmth of her, she was heaving, heaving, holding still and stretching, moaning, heaving again and again. He felt strangely remote from her, letting her thrust against the hardness of him, Kate darling, how much I miss you, she was heaving again, she cried out, panting, each breath a sobbing gasp, at last the unbearable delight of his sudden, scalding agony.

They were curled up together, their breathing changing from sobs to gasps, to quiet. "It's been two months," she said.

He drove her back to the Waafery and when she got out of the car she laid a cool hand on his cheek, pecked a kiss and was gone. Neither she nor Tony mentioned meeting again.

"I never thought, darling, that I could stand Worcester without you, yet somehow I'm managing." On the morning before Rostock there was a letter from Kate. "The Waafs here are a bright bunch and the course is interesting, that helps a lot. Although last night in the hut I was sitting on my bed laughing at something one of the girls had said and then I thought, how can I be laughing, Tony could be taking off for what you call Happy Valley, Valley of the Shadow, I call it. Darling, don't be brave, please? Just do what has to be done and come safely back to me.

"There's something, my dearest, I have to confess to you. I asked for this posting to Worcester." Not that Tony hadn't guessed. "There, I've told you now and I feel so much better. I hope you aren't angry with me but like Beryl I couldn't go on thinking every time we kissed goodnight this might be the last time I ever see you." Felt the same, Kate, darling.

"Bill—Kate sends you her love."

"Oh." Not much Flaming Interest. "Give her mine."

Rostock on fire on the horizon, incredible sight, they flew towards it from the sea. Now the city was blazing beneath G George, a mass of fires, target well and truly clobbered, all right, admire it later, bomb doors open.

"Steady. Steady." Take your time, Bill, no burning Wimpeys, skies empty of flak, no tracer, no fighters. "Steady."

"Steady. Steady." Well, don't take all bloody night.

"Steady." Come on, Bill, press the tit, soon we'll be running out of Rostock. "Steady."

"Steady." Come on, come on.

"Steady. Bombs gone." Operational egg, here we come.

Eleven done. Nineteen to do.

★ ★ ★

Never before a raid like Rostock, they were saying, the whole city alight beneath the bombers. All the squadron had come safely back (lot better than Bochum, they'd lost three in the light of the full moon), the afternoon Crew Room was all a-buzz. "You could pick out the streets like a guide book, old chap, all of 'em on fire." "Brock's bloody benefit . . ." "So much light from the flames, I just stooged around reading the *Daily Mirror*." Shouts of "Who's got the Line Book?"

Grimy windows pattered with rain, the sky loomed blue-black, even the seagulls were walking, out on the airfield a quartet of them stood around a gigantic puddle, seaside visitors on a wet Bank Holiday, trousers rolled up, knotted-hanky hats, no chance of ops tonight. "Shouldn't mind going out, though, to see them get another bashing like that." "Yup, a few more of those, Adolf's had it."

Never before an op like Rostock, suddenly it seemed worthwhile to put your life on the line; for the first time ever and about bloody time, too, Bomber Command was beginning to make a bit of sense. Maybe Dick's Glenfiddich father was right, after all, maybe bombing could win the war. Drop enough bombs, big enough bombs, Germany and then Japan might surrender before the brown jobs had to go in and die on the beaches, in the fields and in the streets. Maybe yes, maybe no, but hurrah for us, everyone was in excellent nick.

Except Bill. "Can I talk to you, Tony?"

At last, thank God. "Yes, of course, Bill. Fire away."

"No, not here, not in the Crew Room. Somewhere outside." Here it comes, whatever's been on his mind, at long, long last.

They walked in the pelting rain, Tony neat and officer-like in trench-coat and peaked cap, Bill, to remind him he was an NCO, in useless side-cap and sweaty waterproof cape. Five nights ago F Freddie hadn't come back from Bochum; behind the hardstanding of its dispersal were trees and some sort of shelter. Bill said, "I'm packing it in," a pheasant rattled noisily away from a clump of bushes.

"Sorry, Bill, don't think I heard you properly."

"I'm packing it in, Tony."

"Packing what in?"

"Ops. I can't go on."

Can't go on? Oh, God, he couldn't cope without Bill in G George, he couldn't be expected to go on without him, not with those layabouts, Sills, Ramsarse and Eckersley. "Bill, you can't, you've got to—"

Eyes on the ground, low voice, hard to hear above the rain clattering on the leaves. "I have to come off ops, I'm seeing the Wingco. I've thought about it, good Christ, I've done nothing but think about it. I just wanted you to know before—"

His own worries gone, what an absolute sod of a time Bill must have been having, "Have you thought what they'll do to you, Bill, if you go LMF?" Confess to Lack of Moral Fibre and you were in for a fate worse than death.

"Yes. And what it will do to my father, he won the Military Medal in the last war. But I can't go on, Tony. Not after last night."

"Last night? Last night was bloody marvellous, best show

ever—look, Bill, we're all frightened, all shit-scared but—"

"Of course we're all frightened, all the time. My stomach always heaves when I see the bomb trolleys going out and I taste vomit every time the Tannoy clicks. But I can take that, like everyone has to. What I can't take, Tony, is what we did last night."

For the first time Bill, his face a rain-streaked mask of stone, looked directly at Tony. "Before last night, had you ever heard of Rostock?"

"No. But I've never heard of half our targets. Why—"

"There's nothing there in Rostock, Tony, no factories to speak of, no docks, no railways, nothing. Just a town full of people, men, women and children. Know why we bombed it? Because it's a mediaeval city built of wood and we were sent there to start a bonfire. To light a bonfire of wooden houses, full of women like my Beryl and kids like our Shirley and Norm, all of them burning down there."

Bill made an odd gesture, wiping something away from before his eyes. "We set them on fire for newspaper headlines, for the BBC news. Did you see the papers at lunchtime, 'Bomber Command Blasts Rostock,' hear all those BBC lies about factories, communications, naval harbours? All that gloating about a lake of fire, just as if the RAF were winning the war, when all we're doing is burning ordinary people down there, not even soldiers and sailors, but women and kids."

Tony said, "Whoa—steady on, Bill. We're under orders. We're doing our duty. We didn't start this war, nor the bombing. We don't make the decisions. We do what we're told to do. We carry out our orders."

Earnestly, "Believe me, Tony, I've tried that way out. Day after day, night after night, I've tried all those arguments. Maybe if I'd been your age I'd have convinced myself, if I hadn't been married, hadn't got kids of my own—if I'd been like you and almost all the rest of the squadron.

"Don't forget, I'm getting on for ten years older than most of you. God, I can understand you and the others, you've hardly left school, good boys, doing what you're told, you've been ordered about all your lives. By schoolmasters like me," he added bitterly. "Question what we say and you're caned for impertinence.

"And, yes, I've told myself that bombing is the only way we can get at the Germans, that we've got to bomb cities and not military targets because that's all we can find with our protractors and maps, always supposing we can see the ground. That we go out night after night to show America and Russia we're still in the war. And to cheer our own people up with those headlines, too.

"I've tried to tell myself that the Germans bombed us first and they're only getting what they deserve. That we're doing terrible things to stop Hitler and his—his guttersnipes from doing things that are even more terrible. I've tried them all, all the arguments."

Noisily, Bill swallowed. "Know why I took you three times over Bochum, if it really was Bochum? I could see railways down there in the moonlight, dozens of them, a marshalling yard and I said to myself, no women and children in goods-yards. So I just kept taking you round until I had the railway tracks in my bombsight. Know why I took so long over Rostock?" Bill swallowed again.

"I took you well past the town and dropped the bombs in open country. Last night we didn't kill anybody, yet all the way home I was thinking, you'd risked your life, and so had Sills and Ramsbottom and Eckersley and because of me it was all for nothing."

Bill pressed the heels of his hands against his eyes. "That was the end, Tony, when I saw the flames eating up Rostock, that was the finish. I'd stood it this far because I couldn't leave you here to go on without me. But now, no more, I've even got to do that, to betray you.

"I can't press that bomb release ever again over a city, over ordinary people in their homes, over women and kids. Perhaps if each of us killed by pushing a thumb on a button, instead of just one to a crew, more would feel like me. Who knows—but even if you don't understand, Tony, I've got to go and tell the Wingco that I'm not flying another op."

Tony said, slowly, "I'll come with you."

* * *

He wasn't Twinkletoes any more, he was Wing Commander

Kincaid, Distinguished Service Order, Distinguished Flying Cross and Bar, Officer Commanding a Wellington squadron of Royal Air Force Bomber Command. From behind his desk, "Sit down," he ordered in a voice like ice crunching the *Titanic*. "I don't mean you, Wilberforce, stay at attention. Now, Marlowe, you've heard what this coward has to say—"

"He's not a coward, sir."

"Don't dare to interrupt me, Marlowe. He's a coward. LMF. Know what that means, Wilberforce?"

"Yes, sir."

"What does it mean, coward Wilberforce?"

"Lack of Moral Fibre, sir."

"Know what they do to fighting men who run away?"

"Sir, I—"

"They shoot them, put them up against a wall, that's what they do to cowards, coward Wilberforce. The Royal Air Force thought you were special, Wilberforce. Trusted you. Spent thousands of pounds training you, trusted you with the responsibility of an aircraft that your country—not that your country means sod all to you, Wilberforce—invested thousands of man-hours to build. And how did you repay that trust, Wilberforce?"

"Sir, I—"

"Shut up, coward Wilberforce. Complete and utter shit Wilberforce. You're a disgrace to the men on your squadron who have died doing their duty. And to the men in all the Royal Air Force who are going to give their lives in the future. Maybe I can't have you shot, disgrace Wilberforce, but by Christ, by the time I've finished with you, you'll wish you had been. Now, your whine is that you're afraid to bomb cities—"

"Not afraid, sir. It's just that I don't think we should—"

"You imagine you've got the right to think, Wilberforce? With your country and the whole bloody world just about at the mercy of a maniac like that swine Hitler? Or maybe you want Hitler to win this war? To do to your countrymen, your family, your friends, what he's done in Poland, Holland, Belgium, France?"

"Sir," said Tony.

"Yes, Marlowe."

"He's not a coward, sir."

"You've got thirty seconds, Marlowe. If you haven't convinced me by then I'm calling in the Royal Air Force Police to frogmarch Wilberforce to the guardhouse."

"We've done eleven ops together, sir. He's a first-rate navigator. And he's no coward, last week he made three bombing runs over the Ruhr to make sure of his target—"

"He may not have been a coward last week," Wing-Commander Kincaid reached for the phone. "But he's a coward now. Ten seconds, Marlowe."

"If you put him under arrest, sir, you'll have to arrest me, too." Tony tried to keep the break out of his voice, couldn't. "I'm refusing to fly if he's unjustly accused."

The Wing-Commander, hand on phone, held Tony in his gaze; shook his head, took his hand away.

"Very well, Marlowe. That's a stupid threat but it shows how deeply you feel—oh, sit down, Wilberforce. Now, you say you don't like bombing cities, right?"

"Yes, sir." Bill was coming alive again.

"And you, Marlowe, are convinced he isn't a coward and are prepared to make an idiotic gesture to prove it. Well, let's see if you're right. Wilberforce, if you're not keen on bombing cities, have you anything against other targets? Ships, for example?"

"No, sir, it's only—"

"Yes, yes. Well, here's your chance to prove Marlowe right and me wrong. There's a squadron of Beauforts. Torpedo bombers. A tour with them is three ops—three torpedo strikes. Three, and I've never known anyone finish a tour. Suppose I were to post you to that squadron—"

"Thank you, sir. Thank you very much indeed."

Bill had gone, stamping a noisy, jubilant salute on the bare boards of the office floor. "Sentence of death," marvelled Twinkletoes, "and all he does is say ta very much. That's my brother's squadron," half-proudly, half-sadly, "sinking German convoys in the North Sea. Each convoy has an escort of flak ships, they fire splash. Don't have to aim. They just shoot into the sea in front of the low-level Beauforts, wait for them to fly through what you might call a curtain of steel. Now and again a Beaufort comes out the other side."

He sat silent for so long that Tony thought it was time to go, saluted, was halfway to the door.

"Tony—"

"Sir?"

"Did I tell you how I won the war?"

Startled, "Sir?"

"Well, me and a few other intrepid birdmen. It was soon after I started flying on ops, on Wimpeys. It was late in August 'forty, when the Germans had the Battle of Britain as good as won, it had finally occurred to Fatty that the thing to do was bomb our fighter airfields. Making a good job of it they were, too, just about knackered Fighter Command.

"Know what happened then? The RAF sent out Wimpeys, and twenty-odd of us, me included, bombed Berlin for the first time ever. Probably the most important op of this or any war because it drove old Adolf right up the wall. Had him raving, mouth full of carpet, he tells Fatty, no more bombing airfields, get cracking, blast the hell out of London, pay us back for bombing Berlin.

"So the Luftwaffe unloads its bombs all over London and leaves our airfields alone. Fighter Command pulls itself together, soon the Spits and Hurries are up there again, clawing the Germans out of the sky. Soon, no more German bombers, Adolf calls off the invasion of Britain. And now the Russkies are grinding away at the Germans like a mincing machine and the Yanks are building up the most powerful army the world has ever seen, ready to clobber the bastards. All because of me and a handful of Wimpeys.

"Ask me what's Bomber Command done, never mind all that meandering about looking for targets we never find, and I'll say we stopped Britain—and the world—losing the war. All right, Bomber Command's a shambles but one thing I know, and that is we'll muddle through in the end.

"As for what Wilberforce says, I'm with him, hell, I don't want to kill women and children. But if some women and children have to die so that bastard Adolf and the shits around him don't end up running the world, all I can say is, tough titty.

"Tell you something else, Tony, that crap about not killing Germans in their homes—a German making guns takes his chances, right? He's trying to kill us just like a German in uniform, right? He's got blood on his hands, just like a girl who puts explosive in a cannon shell.

"So when does a German stop being an innocent civilian and become a military target? When he gets on his bike to ride to Krupps? When he pedals through the gate?

"Oh, fuck it, Tony, when you look at clowns like Air Commodore bloody Allardyce, you think the RAF doesn't know its arse from its elbow. But my motto is, press on. We'll win this war in the end even if all we do is keep Adolf chewing carpets. So press on, Tony." As Tubby says, ponder and you go round the bend. And if what we're doing doesn't bother the Padre, why should it bother us?

Clowns muddling through. Or maybe there really was a headmaster somewhere, someone heavy with scrambled egg, who knew what he was up to. Nothing else a birdman could do, after all, but press on.

"Press on regardless," said Twinkletoes.

"Yes, sir," said Tony.

* * *

Nobody was going to stamp that damning "LMF" all over Bill Wilberforce's documents but Twinkletoes saw to it that he didn't hang around, within twenty minutes of Tony leaving his office the Tannoy sounded, "Sergeant Wilberforce report to the Station Orderly Room," a clearance chit was waiting for him with a railway warrant to his new RAF Station Somewhere in Scotland.

Tony drove him around the hodge-podge of offices and stores in the still-pouring rain to get the chit signed, they had the whole lot done in a record hour and ten minutes. Bill got himself packed, didn't take long and by then it was past five o'clock and Tony was free to drive him to Lincoln to pick up a six-sixteen train.

The buzz had gone round the Crew Room that Bill had been posted, nobody knew why or, frankly, bothered. As Chalkey had said, people come, people go. One way or another. Fat chance, of course, of Sills, Ramsarse or Eckersley taking the trouble to see Bill off. Round the corner came the 6.16, up it chugged to the platform. Bill said, "Thank you, Tony."

"Thank me? For what?"

"For what we've been through together. For what you said to

the Wingco." His voice faltered.

Tony helped him heave the two white canvas kit-bags up on to the luggage-racks of a crowded third-class compartment, looked as though Bill would be standing in the corridor for the next several hours, pity he wasn't an officer, travel First. The train hissing, jolting, jerking, moving off, Bill shoved the window down, the train was gathering speed, Bill's head out, he was calling, "Tony! Tony!" Too late, "Tony!" the train was far down the platform.

"I say, old boy, do you mind? Don't seem to be any porter cheppies around." He was a Flying Officer navigator with a pile of luggage, his black moustache too ambitious, likewise his accent. Thoughts elsewhere, Tony picked up two of the suit-cases and they set off together down the platform.

"Wouldn't know how I get to Onley Market, would you, old boy? Just been posted there. Should be transport waiting for me but you know what these Transport cheppies are like, never can trust them to get their fingers out."

Tony's mind was on Bill and his long lonely journey north to his new squadron, now and again a Beaufort comes out the other side. Trying not to sound grudging, he offered Cheppie a lift. "Oh, I say, old boy, that's frightfully decent of you."

As they tramped along, "Smashing piece of grumble, that, wouldn't mind getting across her, I can tell you." The girl heard him, looked round, tracks of tears on her cheeks. Just seen some aircrew bod off probably, Bomber Command stations were thick on the ground all around Lincoln.

"This yours, old boy?" They had arrived where Tony had parked the Morris Eight. "Handy little runabout. Drive an M.G. myself. Leave it in the garage nowadays, petrol rationing, you know."

Tony asked, "Series T.B.?"

"Yes."

"What's the horsepower?"

Hurriedly, "Twenty."

Bullshit, but Tony didn't bother to contradict. Beauforts, torpedoes, shipping. Jesus, poor Bill.

He called in at the Good Pull-Up, siphoned a tankful, filled his spare can. He wondered, not seriously, whether Cheppie—his name was Fuller—would chip in. Not a hope. One way and another, Tony was very bored with Flying Officer Fuller when they reached Onley Market after the half-hour drive. If he were called Old Boy once more, he'd strangle Flying Officer fucking Fuller.

In the Mess, a folded slip of paper in Tony's box. "P/O Marlowe. Telephone call. No message. Will ring again later." His heart jumped—Kate?

"Pilot Officer Marlowe—telephone."

Wasn't Kate. "Hello Tony, it's Dick. Wanted to tell you there's a bod posted to your mob from Flaxfield. Avoid him like the plague. He's off a crew we had here that got broken up—the radar people got suspicious, suggested they were cruising up and down the North Sea and dumping their bombs overboard. Couldn't court-martial them, not enough evidence. Looked devilish fishy, though."

Tony asked, "Is it a cheppie named Fuller?"

"Yes, how did you—"

"I've met him" said Tony.

Next morning at breakfast, powdered egg, soggy toast, Twinkletoes tapped Tony on the shoulder. "Pop in my office first thing, there's a good fellow."

Huge shoes up on his desk. "Got a favour to ask you, Tony, say no if that's how you feel. We've a problem on our hands, name of Flying Officer Fuller—oh, you've come across him. Well, Fuller calls himself a navigator, comes from a crew they took apart at Flaxfield—"

Tony said, "I know."

"How—oh, yes, Allardyce's boy. Well, even in the RAF you're innocent until proved guilty but I'll give you ten to one that Fuller and his merry men stooged to and fro and chucked their bombs into the oggin rather than venture across the coast into all those nasty bangs over Germany.

"Now I can call around the OTU's and ask one of them to post in a sprog crew without a navigator and then fix them up with him. Or I could take the horrible little man and put him with someone I can trust to handle him and show him all the joys of flying over Germany. That's what I'd rather do, sprogs having enough on their plates without having to cope with someone like our chum Fuller.

"Bod I had in mind, Tony, was you. Not because Wilberforce has conveniently gone into a new line of business, poor bastard, but because I reckon you're the type to stop any bloody nonsense Fuller may try to get up to. But you don't have to have him. Up to you, shall I put him with sprogs or will you take him over?"

Ops were going to be bloody without Bill, anyway. Besides, Twinkletoes had turned down a promotion to Group Captain to do a third tour of ops. Hard to deny him anything.

"Looks like I've got a new navigator, sir."

"Good show, Tony. Thanks."

* * *

Dick peered into his Whitbread's as if the answer to some unsolvable problem were swimming around in his pint. "Told your Wingco straight out, did he? No more bombing women and children?"

"That's right. And afterwards Twinkletoes told me how he won the war—"

"So you've said, Tony." Dick swallowed the rest of his Whitbread's in one gulp. "I'd like to have met your pal Wilberforce." He beckoned the bald barman of the Wheatsheaf. "Whiskies. Doubles."

Baldy, enjoying himself, turned slowly and pointed to the sign above the bar, "NO SPIRITS."

A fistful of grease-spotted shirt ripped noisily, he was spread-eagled across the bar, nose an inch from the counter. Dick said again, very quietly, "Double whiskies." Twist of a wrist, the barman made a choking noise.

"Yes, sir," he croaked. "Double whiskies."

A glass teetering on the edge of the bar tumbled off and splintered on the floorboards and everyone in the Saloon Bar began talking again. But Tony didn't ask Dick why he'd manhandled Baldy. Don't pry. Don't brood.

* * *

"Good boys, doing what you're told," Bill had said. Made you think. Tony scraped lather from cheek and chin and checked in the mirror for remaining stubble, not likely, he really only needed to shave every other day. The two scars still showed faintly, the little semi-circle left by the stud of somebody's boot, the thin line of a slash from someone's heel, souvenirs of eleven years of School rugger. No scars, yet, touch wood, from eleven ops.

Eleven years of rugger, "Get the ball away, Marlowe!" Eleven years of English, French, History, Geography, Phys., Chem., Biology, Algebra, Geometry, Div., Latin, Blotto's mottoes. Eleven years of classrooms, of being stuffed with largely useless facts. Far less trouble than not to sieve through those remember-for-a-time notes, to scribble reasonable answers to end-of-term exams, to the Oxford and Cambridge General Schools, to the Higher Schools Certificate.

Answers about the dull acres of *Westward Ho*! and the somewhat winsome goings-on in *A Midsummer Night's Dream*, about the irregularities of "aller", what was the Diet of Worms, name the industries of Madagascar and how about the atomic weight of nitrogen. Eleven years of being blotting-paper, of being bored by Julius Caesar overcoming the Nervii, pistils and stamens, simultaneous equations . . .

Doing what you're told. All done to please the grown-ups? Well, thought Tony as he rinsed his razor, nowadays one of the grown-ups he most looked up to was Twinkletoes. Press on regardless.

Regardless of whom you were dropping bombs on, regardless of hardly ever finding your targets, one out of four within five miles on full-moon nights, one out of twenty when there wasn't a moon, and those were the picked crews. Only by staying regardless could you possibly hope to finish a tour.

"Forty minutes to base, old boy."

It could have been a re-run of one of Tony's early ops, back before the spinning firework, back when flying a Wimpey had seemed no more exciting, no more precarious, than a flight over Wolverhampton. Tony had lifted G George off the Onley Market runway, climbing through darkness into the clag at about five thousand feet, staying cloudbound all the way to clear skies at fourteen thou. P4 compass, gyro, ASI, altimeter, artificial horizon, revs, fuel, oil temperatures, oil pressures.

All nice and quiet, no threatening flak, no fighters to be seen on this take-it-easy trip, Tony's first with Flying Officer Effing

Fuller. In fact the only sign that the Germans weren't all that pleased to see them was after G George dumped high-explosive and incendiaries through the icing cloud below on to, perhaps, Cologne, on Fuller's DR; when Tony pulled up the lever that closed the bomb doors, he caught a glimpse of shell bursts in the sky about twenty miles ahead.

After which the flight back had been quiet and uneventful, Green Line, not that Tony was lulled into day-dreaming, not with all those ops behind him—coming up to number twelve—and the prospect of sudden tracer whipping towards him always in his mind. Only thirty-eight minutes' flying time to the good old operational henfruit.

Stooge on, same old routine, P4, gyro, ASI, altimeter, artificial horizon, Kate kneeling naked over him, laughing, his hands reaching up, sliding down the curve of her hips, wake up, Marlowe, day-dreaming prohibited, don't you know there's an op on, that the danger is thinking that any moment isn't dangerous?

"Pilot to navigator—"

"Oh, er, hello, yes, old boy?"

God how he missed Bill. "Fuller, is it time to start our descent through cloud?"

"Oh, I suppose so, yes, old boy." Lucky Tony had reminded him.

With the tiny aircraft sitting just so on the dial of the artificial horizon, with the needle of the Rate of Climb indicator steady on a descent of five hundred feet a minute, they broke cloud over the sea at a comfortable three thousand. Sooner than he expected, Tony saw the coast of England ahead, the aerial lighthouses of the pundits flashing their single-letter signals, the reds of the airport beacons winking their double letters.

He waited for Ramsarse in the front turret to make some sort of announcement—a pundit remarked upon, perhaps, or a beacon noticed? Not a murmur. Christ, thought Tony, do I have to do every bloody thing myself? "Pundit ahead, navigator. Flashing Q Queenie."

Seemed to take a long time for Fuller to find pundit Queenie on the rice-paper list he was supposed to eat if someone shot them down. And longer still to work out a course for Onley Market. Finally,

"Course 328. ETA in 16 minutes."

And then, wonders never cease, Sills came up with a QDM on his radio, magnetic track to steer for Base, but it was a whacking eighty degrees different from Fuller's course. But not to panic, they were over the coast by now and below Tony was the unmistakable nose of Flamborough Head, sixty-two miles from where they should have been. So he told Fuller, who was amazed.

Feeling like a shepherd with an idiot flock, Tony enquired gently about the night's letters of the Onley Market beacon and once again Fuller, whose job it was to know such things, had to rummage about before he came up with the answer. AJ. All bad things come to an end and here at last, dit dah, dit dah dah dah, Onley Market.

Tony chucked his harness in the back of the van as Flying Officer Fuller hurried to appropriate the front. "Hello, you beautiful creature," said he to the WAAF driver.

"Oh, fuck off," said My Brother Sylvest.

Nice to be home. Bit odd, though, that they were first back, particularly after all that buggering about at Flamborough Head. Oh, well, the hell with it.

"Bombed on DR? Good show. Bombed primary, Cologne." Gold pen. Greek "e"s. Twelve done, eighteen to do.

* * *

"In three weeks, three days, fourteen hours, sixteen minutes and twelve seconds all of us on the course are getting a forty-eight and I've wasted umpteen coupons on a fragment of nightie I hope I won't have a chance to wear, darling, when I'm with you 3 wks 3 ds &c from now because SOMEHOW we'll be together . . ."

With her letter Kate had sent him a photograph and when he looked at it he laughed aloud. She'd told him she hated having her picture taken, she was staring at the camera cross as two sticks but even scowling—

The corporal armourer let out a long, low whistle. "What's she starring in, sir?"

"My life," said Tony, snootier than he meant.

But it had been more than two hours ago that the corporal had handed over the beribboned security pins and now God alone knew where Fearless Fuller had navigated G George, certainly nowhere near Emden, although if any targets anywhere were possible to find, coastal cities were the most possible. Particularly on a night like this, cloudless with quite a bit of moon riding high above.

No flak, no searchlights, no sign that Bomber Command was out in force—three hundred kites on this do, they'd been told at briefing. Odd how often you could fly a whole op and never see another bomber, unless it was being fired at. Nothing, in fact, to be seen anywhere, vacant sky all around, anonymous countryside below, nothing to check against the map that Tony pulled out of his flying-boot. Miles and miles of SFA.

They should, if Fuller knew his job, have been coming up to the wide estuary of the Ems, on the other side of which was Emden. No sign of the sheen of water; nothing; they must have been at least twenty miles south of track.

"Five minutes to ETA, old boy." For God's sake, here was Fuller, pushing his way past Tony's seat to the bomb-aiming compartment up front and the realisation hit Tony like a physical shock, what an idiot he'd been not to have grasped it before, why he'd seen all that flak far ahead on that last op, why they'd been first back at Onley Market: Flying Officer Fucking Fuller had turned them back long before they reached Cologne.

Angrily, Tony stretched out a hand to grab at Fuller's Irvin jacket, couldn't reach. He jerked the control column, G George tilted clumsily skyward, dismayed voices chattered on the intercom, Fuller tottered across the cockpit to jar against Tony's shoulder.

Tony stabbed a finger at the intercom socket, waited while Fuller plugged in earphones and connected up his oxygen tube.

"Just where do you think you're going?"

"ETA coming up, old boy, going to drop bombs on DR."

Tony thrust the stick forward, the horizon of the dark, empty landscape climbed further and further up the windscreen. "Do you see the target? Shut up," he snapped as the intercom filled with protests, no question tonight of the crew being all pals together.

Fuller said, "ETA coming up." Incredibly, he sounded puzzled.

"Time to bomb and get out." That was Sills. "Bomb on DR and get out. Can't hang around—"

Inelegantly, "Shut your trap, Sills." To Fuller, "We're turning north, towards the coast. To look for Emden."

"But—"

"Get your map out and get on with your job."

So what the RAF suspected about Fuller was true. Ten minutes later moonlight glinted on a north-and-south river half a dozen miles or so ahead. Right, that was the Ems. No glad cry of recognition from doughty Ramsarse in the front turret.

"See the river?" Tony asked Fuller, still standing beside him, map in hand.

"What river?"

"That river," said Tony, and thrust the nose of G George down, down, down. Height reeled off the altimeter, thirteen thousand, twelve, eleven, ten, nine—

Fuller's eyes were wild as Tony pulled out at eight thousand feet, "For God's sake we can't stay down here—"

"See the river now?"

They were so low they could see the water creaming at the bows of barges, the wakes sparkling silver, lorries on the bridges.

In cold fury, the intercom silent, Tony banked G George and followed the river north and then west as it turned towards the city. Sooner or later the guns would open up, all the guns, they had the target to themselves, no other aircraft overhead right now and, frankly, in his present mood, Tony didn't give a damn.

Down here at eight thou G George was in range of the light stuff and when it finally came up it was a wall of tracer, not aimed, just poured up in front. No point in jinking or dodging, best to go on straight and level, get the other side of it with the least possible delay.

Roofs and streets a moving procession below, "Looks like Leer," Tony's finger was on the map he held up before the horrified Fuller, whose eyes were hypnotised by the interlacing patterns of orange and white tracer. Now the flak was left behind, the river was leading them towards a city patterned by a herring-bone of docks. Emden.

"Not yet," snapped Tony as Fuller made to unplug himself

and go forward. Not giving him the chance to chuck the bombs down short of the target. Nobody was firing at them. Not yet.

Centre of Emden coming up, still no flashes in the sky, Tony punched Fuller's arm, he just had time to stretch out at the bombsight before the dazzling shafts of searchlights fenced in G George. Two solid columns of light tumbled past the windscreen, a third beam fastened on, one after another straightedges of blinding light angled up from the ground, G George was a fish swimming in a sea of eye-searing white.

And then the flak began, bursting in black smudges, a continuous never-ending firecracker rattle, smell of cordite wafting through the cockpit. "Bomb doors open," said Tony. Either they were going to fly out of all this crud or they weren't, what the hell, nothing whatever to do but sit it out, no such thing as time; what was left of it was a dazzle of firecracker eternity, Christ, that was close, fewer firecrackers now, searchlights sliding behind, going out one by one, G George alone in a blank black sky, why hadn't he felt the kite lift—

"I didn't—so much flak, I didn't drop—"

"Have another go," said Tony. Hard one-eighty degree turn, over Emden again, height spinning away on the altimeter, below five thousand now, G George lifted, bombs gone, bomb doors up, balls-out, diving for speed, no guns, no searchlights, caught them on the hop. What he'd done and the chances he'd taken caught up with him as G George flew home over the sea. Drenched with sweat, Tony couldn't stop his feet from trembling.

"Went round a second time," said Fuller. "Dropped 'em bang on target." The Intelligence Officer nodded, more of those pretty Greek "e"s on the Debriefing Form. Chaps like this at the bombsight, war will be over in next to no time.

* * *

"There I was," said Tony, "upside-down in cloud, fuck-all on the clock and still climbing." Which, in the esoteric jargon of the bomber's trade, was the classic reply to squelch a bod who was shooting a line.

He'd used it on Fuller this afternoon, the third time the Cheppie had told the Crew Room, "There I was over Emden, old boy, flak and searchlights everywhere, couldn't get the docks in my bombsight, so round I went again—"

Shortly afterwards Tony was thanked by a pilot called Overton. "If you hadn't shut that cocky bastard up I'd have belted him one." Overton was a bit upset, shaky do last night, front turret hit by flak, gunner strawberry jam.

Eighteen of the squadron's Wimpeys out last night, two crews missing; sprogs, one on their second op, the other on their fourth. Everybody was sorry, of course, great shame really, but little gloom hung over the Crew Room. People come, people go. It was only when a crew well on in their tour didn't come back that the pontoon schools were less noisy, the chatter subdued.

Who in the Crew Room except me still remembers Hickey and Tinker, Tony wondered. The just-arrived issues of *Aeroplane* and *Flight* had been going round the Crew Room, well-thumbed already, especially the pages which carried the latest Air Ministry list of aircrew casualties. There they were, Hickey, Tinker, Phil and Geordie, their names scattered alphabetically amongst the long columns, "Missing Believed Killed in Action."

Other names, too, Tony recognised. Someone from school—Jameson ma. would never keep wicket again—two or three crews he'd known at Littledale OTU, several, of course, from his first week or two on the squadron. Too early for Tich, probably be in next month. Well, doesn't do to brood. To cheer himself up, Tony opened the letters he'd brought over from the Mess, no fewer than three today, plus a postcard.

Picture of Worcester Cathedral—"2w, 3d, 11h, 4m, 21s, X K." Mum and Dad hoped he was well, they were all fine, lovely blossoms still on the apple tree, Trixie in disgrace, buried bone in lawn, Love. Dick: coming over on Tuesday evening, 8-ish, all other things being equal. Got a surprise for you. Yrs, D.

Surprise? Good show. Tuesday's today, isn't it? "Ramsbottom—what's today?" "Gosh, Marlowe, I don't know." Tuesday it certainly was, however, information volunteered by Dicky Bird, Twinkletoe's rear gunner. Who added, "And the big hand's on the ten and the little hand's on the four."

Unrecognised writing on the other letter. Turned out to be

from Chalkey White, who'd ever have thought.

"Dear Tony, Well, here I am at OTU, it's a bastard. Sight more dangerous than ops, believe me. All the kites are clapped-out and keep falling out of the sky, five written off last month. Lost four screened pilots." If you were screened, jargon again, you were an instructor, just off ops. "Fact is, I can't wait to get back on squadron, but once they've got you instructing at OTU they won't let you go for six months. It's a laugh the way the RAF calls OTU a 'rest' after a tour of ops, take it from me."

Decent of Chalkey to write. Click of Tannoy, not much to worry about, not after ops the night before and anyway, it was late in the afternoon. Sure enough: "LACW Hooper two-eight-nine report to—" Across the Crew Room Tony caught Fuller's eye, was given a glance of sheer hatred. Fuller was aching for revenge, he was at a corner of the table with Ramsarse and Eckersley, no band of brothers we, Tony knew that his crew looked upon him as a dangerous maniac, well, if they wouldn't work with him, they'd work for him. Have to watch his step, though. First chance they got to humiliate him, they'd grab.

Eight-ish, Dick had written, but there was nothing ish about quarter to ten. Tony was almost alone in the Mess, there had been a general emptying about an hour and a half ago, what with the ENSA show on tonight.

Didn't seem much point in hanging around any longer. Pity, had been looking forward to Dick's surprise. All other things being equal meant if neither of us is on ops and maybe Dick's squadron over at Flaxfield is going out tonight. Tony finished his glass of gnat's piss and unscrunched himself from the shabby green armchair.

The only other chair occupied held a pilot called Durrel who was pretending to read the *Daily Mirror*.

"Just going over to the Every Night Something Awful. Like to come?"

"Oh. No, no thanks, Marlowe." Broody. Chop written all over him.

The Station's theatre-cum-cinema was jam-packed (tomorrow was the Other Ranks' fortnightly pay-day) but Tony found a place to lean right at the back. A comedian was making jokes about senior NCO's—as always, he'd found out beforehand the Station Warrant Officer's name—and about the RAF police. He then told several more in less careful taste about virgins, Waafs and mothers-in-law. He made a slighting remark about Hitler and was somewhat critical of Goering.

"And then there's Goebbels, you all know Goebbels, proper little b-b-b-b-basket, 'e is, in't 'e? In't 'e, eh? Ur, proper little basket. Well, Goebbels, see, 'e dies, yersee—you've 'eard it? You've 'eard it? Nah, I thought you 'adn't, Goebbels dies, and there 'e is, standing outside them Pearly Gates, the Pearly Gates.

"So Goebbels, 'e knocks on the Pearly Gates and out comes Saint Peter—wait for it, wait for it—and Saint Peter, 'e says, Saint Peter says . . . 'Vat you want?' " He got a generous round of applause that warmed the cockles of his heart, best audience since the New Cross Empire back in 'thirty-two.

An elderly lady scraped Eine Kleine Nachtmusik out of a vinegary cello and was listened to with respect but not without muffled giggles from around Tony where some wit had whispered, "Watch the spike! Exhibeesh!" Now two creaky dancers were prancing and poncing about the stage, one in approximately forty square yards of flowing drapery, the other in plum velvet doublet and green Robin Hood hat. What the hell, it was free.

Up till now it had been a typical ENSA show, no better, no worse, but as tepid applause died away the curtains drew across the stage and on came the Station Entertainments Officer, a grey-haired twenty-three-year-old who'd survived two tours of Hampdens.

"And now ladies and gentlemen, it's my pleasure to introduce, bringing us her speciality straight from London's famous Windmill Theatre—" ho, ho, so this was Dick's surprise "—Miss Judy Gale!"

Every light in the theatre went out. A drum began to tap, slowly, tantalisingly. A single spotlight threw a glaring white circle, a leg, gloriously long, deliciously bare, slithered between the curtains and a high-heeled shoe tapped once, twice, three times, to the beat. Roar of applause. The leg slid back. Six beats later it reappeared, kicked high and let the shoe drop. Scarlet-nailed toes wiggled in greeting.

Curtains swished open on a darkened stage, more spotlights flicked on and there was an audible gasp from the packed audience. All she did was stand, serenely still—Judy Gale, but so much more than Judy Gale, her presence filling the theatre, pin-drop silence as she stood in a dark-green velvet gown and long white gloves, vivid red hair piled high.

Tap, tap, tap, a new rhythm and, gravely, she began slowly to peel off one glove, then the other and drop them on a chair beside her. She began to sway, side to side, in time with the tapping drumbeats, her face dreamy, demure. Her hands reached behind her, she pulled a zip, stopped, then pulled again. A flurry of green velvet twirled through the air to fold itself over the chairback. Again she was still, standing in a wisp of black-and-white lace.

Awed whisper in front of Tony, "Goes straight to the balls."

A muted trumpet sounded softly behind the drum and now the trumpet snarled and as the bump-and-grind music started Judy, was it really Judy up there, wasn't wearing lace any more, just three heart-shaped scraps of black.

She reached up and her red hair flowed across her shoulders and she began to twist and thrust the near-nakedness of her writhing body to the crashing beat of drums and cymbals and the yearning of the trumpet.

Not a sound in the theatre as the throbbing of the drums died away, as she knelt on the stage, her hair tumbling before her, skin of her back and shoulders glistening in the spotlights, silence as the stage went black and the curtains closed.

Spotlight. A bare arm came through the curtains, waved, and three heart-shaped scraps of black were whisked out into the audience and that was when the cheering and stamping and whistling began.

"First time," someone was saying, "that I saw a girl shagged by the Invisible Man."

* * *

"No, sir," said the white-jacketed waiter in the Officers' Mess, the tiny wrinkled ancient they called Low Forties after his RAF number, he'd been in since Pontius was a pilot. "No message for you." Nothing from Dick, so what to do now was to find Judy and get her away from the ravening mob, one can only try. "Did you see that girl dancing, sir? They tell me there wasn't a dry prick in the house."

"Low Forties, you're a dirty old man."

"Thank you. Sir—if I was your age, I'd be over at the Sergeants' Mess. That's where the ENSA company's gorn. Everybody's invited."

No All Ranks Dance in the Sergeants' Mess tonight, no Kate, no Chalkey White, but chatter, chatter, chatter, too many uniforms, the two aged prancers, the gnome of a Cockney comedian, the elderly lady shaped like her cello and disappearing under a waterfall of blue shawls.

No Judy.

But a "Pssst" and a tug at his sleeve and Assistant Section Officer Cynthia Dayton-Jarvis whispering, "She's asking for you, Tony. We've holed her up in the WAAF loo. Hiding her from the Perambulating P."

"Thanks, Cynthia, thanks a lot." Good of her, especially as Tony had thought that he and Assistant Sexual Officer Dayton-Jarvis still weren't speakers; on his second, pre-Kate, evening after arriving at Olney Market he had lured her into the Morris Eight, no dice and an elbow in his ribs.

Cynthia wrinkled her Tatler brow. "You really should," she admonished, "put bromide in your morning tea."

Tony was not allowed in the WAAF quarters of the Sergeants' Mess but then neither, on unofficial business, was the Perambulating Prick, they passed each other, eyes averted, in the corridor. Round a corner an arm reached out from the doorway of the loo and snatched Tony in to a dark Yardley's Talc haven of brass-buttoned overcoats. Sound of footsteps approaching, stopping at the doorway. "He wouldn't dare," outraged whisper from an indistinct Judy.

More footsteps, Cynthia's Mayfair voice, she ektually came from Ealing. "Hello, Group Captain, on your way to the party?" Footsteps again, receding. A pull at Tony's tunic, "Follow me." Loom of cubicles in the pitch dark, fingers fiddling with a blackout screen, click of a catch, a window going up.

Tony holding Judy's waist, lovely handful of girl, heave, she was through, he was scrambling after. They stood for a moment amid rose bushes.

"What's Group Captain? Someone important?"

"Enormously."

"God's little brother Alf? Then why does he make popping noises in his nose? Hello, Tony." She hugged him, smackingly kissed his cheek. "What shall we play now?"

"We could play sitting in my car."

"Oh, dear, Cynthia did warn. Haven't got a cheese sandwich, have you?"

Later, "Branston pickle," gleefully. "Buzzard." He'd worked miracles of organisation, parked her in his car among the trees outside the Officers' Mess while he conjured sandwiches out of Low Forties and bottles of beer from the Bar, not forgetting the opener and all in about ten minutes.

"Not buzzard. Wizard." He waited while she tip-tilted a bottle of Watney's and let out a long, low "Aaaaah." He asked, "Where's Dick?"

"He'll be along." Again Judy guzzled noisily. "About midnight." Tony glanced at his watch: twenty to. "He got a call at the hotel this afternoon, had to take off to help Air Sea Rescue look for a Wimpey that crashed out at sea."

Must have searched the sea till dark, long flight home. What hotel where, he wondered, probably the Eastleigh at Flaxfield, decided not ask, mind his own business. Judy said, "Like my dance?"

Tony made a slurping sound, indicative of indescribable lust. "Buzzard," he said.

"Positively my last ENSA appearance, steam will come out of Basil Dean's ears. Second and last, Flaxfield last night, Onley Market this." She belched alarmingly, like a Bofors. "Had a few days off from the Windmill. Buswoman's holiday. Girl I know asked me to take over for her, husband's back from Africa. Wounded," she added sorrowfully.

"Show must go on."

"Indeed, Tony, indeed, and it gave Dick and me a chance to be together. And for me to see you," dancer she may be but she was also an extraordinarily accomplished actress, he was quite shaken by the look she gave him of frustrated sexual longing. "Buzzard to you," said Judy.

"How is Dick?"

"Bit ho-humish." Oh, God, not going broody. "I think that awful father of his gets him down." Hope that's all it is.

Judy said, "Dick doesn't much like bombing."

"Nobody does. Chilly. Boring. Frightening."

"But Dick," began Judy, a pair of dim headlights wavered between the trees, a car, an Alvis, turned up the drive towards the Mess, Judy was out and running.

Tony waited a decent interval. As he came up, Judy and Dick disentangled.

"Wotcher, Dick. Did you find the Wimpey?"

"Bits of it." Dick's eyes were heavy with fatigue. "Thanks for looking after Judy." His voice sounding strange in its tiredness, he added, "Mind you both always look after each other."

Curious thing to say. Judy was pressing something into his hand, a slip of paper, on it a scribbled telephone number. "Any time, Tony."

Hurry of goodnights, a varoom of Alvis; a puzzled Tony stood listening until the sound of the engine died away in the silent Lincolnshire night.

★ ★ ★

In ordinary life, no doubt, one had plenty of time to ponder this, that and the other. You could have a nice quiet sit and ask yourself how Bill Wilberforce was doing in his Beaufort against those flak ships firing splash and why Dick had half-throttled the bald barman and why the hell you kept on wasting your time stooging over Germany.

Trouble was, on ops, there wasn't room inside your head to do more than daydream about Kate and keep the fear of the ops to come (seventeen) locked away, slam the door on the tiger. On top of which, what they didn't tell you about ops on a squadron was how incredibly tired you got, absolutely shagged out.

Two scrubs on two consecutive days, that really gave you a beating and yesterday night's had been an absolute bastard, take-off postponed for one hour, then for another and then yet another hour spent waiting in the cockpit of G George, which Tony with apologies had privately named the Deadbeat Express. You could chop up the atmosphere aboard the kite with a butter-knife; with the rest of the crew, Tony was definitely not popular.

The damp chill of an unseasonable mid-May night coated perspex and engine cowlings with a clammy film like the sweat you wiped from your face as you splitarsed away from the guns of the target, if that's what it was. A film on the windscreen you could write on if you'd nothing better to do, finger tracing out the letters: KATE. Nothing better to do until the word came and it might come at any moment—start engines, the flak and fighters of last night, Mannheim, tonight, Kassel are waiting for you less than three hours' flying away. Or until now, at 0130, someone waggled a torch and out you get, no op tonight. Twice in a row.

0200 and a scratch meal, no egg, in the Mess with the other exhausted aircrews, swamped once again by the guilty relief and the frustration of long hours of wasted work, NFT's, briefings and, especially, wasted emotion. Off to bed in the dusty, fuggy Nissen hut with its concrete floor and blacked-out windows.

Into your pit with the secret joy of not being in the dark high above Germany, nerves tight with the strain of watching the green-glowing dials, ready to haul and heave the Wimpey about the sky at the first sign of a hunting fighter or the sudden leap of the questing searchlights and all the time the worry of listening for a stutter in the roaring engines and the wonder, what sort of a balls-up is Fuller making tonight?

Yet sleep comes almost at once, no time, no energy to think, an escape from the shrieking arithmetic of the squadron's losses, three out of seventeen over Cologne and two out of eighteen over Emden in this past week.

No escape, however, from the day ahead. On the way to the Crew Room at two the next afternoon Tony saw the bomb trains snaking towards the Wimpeys at their dispersals and there they were, typed on the Battle Order, P/O Marlowe, F/O Fuller, Sills, Ramsbottom, Eckersley. NFT: 1500. Main Briefing: 1630.

The last two scrubs, in all conscience, had been bad enough for Tony but they must have been sheer hell for Stuffy McAllister and his crew. They were waiting to do their thirtieth, their last—Tony checked himself—their final op, a hell of a strain, poor sods.

Back once more in the Briefing Room, a shabby theatre with its scruffy cast of characters ready for the night's performance, so often presented before, its script a terse dialogue of compass courses and times, its action monotonous and boring, its drama sudden and frequently fatal. Curtain Up, the map of Europe, red wool stretching from Onley Market across southeast France into Italy and Stuffy and his crew whooping and slapping each other's backs. Milan. Piece of cake.

Better than that. A joy-ride. No searchlights, no flak, no fighters. Met wind must have been spot-on, too, not that there was much of it, not even Fuller could manage to get lost, not with an anti-cyclone squatting gigantically over the Alps as the Wimpeys and the Stirlings and the dicey Manchesters flew above the white peaks reaching sharply up towards them, five, four, three thousand feet below. Cook's tour. No wonder the Eyeties went in so much for opera, couldn't help it with this kind of scenery. Lovely, the mountains, of course; but too much of everything, too much snow, all that dazzling white laid on with a trowel, and high in the sky, much too theatrical, a shining, sharp-edged sickle moon, whole shebang one hell of an extravaganza. Sight to see, though.

Peaks dropped further and further below, the snow gave way to a countryside black and corrugated. Now the land below had flattened out and far in front Tony could see the target. The first aircraft were going in, his stomach tightened with the familiar bomb-run symptoms.

Up ahead the flak was starting but it was weak and widely scattered and the searchlights weren't giving the gunners any help to speak of, beams sliding aimlessly, none of the vicious decision that was so menacing over Germany. Incredibly, some lights were switching off, others stilled at odd angles, the flak was dying out. They wouldn't stencil a bomb on G George's nose for this op; someone would paint on an ice-cream cone.

The target was undefended as Tony brought G George, bomb doors gaping, over Milan as Fuller made cooing noises at the bombsight.

"Bombs gone! Bleeding fantastic, eh?"

Wasn't so beautiful on the way home, the moon sinking lower in that vast sky. They'd come a devil of a long way with half a continent still to cross, but no flak, searchlights or fighters, the struggle was only to stay awake, keep alert; incredible to remember that, once on an op, he'd daydreamed about blossom, Christchurch Road and Mum at her flowerbed.

Dawn broke while they were over the Channel and it was strange to see so many bombers in the sky. Bright daylight when they crossed the English coast and not even Fuller could miss seeing the Wash. Sills, when it wasn't needed, came up with a QDM with ample time to spare. Nothing to the daylight landing, so, naturally, he bounced the Wimpey twice.

Christ, he was tired. So was everyone else, debriefing was unusually quiet. Perhaps not just because of fatigue. Perhaps for the reason why Tony was glad Bill Wilberforce hadn't been on this op. For the Eyetie crews had run from their searchlights and guns, tonight Bomber Command had not fought its enemies, the flak and the fighters. They'd attacked the men, women and children in their homes in the city below—but tired, sweaty and grimy, Tony was between the sheets and sleep came in a rush and took all thought away. Even the memory that somehow on this ice-cream op Stuffy McAllister and his crew had gone missing. You expected the sprogs to go for a burton but when the old-timers got the chop you had to be careful not to ponder.

* * *

Forty-six not out, Tony spun the bat in his hand and gazed round the field. New bowler coming on.

Two slips, gully, deep third man, cover-point; mid-off and mid-on both moving deep; a fielder near the boundary at long-on and now a third slip taking up position. Wicket-keeper's a lot further back, stand by for a speed merchant.

No ops tonight and the war had stopped for the squadron for a day in which the aircrew joined in the peaceful, you couldn't really call it peacetime, life of the rest of RAF Station, Onley Market. For if you didn't fly, if you were one of the two thousand men and women of the ground staff, the airfield with its hangars and workshops and offices was nothing more, nothing less, than the same old Wimpey garage where you put in the day's graft with tools, typewriter or scratchy pen.

Mind you, no pre-war union would ever have sanctioned the

conditions of work, no foreman would ever have got away with all that buggering-about you got from corporals and sergeants and that bastard of a Station Warrant Officer. Couldn't call your soul your own—why, this very cricket match on this chilly, cloud-covered afternoon, Ground Staff v. Aircrew, was the Groupie's idea (feller's Station is often judged by the standards of its Sports).

Plenty to grumble about, don't you know there's a war on. The cooking in the Airmen's Mess or the NAAFI wasn't a patch on Mother's or The Wife's; nor was the draughty Nissen hut where you slept on straw biscuits what you might call comfortable. Everybody grumbled all the time, especially those who were married; but some of the older ones didn't put their hearts into it, remembering the Slump, knowing that tomorrow wouldn't find them lining up at what they always called the Unemployment Exchange.

And in the backs of the minds of even the most cheesed-off members of the Ground Staff XI was the thought: this won't be my last game. Tony took a new guard, two legs, and hacked his block. The speed merchant paced out his run, dug in his heel, stopped, stood looking skyward.

The Wimpey was coming down through scattered cloud, now you see it, now you don't, but you could hear it, an unhealthy rumble. In trouble. On one engine. Clear of the cloud now, it lumbered low over the cricket pitch, awkward, black, graceless, its motionless starboard propeller like a stuck-on decoration.

Tony remembered another Wimpey, another time, Kate beside him. He read the letters on the fuselage—that was a Littledale OTU Wimpey, crewed by sprogs, turning towards the runway half a mile ahead, the pilot, poor bastard, must be shitting bricks.

Long, low approach, wheels coming down, over the runway now, the Wimpey vanished behind the hangars, the giant black tree of oily smoke began to grow before they heard the muted whoof of the explosion. "Play," called the umpire at the bowler's end.

Fastish ball but short of a length and a foot wide of the off stump. Tony caught it in the meat of the bat, it streaked away past cover-point, boundary all the way.

Fifty.

* * *

Duisburg, Mannheim, Essen, Hanover, Münster, Wilhelmshaven, Osnabruck, Homberg, Oberhausen, Bochum, Rostock, Cologne, Emden, Milan, fourteen ops. Fourteen targets. Admittedly the tit had usually been pressed over a dot inside a square drawn on a chart but as far as Bomber Command's fatuous statistics were concerned Tony had unloaded his bombs over thirteen city targets and hit for certain one enemy airfield (not the primary target. Black mark?).

He was mildly glad the fourteenth was over and done with, for that was the one, not the thirteenth, dreaded by the more superstitious crews on the squadron. All the fault of Fishy Rowe.

"Simple matter of arithmetic," Fishy had said. "Count up the number of Wimpeys that have been sent on ops since I came to Onley Market. Two hundred and thirty-eight. Seventeen haven't come back. Exactly one in every fourteen."

And then as if to prove his point Fishy bought it on that Emden op, his very own fourteenth, bit of a giggle, that. Until you remembered at the time that you hadn't done your first fourteen, let alone the second fourteen of the thirty of even your first tour. Didn't do to brood, though.

What was alarming, however, was Twinkletoes telling Tony, "You'll be carrying a camera from now on." Flattering, maybe, especially considering the crew that Tony was flying with, but highly disturbing to the apprehensive airman. Trouble was, if you'd got a camera you dropped a photoflash with your high-explosive and incendiaries and then you had to stooge on straight and level for twenty long seconds until the wretched thing went off and the picture got taken.

Nobody but a maniac would fail to yank his Wimpey into a splitarse turn as soon as "Bombs gone" so long as he had a choice. What the flak gunners down there prayed for was a kite flying steadily on for that third of a minute, as they pooped up their 88mm shells to reach just where their radar predictors promised your particular kite would be.

No chance to dodge, you see, that was the trouble, while you were waiting for that flash and wondering if you'd be keeping an appointment with an up-and-coming burst of flak. Which was one reason for looking forward to tonight's op (Hanover again) with even less than usual relish.

"ETA Hanover," said Fuller's voice, tinny against the rumble of G George's engines. "Coming forward to bomb."

As insurance against Effing Fuller's parlour games, Tony had checked the Estimated Time of Arrival with Tubbs. "Good idea," Tubby had said, stouter than ever in his fur-lined Irvin, "Don't trust that bastard further than you can throw him." And then Tubby had kindly marked up a small, handy Captains of Aircraft chart for Tony. "Never fly on ops without one." Well, you live and learn, And you have to learn, to live.

Four minutes early for the expected ETA but Fuller could have found—doubt, really—that the westerly wind was stronger than the Met forecast. Perhaps Hanover really was beneath them under the cloud.

"Stay back where you are, Fuller. We're going down to take a look."

"But we're at DR Hanover—"

"Shut up."

Sometimes you felt that there was nothing to life but fear and fatigue and fucking Fuller in the night sky, the dials ready with the threat of disaster, sweat and spit in your chafing oxygen mask, taste of rubberised air. G George slid out of the base of the cloud, blank darkness below but up ahead to port, bright sparkles in the sky.

"Fuller, I'm altering course twenty degrees to port, there's flak over there, about twelve miles to go." Four minutes early, more or less. Time taken to fly twelve miles. Significant.

"But we're at DR Hanover right now—"

"Fuller, for Christ's sake, belt up."

Four minutes, two hundred and forty seconds, two hundred and ninety heartbeats, bags of flak coming up, quite a few searchlights slithering across the sky, beams crossing, dozens more suddenly shining up, at their apex a brilliant tiny four-engined Stirling, more beams, flak all around, flak stopping, tracer, whoomph of smoke, bagged by a fighter.

Drifts of cloud beneath, clouds clearing, far below blazing squared-off lines like a crossword puzzle on fire. "Hanover ahead, Fuller. Come on up and bomb."

Left, left. Steady. Right. Steady, steady. Just sit here, sod all you could do against the flak, hear it, dicey, smell it, shit creek, sharp tang of cordite, sit it out. Steady, steady. "Bombs gone."

"Fuller, did you remember the photoflash?"

"Oh. God, no. Dropping it now."

Straight and level. Radar's locked in on our height, flak bursting alongside, radar's got our track and speed, they're feeding in the shell with G George's name on it, bursts noisier, tang of cordite constant now, not just whiffs, there goes the flash, diving splitarse turn, just in bloody time, sky's full of stuff where we were going to be.

Another van was waiting beside My Brother Sylvest's at dispersal, from it a bod dashed out to unload that sodding film.

Gold pen. Greek "e"s. "Bombed primary. Good show, chaps." Well, thought Tony, that showed Fuller and the other stupid bastards where they got off.

Twinkletoes at their debriefing table, scars of melted black rubber on his cheekbones, "Sorry, Tony. Bad news." He slapped a still-wet eight-by-ten glossy photograph on the table: network of white lines against solid black. "That's not Hanover. It's a decoy target. The Jerries lit up a criss-cross of bonfires—"

When Twinkletoes had gone, "Might just as well have dropped on DR," said Fuller. His laugh was a triumphant insult, so were the giggles of Sills, Ramsbottom and Eckersley.

* * *

Fifteen ops done, half of your first tour, enough to leave you completely whacked out. Wasn't the sheer slogging hard work of ops, the accumulating strain, the draining away of the capital of your courage, what really took it out of you was the utter uselessness of it all, grinding out night after night with fuck-all to show for it.

They stopped talking suddenly, Fuller, Sills, Ramsarse and Eckersley, as Tony came into the Crew Room, obviously they'd been discussing him, he'd heard Fuller's high-pitched laugh, very funny, no doubt, Tony taking them last night to that decoy.

Tony was cheesed, brassed off, browned off, on the edge of brooding. He listlessly pretended to read, hiding behind a paperback. Should have bombed on DR, better than buggering about looking for decoys; they were openly jubilant about his balls-up. He'd never been so miserable before, never in all his nineteen years.

He'd been sandbagged all of a sudden by a terrifying despair, it had come over him out of nowhere, nothing seemed to matter any more and when Twinkletoes a bit later in the morning appeared with the announcement of a stand-down, ten-tenths clag covering all of Europe, it was only by reflex action that he got into the Morris and drove out of the camp, never end up sitting behind a bullet-hole.

Almost to his surprise he found himself in Lincoln, he hardly remembered the drive in. Lucky Kate couldn't see him like this, no aims, ambition or flaming interest; he was in a call-box, hardly knowing what he was doing, reading a scribbled number on a crumpled slip of paper, clanking in the coins the operator told him, pressing Button A.

Judy said, "Buckingham Palace Laundry."

He floundered, made what-did-you-say noises.

"Oh, I'm sorry. I was expecting a call from Arnold."

Stupid, confused, he asked, "Who's Arnold?"

"Arnold Kimber, only man I know who wears hairy tweeds with Chanel Number Five. He's a theatrical photographer, took some pix of me, thought it was him ringing to say they were ready. Hello, Tony."

He didn't speak, surprised she should recognise his voice.

"Tony?"

"Yes?"

Worried, "Where are you?"

"Lincoln Station."

"Is everything all right? You don't sound like you, somehow."

"I'd like to see you," he said, dully.

A moment's silence. Then, "Tony, it's ten past eleven. There's a train to King's Cross in twelve minutes. Platform Four. Got that? It's the one I often catch. Platform Four, eleven twenty-three. When you get to London, hop a taxi to Fourteen Pembroke Street, that's a few minutes from the Windmill.

Now, say that back to me."

He repeated her instructions, a lesson learnt like a schoolboy.

Decisively, "Right. Off you go. Platform Four. In eleven minutes. I'll be waiting." Buzz in his ears, she'd rung off.

At 14 Pembroke Street, three bells, one above the other, the top one marked "Gale."

He rang, up above a window opened. "Tony—catch!" He made a futile grab, keys jangled on the pavement. He opened a door, climbed one flight of stairs, started on a second, Judy was coming down to meet him.

"Tony, love—" she stopped as she saw the taxi-driver behind him.

"Could you lend me—I've only got a shilling or two—"

"Just a moment," she said, over Tony's head. She ushered him into her flat, collected her purse. "Thank you, miss," on the landing, "thank you very much."

Tony was standing where she'd left him; she put a flat hand on his chest, pushed him down into an armchair. She asked, "Do you want to cry?"

Startled, "No. No. I don't think so."

Judy nodded. "Then drink this." In his hand, a tumbler. Brandy. He gulped, coughed, gulped again. She said, "Down the little red lane. All of it." Gulp, gulp, fiery in his throat, his stomach; he took a deep breath. "Judy, I'm sorry to bust in on you like this—"

"Hush. When did you last eat?"

"Ten past seven," he said, pedantically.

"Steak? With an egg on it?"

"How did you—"

"I've a friend who has a friend who flies in the USAAF Transportation Command. Fried potatoes?"

"God, yes," said Tony.

"Drink this." Same tumbler, full of red wine.

Later, a wooden chair at the wooden table in the tiny kitchen. She put a plate in front of him. "Don't touch. Scalding hot. Eat," she commanded. She refilled the tumbler.

Steak. Fried egg. Fried potatoes. Tomatoes. Button mushrooms. She watched him as he ate, she was coming into focus, green eyes, red hair tied back, yellow dress. Everything was coming into focus.

"You're starting to look like Tony again."

He stood up, thanking her, gathering knife, fork and plate.

"Leave that." She led the way into the sitting-room, gas fire, weary carpet, two armchairs in faded maroon, one of those sofas which make up into a bed.

Tony said, "Eat me. Drink me. Just like Alice in Wonderland."

She was laughing up at him. "Kiss me."

He touched her lips with his, chastely. Her tongue slid in, slid out. He was a bit hazy but nowhere near drunk enough to—"Dick," he said.

Her tongue darted between his lips. "There was a Wimpey on fire, remember? Look after each other, he said." She was twisting the brass buttons of his uniform, sliding her arms beneath his tunic, quick little kisses. The sofa had become a bed, Judy wasn't wearing a yellow dress any more, he was losing himself inside her, finding himself, brooding, who's brooding—

* * *

No waving torches scrubbed tonight's op, no coded signal, however eagerly awaited by Sills, recalled the Deadbeat Express from over the North Sea.

The long needle on the altimeter arced slowly round: 13,700. At 14,000 Fuller was due to give him a new course for level flight. 13,800. Was Fuller's finger, as usual, well in? 13,900. Tony bet himself an odds-on yes and decided to treat himself to a piece of barley sugar, aircrew flying ration, if he were right.

14,000.

You kept your left hand on the control column, unclipped your oxygen mask, held one end of the wrapping by your teeth and twisted your right thumb and forefinger to denude the delicious sweetie. Back on with your oxygen mask, move the barley sugar into your cheek—used to do this for secret, forbidden pleasure in Stinks's chemistry class. "Boy! Are you eating?" Gulp. "No, sir." Click down the microphone switch.

"Fuller—"

"Yes?" Pompous, very full of himself.

"You owe me a new course at fourteen thousand."

"Oh." Not so pompous. Long pause, heavy breathing, forgotten to switch off his mike. A wait. A long wait. "224."

"Oh, Christ, Fuller, pull yourself together. That's probably the ground speed."

"God, just a minute . . . 125."

Eyes moving automatically along the green-glowing dials, air speed, artificial horizon, gyro, then sweeping the dark sky ahead, port to starboard, up, down. Gyro, petrol gauges, oil temperature, oil pressure, business as usual, flying a Wimpey, making his calls.

Starboard engine revs slightly low; a touch of throttle; needle steady on the dial.

Krefeld.

It was down there now, after the eternity of instruments, horizon, instruments, horizon. The Rhine glinted below, the black fingers of riverside docks thrusting out from the western bank. Mumble, mumble, from Ballsache Fuller up front at the bombsight, must mean time to open bomb doors. Down with the handle, fight the spasm of the control column as the doors crank down to bite into the airstream as G George bucks and lurches. Bags of flak to port. Over to starboard, some poor bastard catching it, a brilliant glitter at the apex of ruler-straight beams, a Wimpey in silver silhouette, twinkling flak flickering all round.

"Steady, steady." Come on, Ballsache, can't you find the tit? Bladder near to bursting, cold as charity and that's fucking chilly but not so cold as our poor Willy—Jesus, they've got him, blinding red flash, a billow of black smoke in the searchlight beams, reddish puff where the Wimpey flew no longer. "Steady, steady."

That cone of searchlights was gone as if dowsed by a single switch. "Left, left," looks as if he'd tamed Fuller, no more leaping up front and pressing the tit right away, a touch on the rudder pedal, "Steady." A blue pinpoint of light winked from the ground, the cockpit was suddenly alight in a brilliant flash, the radar-guided beam of the master searchlight had come and gone, flicking over and past G George.

Christ, it's back, everything dazzling bright in the cockpit, instruments lost in the glare. Now other beams leapt skyward as the radar beam locked on, as huge solid pillars of light wheeled up to seize on G George, instantly flak everywhere.

Voice yelling on the intercom, "Flak!" Thanks a lot, so helpful, ears ringing with the whipcrack of the explosions, unbearably loud, lights blinding, G George flung about the sky, Tony's wrists aching as he battled the crazily jerking control column, no time for thinking, just keep G George up in the sky—sledgehammer blow on the fuselage just behind Tony, G George reared up, sickening drop of the port wing, explosions all around, a rattle again, flak stopping, searchlights out.

Teeth clenched, every muscle straining, Tony heaved with all his strength at the handlebars of the control column; gradually G George rolled back to straight and level. Slowly Tony's night vision came back, the instrument panel was a blur, then a row of indistinct dials, then needles and numbers.

Hell of a bitterly cold wind howling through the cockpit but Tony was alive and G George was still flying, that's all that mattered, even if we've lost a hell of a lot of height. He could see everything clearly now in this scarlet light. What scarlet light?

To starboard an aircraft on fire was flying alongside. Better them than us.

His head was clearing now after the battering of the flak, the searing eye-staining ache of the lights, the disorienting acrobatics of G George—what idiocy was this, scarlet light, formating aircraft? He looked again to starboard and the sight he saw was so terrible he turned his eyes away, refusing to see. He forced himself to look again, half hoping, half believing, that it couldn't be true.

The starboard wing was on fire, that was true, that was why the guns had stopped, the searchlights gone out. Flames floated over the entire upper surface of the wing, cascading behind to a scarlet banner in the slipstream. Thumb stabbing the port fire extinguisher button. Useless. Into his microphone Tony yelled, "Jump, jump, we've had it!" Better switch the bloody thing on. "Abandon aircraft! Abandon aircraft!"

Now Tony understood the significance of the howling bitter wind. The parachute hatches were open. They'd gone, Fuller and Ramsbottom—Sills? Tony looked behind, couldn't see all the way into the radio compartment but there was the gaping hole in the side where the flak had hit and something, maybe leaking hydraulic fluid, maybe not, was splashing around on the floor. Eckersley? Probably first out, spin his turret, drop clear away. Out, out, out, out, out, shouting in Tony's mind, out before G George explodes in a black, smoking thunderflash, out NOW. Helmet off, that wire can strangle. He had it half off, could hear the wind whistling, the sound of something rolling in the radio compartment, heard the voice in the earphones, "It hurts."

Trust bloody Eckersley, Tony thought, his only feeling something like exasperation. He pulled his helmet back on and reached for the starboard petrol cock. Off. Hadn't remembered turning it. Press starboard feathering button, propeller blades stark and still. Jesus, still got the bombs aboard. May as well get the job done, Krefeld was still down there, the bomb doors were open, only take a moment. Jettison handle, tug, G George lurches, bombs gone, needn't bother about the photoflash.

"It hurts. It hurts." Pull out the intercom plug, ram the port throttle through the quadrant, full boost, control column hard forward, Christ, yes, close bomb doors, down we go.

Balls-out dive straight for the deck, if the wings come off, the wings come off, if G George doesn't pull out, it doesn't, down, down, down, airspeed right off the clock, down, down, wind blasting through from the open escape hatches, down, down, eyes on the blazing starboard wing.

One moment the flames covered the wing, the next they were a crescent of fire floating behind, whisking away, a fireball, gathering, disappearing. No time to cheer, no time to think, terrifyingly close the dim pattern of rooftops, streets and cross-roads and the voice in his mind saying, you're going to die, you're still going to die.

* * *

Fields below now, empty in the darkness, treetops, a road with a line of lorries, glint of shielded headlights, a farm with out-buildings, wallpaper on the windscreen, Tony hauled at the control column, pulling at a great unyielding weight as the countryside raced up towards him. More rooftops, more streets, a maze of railway lines, now the control column was coming back, slowly, slowly, sweat poured into Tony's eyes, his whole body one aching muscle, beginning to hope now, nose of G George lifting up, the town below tilting away. G George was straight and level, a factory chimney whipped past above the starboard wing, past the lethargically revolving propeller of the dead engine.

Hill right ahead, back with the control column, up and over, flak, silver tracer leaping up from the ground, glint of rails just below, through the steam of a puffing locomotive, hug the deck, orange balls all around, all at once a flak-free sky.

A parallel row of beaded lights, Christ, a Luftwaffe runway, above G George a Ju 88 crossing over, undercart down, huge swastika on its tail, out go the lights, a stream of orange, yellow, white, green balls climbs up, falls behind.

Empty fields. Tony wiped the sweat from his eyes, rubbed his hand dry on the leather of his Irvin jacket. Course—what course was he flying, no time to check: 005, almost due north. Automatically he began to turn on to 280, due magnetic west, Bomber Command's favourite course.

Empty fields.

To starboard, tracer arched indolently up and then whiplashed past the wingtip, Tony was too emotionally drained to care. Think. Think now. Estimate the track for home. Right. Say, 290. Variation west, magnetic best, 9W: 299. Deviation east, compass least, he leaned forward to see the card, 3E: steer 296. Set the P4. Set the gyro.

Intercom plugged in. Sound of heavy breathing, breathing with a bubble in it. Spit, let's hope, not blood. Click the mike switch.

"Eckersley?" Nothing but the sound of breathing. "Eckersley?" No answer. Pull out the plug—no, Eckersley may come round, leave it in, he'll need a reassuring word.

If there's one to offer. If we don't hit a hill. If we don't run into more flak from Luftwaffe airfields. If G George doesn't fall out of the sky, this kite's been bashed about enough, God knows. Please don't let Eckersley's breathing stop.

One thing, down here, on the deck, they were reasonably safe from marauding night fighters, anyone who had a go at G George stood one hell of a chance of writing himself off so low down, any Me 110 that tried a squirt at them only had to misjudge a fraction, wham, straight in. Tony, too, of course, could also misjudge. And down here G George was safe from radar, it can't work so low, blip gets all mixed up with reflections from the ground. So tired.

So tired, tired beyond belief. Wrists aching with the strain of holding G George in level flight, eyes grating with the effort of staring ahead into the darkness. Reaction setting in now, so much happening so fast, starting not to care.

Not to care, watch it, watch it, Griffin, lost, flying over the Ruhr in daylight, if they want me they can have me, they had Griffin in the end, keep caring, don't surrender,

Got to keep caring, nursing G George along, manhandling the tough old kite as it flew gamely on, hold her on 296, stay awake, fully awake, watch out!

Stay awake, saw those pylons at the last second, invisible high-tension wires stretched between them, touch those, a yellow flash, that's it. 296, good old 296, we should hit England if G George doesn't hit something else first. Where the hell are we? Know it's an effort, got to be made. Map in flying-boot. This map? No, that's Lincolnshire—local half-million, hot from the oven. This map. Think. Must be reasonably on track, hardly any wind down here, steam from that train was rising straight up.

You there, Marlowe, don't lounge at your desk, what time did you leave Krefeld? Sorry, sir, don't know, sir, busy at the time, sir. Look at your chart, foolish boy, you marked the Estimated Time of Arrival at the target, didn't you?

Here it is, ETA 0207. Got there more or less on time, hardly any wind, that's why. Fuller doesn't like winds, they interfere with his navigation, where's Fuller now? And Ramsbottom? Know where Eckersley is, he's breathing in the rear turret. What's the time? Can't be. Watch must have stopped. Don't hold it to your ear, fool, never hear it ticking through your helmet.

Check the second-hand. Moving. 0212. Five minutes since we were coned, since we caught the flak, since the blazing wing, seems like the day before yesterday.

Not much scenery around here, all the better, thank God. Empty fields still, can't check position, but at least there's nobody shooting. Navigation. No chance of a pinpoint.

Navigate by DR. Krefeld to Dutch coast, stretch finger and thumb on the map, check the scale; say, 100 miles. Indicated air speed 140, we're at ground level, so that's our true air speed. No wind, so that's our speed over the ground. How long to fly 100 nautical miles at 140 knots? Pencil.

Oh, God. Point's broken.

Right. Pull yourself together. Mental artithmetic. 60 into 140—that's about two-and-a-half miles a minute. Two-and-a-half into 100 goes—spot on, 40. 40 minutes. 40 minutes from 0212—watch it, 0207. ETA Dutch coast 0247.

More sums. Wide river should come up, let's see, 0215. That'll be the Maas.

Countryside all empty, doesn't anyone live here? Flat as a pancake, good show, no hills. Christ, so tired. Keep G George steady on 296, steady, show some guts, Sills must be showing his guts, Jesus, didn't mean to think that, squidgy things on the floor back there, something rolling about, keep your mind clear, concentrate on 296, shut out what you don't want to think, had enough practice, for God's sake, been doing it ever since you started on ops. Think about nothing else but 296.

Don't look at your watch until you see the River Maas. Check the P4, gyro may have wandered. Compass 300. Reset the gyro to 300. Right. Now back to 296.

Press on. Press on regardless.

Must have passed over the Maas, must be well after 0215. Give it a few minutes more.

Must have missed it. Check the time. 0214. Second-hand moving.

There was the Maas, promptly at 0215, slate-coloured against the black a thousand feet below and over to port the runway lights of another Luftwaffe airfield—oh, Jesus, Venlo.

Two minutes later, a small town. He was pretty sure it was Horst, he was checking the map when the arms of the windmill leapt suddenly up out of a black nowhere to pass barely a dozen feet below G George's battered fuselage and then Tony decided, no more map-reading; after all, somewhere up front was the coast of Holland.

He flew on, concentrating, unconscious of time, watching for every fold in the ground as the night thrust the occasional church steeple up towards him but mostly beneath G George were vast flat empty fields laced with a shining net of irrigation ditches. Once he crossed the impossibly neat ribbon of a canal; more steeples; now a wide river, very wide, studded with islands, the Maas again, now flowing southwest towards the sea. Land again and on the horizon past the dead-still prop, flak high in the sky. Bomber Command on the way home, someone had strayed over Rotterdam.

Almost, he whooped for joy. Thin white creaming edge of sea ahead, 0247. Spot on ETA. Red and orange balls sailing up, he watched them almost with boredom. To turn away or not to turn away? Might as well. Port or starboard? Port, towards the good engine. To the right, a sudden flurry of flickering lights, get hold of yourself, that stuff's lethal, turn the other way you'd have flown straight into it. Must be the last of it now, though.

Oh, Christ, no, so bloody unfair, flak again, a whole kaleidoscope of flak, arching all around, white, red, orange, yellow, curling lazily up, whipping past, a storm of flak between G George and the coast, tracer patterns of machine-guns intertwining ahead, bursts of cannon shells, nothing to do but sit tight and wham the throttle forward, sit tight and take it, better yet, ignore it. Either they'll get you or they won't.

They won't. Out of range now and over the gunmetal sea.

* * *

"Eckersley?" Try again. "Eckersley?"

Only sound, heavy breathing with a bubble in it.

0255. Decent watch this, seventeenth birthday present from Mum and Dad, no RAF issue for pilots, navigators got an Omega or a Longines, lucky sods. Not so lucky navigator Fuller, not if he dropped into one of those fires burning in and around Krefeld. What do the German civilians do to you if they catch you? 0257. Don't keep looking at the watch.

Unbelievably tired.

Stay awake. Treat yourself. A look at the watch. 0300. Done the sums. Should see the coast of Norfolk by 0326. Gyro: good old 296. Sing a song to stay awake. Out loud, nobody to hear, Sills isn't listening. Hey, hey, Cathusalem, Cathusalem, Hey, hey, Cathusalem, the harlot of Jerusalem. Hey, hey, Cathus—

Jesus Christ Almighty, 500 feet on the clock, must have fallen asleep, mustn't drop off again, well'll drop in. Sing. Any song but The Good Ship Venus. Sing.

Goodnight ladies, Sleep tight, ladies, Goodnight, ladies, We're going to leave you now.

Lousy line, that. Merrily we roll along, that's better, merrily we roll along, above the deep blue sea. Deep, all right. Not blue, though. Grey, with gentle white horses. Gentle, balls, hit that grey and it's like hitting concrete. Poor Tich. Thank you, Tich, for G George. Wizard kite. But cold.

Hello, ladies. Warm me, ladies. Warm me, Kate. Warm me with the glow of your skin, the clasp of your legs, the clutch of your hands, warm me against your hard-nippled breasts. Warm me, Kate. Warm me here.

Disciplined glance at the watch: 0308. P4 296. Gyro 296. Height 1500. 0310. Not so disciplined, that. So tired, so cold, so damn lonely. 0312. Fourteen minutes to England home and never mind the glory, At Flores in the Azores, Sir Richard Grenville lay.

Try the TR9 R/T radio, useless, probably, bloody incompetent Bomber Command, why can't we have long-range VHF like the fighters? R/T call sign. Stardust. The memory of days gone by. No, not Stardust. Starbright.

Click, mike on. Press transmit button on the control column.

"Hello, Darky, hello Darky. Starbright G George, Starbright G George."

Try again.

"Hello, Darky, hello, Darky. Mayday, Mayday, Mayday."

Again and again Tony called the odd-sounding distress signals into the silence, into the empty waste of waters, into the never-ending dark; as the minutes ticked by on his birthday watch, he feared his tiredness like a mortal disease. "Hello, Darky, hello, Darky—" Once in the lonely silence he looked at the waves below and they were tempting him to take his aching hands off the control column, just for a moment, to dip down, to sleep beneath the waiting waters.

"Hello, Darky, hello, Darky."

"Jesus," he screamed once, "someone answer—" and flooded with relief when he found he'd left the mike switched off. But if somebody didn't answer—"Hello, Darky, hello, Darky, Mayday, Mayday, Mayday."

"Hello, Darky, hello, Darky, Mayday, Mayday, Mayday—" A girl's voice, low-pitched, caressing, whispering from a pillow: "Hello, aircraft calling Darky, this is Kingfisher. What is your emergency?"

Tony swallowed, fighting emotion, struggling to make his voice normal. Deep breaths, right: calm, casual, this is a girl you can't let down.

"Kingfisher from Starbright G George, receiving you strength four." Deep breath. "Have lost starboard engine. Wireless-operator dead, rear gunner wounded, navigator and front gunner baled out. Over."

"Roger, Starbright, thank you." The voice soft, gentle, a tug on a pyjama cord. "Transmit for fix."

Press the button, call-sign, numbers one to five, Monday, Tuesday . . .

"Roger, Starbright. Stand by."

A man's voice now, rich, deep, confident, friendly. "Hello, Starbright. Your position is 112 miles from your base on a bearing of 117 true. How is your fuel?"

Glance at the gauges. "Fuel OK."

"Starbright, can you make it to Base?" A pause. "I'm afraid the emergency airfields are rather busy tonight."

God, it was tempting. A wheels-up belly-flop to sweat through, perhaps, if the undercart wouldn't come down. Certainly a single-engine landing, dicey enough. Much safer, much easier, to land on one of the miles-long emergency airfields near the coast. But there were other Bomber Command aircraft limping home from Krefeld with wounded and dying pilots, aircraft with controls shot away that would need every foot of the longest runway. Nothing from Eckersley since they dived down over the target—

"OK for Base."

"Good show." Hint of relief. "Steer 299 Magnetic, G George. Best of luck. Stand by."

Faintly in his earphones, another aircraft in distress. "Foxhound to Marigold. Losing height."

Marigold was the call-sign of North Ridley, an emergency airfield near the Norfolk coast. "Marigold to Foxhound. Roger. We're alerting Air Sea Rescue. You're fifteen miles from the coast. Stay up there, Foxhound. Listening out."

Seconds slowly into minutes, "Foxhound to Marigold. We're down to 200 feet. Going to ditch."

"Roger, Foxhound, roger." Urgently, "Keep transmitting. Listening out."

"Foxhound, one, two, three, four, five. Monday, Tuesday, Wednesday, Thurs—" Ahead to port a vivid red flash, red petrol flames on the water, someone at North Ridley saying, quietly, sadly, "Mother of God."

Gyro: 299. Height: 1500. No red lights on the instrument panel.

"Starbright from Kingfisher, how's it going?"

"Starbright. Everything's fine, thank you."

"Good show." That resonant, confident voice. "Stay on 299."

"299, roger. Listening out."

White pundit lights, red flashing beacons. Norfolk. Tony's tiredness lifted from him. Then, "Where are we?" Voice in his earphones, Tony jumped in his skin. Eckersley.

"Almost back at the English coast, Eck, everything under control. How do you feel?"

"Passed out, did I? Feel sort of weak. Been bleeding a lot. You OK?"

"Fine, thanks, good to hear you again. Sills has bought it, I'm afraid, Ramsbottom and Fuller baled out over Krefeld. Sorry you got hit. Is it still hurting?"

Then Eckersley, feckless, irritating Eckersley, Eckersley the complete bloody nuisance, yes, that Eckersley, crouched wounded and ice-cold in the rear turret of a crippled Wimpey grinding home on a single engine with the radio-operator dead in his seat and wind blasting through open escape hatches, a sieve of a Wimpey, that very same Eckersley redeemed himself once and for all. He said, and all right, yes, it's an old corny joke, but coming from Eckersley it was the sound of glory.

"Only when I laugh."

"Starbright from Kingfisher. Stay on 299. Forty-three minutes to Base. Godspeed. Good-night."

The girl's voice smoky and low, soft lights and sweet music. "Good-night, G George. Good luck, darling."

Lights glittering ahead, red and white, as G George flew closer resolving themselves into beacons and pundits, the coast of Norfolk. Smudge of a town below—Lowestoft, further to starboard the unmistakable shape of Great Yarmouth and Breydon Water.

In the blackness of the night a searchlight beam shot up, stayed perpendicular, blinked three times, look at me, swung down parallel to the ground, signpointing the way. As Tony flew on its beam faded, another flashed on to take its place, then another and another, all the way across East Anglia, then a beam pointing over the Wash, another ready on the further coast. And now in line with the final beam, a tent-like criss-cross of searchlights, a brilliant canopy over Onley Market.

This was the real RAF, forget Station Warrant Officers, forget Group Captain Rick-Walker, two thousand men and women putting their lives on the line, easy meat for any intruding Luftwaffe aircraft with bombs aboard, welcoming the risk to bring one of their bombers safely home.

Nav lights on. At once, "Hello, Tony, we see you. Welcome home." Twinkletoes. "Come right in, we're all ready for you."

Light as day in the canopy of lights above as Tony glided G George slowly, gently, down, hold it, hold it—from the corner of his eye a fire-engine and an ambulance racing alongside—oh, Jesus, don't let the kite swing, don't let a spark set us on fire, thank God the undercart came down, meeting the runway, touching down, slowing, slowing, stop, hoses spraying white foam over wings and fuselage and two men in asbestos suits, they'd walk into flames to get you out, were pulling open the cockpit roof.

Rush of air from above, someone with a plastic-windowed hood hanging over his shoulders. A hand carefully easing off Tony's flying helmet.

"All right, sir?"

"Not a scratch," said Tony.

A hand reached down, pulled the pin of his Sutton straps and clicked the release of his parachute harness.

The man in asbestos said, "Ups-a-daisy."

Glorious to feel solid earth beneath his flying-boots and to breathe in the scent of dew-heavy grass after the smell of rubber, metal, oil and sweat. They'd switched off the searchlight canopy but G George, what was left of it, poor bloody Deadbeat Express, was brilliantly illuminated by the incandescent blaze of arc-lamps; men everywhere, swarming over the carcass of the battered Wimpey or standing silently, spectators white-faced in the glaring light.

Twinkletoes was leaning over Eckersley; a face dark with dried blood looked up at Tony from the stretcher. "Thank you," said Eck, with a gallant try at a smile. To Twinkletoes, he said, "It was fucking marvellous, the wing was on fire, he went in to bomb."

The young bespectacled Medical Officer snipped scissors, shearing up a sleeve; dab, dab, on a bare arm a needle sliding in. Eyes closed as Tony laid his hand gently on the blood-encrusted face. Eckersley was in the ambulance, the MO smacked his palm against the closed doors, the white van with dark crosses was gone.

Quietly, Twinkletoes said to Tony, "Well done. Well done, indeed." Louder. "You certainly bent that aeroplane, have to stop it out of your pay."

"How's Eckersley?" as the MO looked long and hard at Tony, not answering. The MO asked, "You feeling OK?"

"Fine. How's Eckersley?"

"He'll mend. We'll patch him up and send him to Ely Hospital." Above the MO's head the rear turret was a shambles, the shattered perspex smeared with blood. "He had a lot of pain, took guts to sit there and take it." Only when I laugh.

Bent, G George was, to put it mildly. You could see clear through the fuselage, the ruined steel girders a skeleton against the arc-lights, the fluttering canvas skin slashed and charred. Inside someone was spewing his heart out. "I kicked it, I kicked it, head on the floor, I kicked it."

"Come on," said the MO. "Off with you. Now." He jerked his thumb at the waiting ambulance. "Right now."

* * *

White horses scribbled the deep blackness of the sea, concrete water was moving up towards him, beckoning him down, the single engine of G George was a rumble in his ears, he couldn't hold the kite up any longer, "No," he said quietly, "no!" and he was awake in Station Sick Quarters.

Peaceful room, green-painted walls, white ceiling, tang of

floor polish, faint whiff of disinfectant. Safe. Eckersley safe, too. Sills didn't make it, poor bastard. Where were Fuller and Ramsbottom? God, this bed felt good. He closed his eyes. Kate said, "Tony, darling."

Wide awake now, he jerked his head on the pillow. On a chair beside the bed, Kate, eyes brilliant blue, huge with anxiety. "You were dreaming." He reached out for her, her arms were around his shoulders, her lips cool on his, hungry, twisting, he was alive, very, very alive.

He uncovered a tunnel of sheet and blanket. "In you pop," he said. A door opened and Sawbones, the Medical Officer, was saying, "—all he'll need is a nice cold gin and a nice warm blonde, oh, God," at the sight of Kate's honeyed hair; Twinkletoes said, "Good-morning, Corporal Elliot. Where should we be, Sawbones, without your profound knowledge of modern scientific medicine?"

"Ars longa, vita brevis est," said the MO.

"Shouldn't be a bit surprised and the same to you. How are you, Tony?"

Still embarrassed, the MO counted Tony's pulse, took his temperature, said, "Ah, yes," in a most professional way and answered Tony's question about Eckersley. "I rang Ely. Doing fine. Out in a couple of weeks or so," and disappeared.

He was back almost immediately with a bottle of Gordon's, four tumblers and a medicine-bottle full of orange juice, the kind the Ministry of Food issued to nursing mothers. "Here's half the prescription, anyway." They sat, Twinkletoes and the MO on Tony's bed, Kate on the only chair. Tony said, "I thought it was going to be one w and three d's—"

Kate looked at the watch on her wrist. "And six h and nine m. But Twink—Wing Commander Kincaid very kindly rang the CO at Worcester and got me a short compassionate leave."

Eagerly, "How long?"

"Well, I've got to be back on the midnight train from London to Worcester—"

"Which means," said the MO, the sort of chap who always had such things at his fingertips, "catching the seven-fifteen from Lincoln."

"Nine hours from now," calculated Twinkletoes. "Is he well enough to get up?"

"I've had a marvellous kip," said Tony.
"So I should think, I gave you a jab, ars longa, you snored all the way through yesterday. Yes, sir, he's fine, time he stopped lying there dodging the column."
"So he's well enough to be told the news?"
"Fit as a fiddle, sir."
"Well, Tony," said Twinkletoes, "when you're in Lincoln, buy yourself a bit of ribbon." Sudden glow in Kate's eyes. The Wingco raised his dark yellow tumbler in a toast. "Just got a teleprint from Group awarding you the Distinguished Flying Cross."
But Tony and Kate didn't go straight to Lincoln. On the way Tony stopped the Morris at a stile, they walked hand in hand across a sunlit meadow embroidered with the yellow and white of buttercups and daisies and into a wood springy with turf and smelling of fern.
"Now for the rest of that prescription," said Kate. What with one thing and another and another, they didn't get to Lincoln and the tailor's shop on the outskirts until almost closing time.
The manager took them upstairs to his flat and his wife fed them tea and gingerbread and Kate, frowning over borrowed needle, thread and thimble, tip of her tongue showing at a corner of her lips, sewed on, as she'd insisted, the purple and silver ribbon beneath the wings of Tony's uniform.
Wizard.

* * *

Back in his blacked-out room at Onley Market, with Kate still on her slow train to Worcester, Tony sat on the unlucky bed, fountain-pen and pad in hand.
Sills, H for Henry, Ramsbottom, E for Edward, Fuller, K for Kenneth, Eckersley, J for James. Jimmy. Odd how none of them had ever used Christian names. Ramsbottom, where's Eck? Fuller asking, lend me a quid, Sills? Using them now for the first time.
Dear Mr and Mrs Sills, I was Henry's pilot and I would like you to know how much I sympathise with you on the loss of your gallant son. All of us in the crew thought very highly of him and he was one of the most popular chaps on the squadron . . .

Dear Mr and Mrs Fuller. Dear Mr and Mrs Ramsbottom. Dear Mr and Mrs Eckersley. Henry, he wrote, had died bravely doing his duty. Edward had stayed by his guns, even though the aircraft was on fire, had baled out only when an explosion seemed imminent. Kenneth had stayed at his bombsight, etc., so had Jimmy at his guns.

Bullshit? Maybe some of it was true. Only when I laugh. Who knows how you'll behave when the crunch comes?

Anyway, thought Tony, unbroodingly, one day someone might be writing a letter about him. Meantime, he had Kate's ribbon to wear. It was ten past one when he finally stamped his envelopes and set off through the darkness to the Mess postbox. There still seemed to be something going on in the anteroom. A thrash?

In the big shabbily-carpeted room with the Peter Scott ducks flying through the tracer and the King and Queen solemn above the fireplace, all the worn green leather armchairs had been piled into a precarious, wobbly pyramid. At its unsteady peak was an upside-down barefoot navigator, held up on one side by an extravagantly good-looking air-gunner, on the other by a huge Wop/AG in the passionate purple of the Royal Australian Air Force.

The navigator had soot on the bottoms of his soles and heels. Carefully he imprinted footprints to continue a line that led up one wall and on across the ceiling.

"Care for a glass of beer?" the inverted navigator asked Tony, politely.

"In the jug," invited the handsome AG.

The Australian said, "Pommy bastard."

Tony found a fairly clean glass and poured Harpic from chipped white enamel. Slowly, the armchair pyramid subsided and its human apex thumped to the floor with the resilience of the rather drunk.

"Very sproggy gong," said the navigator, inspecting Tony's shiny new ribbon; beneath his own brevet he wore a threadbare DFM.

"My name is Jake, delighted to meet you," said the movie-star gunner. "This, inevitably, is Digger, and that clueless navigator answers to Jasper, LOOK OUT," a two-handed grab as a shoe hurtled through the air.

"Play rugger, by any chance?" asked Jasper, with elaborate courtesy.

"Er, yes—"

"Good-oh," said Digger. "God's own country and Judaea versus the Pommy bastards."

Digger maintained that he'd won the toss and elected to kick off. The shoe whacked into the ceiling just by the black footprints, Tony dived for it and gathered it close as Jasper crashed into him with a chest-high tackle. With six-foot-five of Digger sitting heavily on his stomach, Tony said reproachfully to Jasper, "You were supposed to be on my side."

"That's right," said Jasper, pouring beer into the shoe.

Jake was busy over by the fireplace, filling Jasper's other shoe with soot. He poured in a splash of beer, stirred the mixture with his finger, showed the resulting mess to Digger.

"About right?"

"Hero soup," said Digger.

"If there's one thing that lets the Royal Air Force down," said Jake to a helplessly spreadeagled Tony, "it's a shiny new gong." He painstakingly smeared Tony's gleaming ribbon until the bright silver and purple stripes became a soaking blackish blur. Satisfied, he refilled the shoe with beer and took a sooty-lipped swig.

"Pity Our Ern is missing this, he likes a good christening does Our Ern." Jake took a couple more swallows and passed the shoe to Digger.

Squashed flat and short of breath, Tony gasped, "Who's Our Ern?"

"Flies with us, rear gunner, has to doss down, sod it, in the Sergeants' Mess. I'm front gunner," said Jake, "Digger works the radio, Jasper fiddles about with maps." Big, tough, long-faced Digger; handsome, dark-eyed Jake; Jasper, fair-skinned, red-cheeked; all were studying Tony, still stretched flat on his back.

"We were sent here to fly with a new pilot," said Jasper. "Know a chap called Marlowe?"

* * *

Our Ern was a tiny sprightly cocksparrer. " 'Ullo, convict," he greeted Digger in the Crew Room. " 'Oo's this, then?"

"Our new Driver, Airframe." Jasper did the honours. "Name of Marlowe."

"Call me Tony."

"See what you're like with a Wimpey first."

"Ah, you've met." From behind his desk, Twinkletoes grinned at Tony's beer-stained gong. "Now the question is, do you all want to fly a nice quiet practice flight or two to shake down together or would you rather fly on ops right away? There's a do tonight I could put you on."

Jake glanced at Jasper, Digger and Our Ern. Then he looked at Tony. "We'd prefer an op if it's all right with you."

Beam from Twinkletoes. "Good show. In that case, there's a new kite waiting for you. O Orange in Number Two Hangar, just flown in by the ATA."

ATA was Air Transport Auxiliary and they found the pilot who'd brought in O Orange standing with Chiefy Woods and gazing up at it in the hangar. She wasn't much bigger than Our Ern. "Good kite," she said, all jolly hockey sticks, to Tony and his goggle-eyed crew. "Handles well. Hope it brings you lots of luck." Off she went in her dark-blue uniform with the big gold-edged wings.

"Cor," from a carroty-haired flight mechanic in oily dungarees. "Bints flying Wimpeys, whatever next?"

Tony realised he'd acquired no ordinary crew, for immediately they were busy making much of O Orange's ground staff, a friend in need is a friend indeed.

Chums already, they all sat together, cramped inside O Orange. Odd what you found out. One of the fitters was grey-haired, his voice carrying the precision and vowels of Cambridge. He was known as Big Head. "Well, yes, I am actually an archaeologist by trade, but there's not much digging going on just now—" There were Ginger and Wacko and Peek (he was LAC Frean) and, yes, really, Oswald. It was, in fact, Oswald who put it to the assembled meeting that O Orange should have a name and Digger, inevitably, who supplied it. Approval was unanimous and Peek, who was a sign-painter in that curious pre-war world, inscribed very neatly on the nose of the brand-new Wimpey: WANKER'S DOOM.

No ordinary crew. With Fuller, Sills, Ramsarse and

Eckersley, Tony had always carried out the Night Flying Test by himself, taking the Wimpey up with only the regulation ground-crew bod for company.

Luckily they had been given their aircraft early in the morning, otherwise they'd never have got everything done. It was ages before Tony could take off, as Jake and Our Ern made him taxi down to the firing range, where they checked first the sights of the two front guns, tracer zipping into the earth ramparts through the targets and then having him turn Wanker's Doom around to go through it all again for the twin-gun rear turret.

And when Tony finally did get airborne, as soon as he'd finished the engine checks with Ginger, the intercom got busy.

"Navigator to pilot, recommend we air-swing this compass, OK? Looks a bit to cock."

So Tony flew precise magnetic courses over the Lincolnshire town of Spalding, first east, then west, straight and level, dead accurate, then north and south, stooging along with Peek sight-seeing in the other seat and Jasper across his knees, messing about with the P4. Then Jasper had him do it all over again, eight different headings all round the compass, with the inter-com full of natter about something called "GHA Aries" which a mathematical Jake was helping him with up in the astrodome, halfway down the fuselage. Not to mention a barrage of figures from Digger, what the hell was he up to?

"We're also calibrating the loop aerial," Jasper told him. When finally that was over and done with, there Tony was again, flying meticulously straight and level as Jasper and Our Ern chit-chatted away, "Eight starboard." "I make it six star-board," as they checked drift readings from the bombsight and the rear turret.

Nothing was good enough for Jasper. "Bloody P4 was seven degrees out and as for the sodding loop . . ." Even after they landed and taxied to the hardstanding, Jasper was hanging string and a stone from the nose of the Wimpey and muttering something about a lubber line. Not to mention Digger, busy with a wireless mechanic and blaspheming about click stops.

Jake had a big Wolseley and they all piled aboard with their kit after the Meal (stew again) and picked up Our Ern at the Sergeants' Mess and drove out to the thoroughly tested

Wimpey, now ready and patiently waiting for its trip to Mannheim.

So very different, no rush, no fuss, Tony actually felt relaxed as he lined up Wanker's Doom behind the Wimpeys trundling ahead through the solid darkness.

Green light, dash dash dash, winking from the Tower.

"Front gunner to pilot, letter O Orange, we're clear for take-off." Hell's bells, this is a crew and a half, shades of Fuller & Co., they had left everything to Tony, throttles forward, lifting off, up with the undercart—

"Front gunner to pilot, wheels up."

"Navigator to pilot, first course 147 Compass, estimate Great Yarmouth in 32 minutes. IFF on."

"Rear gunner to pilot, Wellington at five o'clock, eighty yards."

Throttles forward, bit of extra speed.

"OK, Wellington's dropping back and below." Sit here and twiddle thumbs.

"Front gunner to navigator, crossing coast at Great Yarmouth."

"Rear gunner to navigator, drift four port."

"Radio to crew. Have just farted."

The white-flecked North Sea rolled sedately below, changed to the dark-against-darkness of Holland and they flew steadily on, Wanker's Doom a thing alive, an extension of the eyes, ears, minds and muscles of its crew. All Tony had to do was sit and drive. Bloody marvellous.

"Front gunner to navigator. Looks like the target dead ahead."

Fires blazing on the ground. "Don't like the look of this," said Jasper. "If that's Mannheim, we're six minutes too soon."

The red flickering below came closer and closer. Now they could see the geometric pattern of the flames, a grid-iron of parallel lines. Crossword. A line of bomb bursts flashed, one, two, three, four.

Jasper said, "It's all much too *formal*."

Tony clicked on his microphone. "Decoy. We're pressing on."

"Front gunner to crew. City ahead."

This was Mannheim, no doubt about it, the flak came up to

glitter around them, three sharp cracks too close for comfort. An Australian voice, "Bugger this for a game of soldiers."

Odd thing was, even during the stomach-clenching concentration of the bombing run, the waiting for the photoflash when the Wimpey was a dead duck for any attentive night fighter, any accurate gunlayer, Tony felt an easiness of mind, a confidence in Jake and Our Ern as their turrets tracked to and fro across the sky, in Digger as he stood in the astrodome, an extra pair of searching eyes (catch Sills ever moving from his seat).

Wanker's Doom hoisted upwards. "Bombs gone!"

"Nothing personal," said Digger.

"Flash gone!" A thousand and nineteen, a thousand and twenty, there it goes, winking white. Dive away from the predicted flak, the gyro spinning round for the homeward course, speed building up to nip smartly away from the target defences. Everything under control.

And everything planned ahead. God knows where they'd be now if Jasper hadn't spent that interminable time swinging the compass, maybe wandering through the flak like that poor bastard ten miles to starboard. This was the way to do a tour of ops—although Tony had to clench his teeth to fight down his fatigue as Jasper busied himself later over the sea, putting in some astro *practice*, for God's sake, shooting sights with his sextant on Spica, Betelgeuse and Polaris as Tony forced himself to fly the necessary precise course, dead straight and level. Bit of a slog, actually.

"Front gunner to navigator, English coast ahead. Pundit flashing V Victor at two o'clock . . ."

"Radio to navigator, QDM Base 325."

"Front gunner to navigator, pinpoint Cromer." Spot-on landfall.

When he'd taxied up to the hardstanding and snapped all switches to off, Tony couldn't believe he'd just flown an op. Weary, yes. But utterly shagged, no. Piece of cake. He'd done seventeen ops. So, by chance, had his new crew. For all of them, thirteen to go.

Jake drove the Wolseley swiftly over to SHQ; with a secret grin Tony saw that they always used the Other Ranks' entrance, with Our Ern. Nice cup of cocoa, dash of rum. Rapid debriefing, Jasper had all the facts and figures for the gold-penned

Intelligence bod. "Primary. Good show." Digger fiddled extra cups from a Waaf who gazed up at him crick-necked, eyes abrim with adoration.

Back in the Wolseley, first to the Sergeants' Mess. "Night, all," said Our Ern. "Nice trip. Nice landing, Tony."

* * *

"Cologne," whispered Jasper, as Tony tok his seat beside him at briefing. "Think there's something special about tonight's do." From up on the stage, Tubby caught Tony's eye. Significant wink.

"Right, chaps," said Twinkletoes. "Tonight's the night we give the bastards one hell of a pasting."

But it was the Perambulating Prick who wanted to hog the occasion. "Tonight Bomber Command is attacking Cologne with a force of over one thousand aircraft—" and a yell of glee went up from the squadron aircrew.

With all of seventeen ops behind him, for the first time Tony felt there was a sense of purpose behind tonight's attack, a new enthusiasm from Twinkletoes (flying tonight, of course) and the squadron-leaders up there on the stage. The audience below followed every word, the familiar boredom and nonchalance forgotten.

"There's no question tonight," Twinkletoes was saying, "of Wimpeys and Stirlings and those poor bloody Manchesters—" laughter, if you were in a Manchester you didn't have to wait for the Germans to kill you—"ambling over the target all night long, the whole shebang of a thousand aircraft is going to be come and gone over Cologne in ninety minutes.

"Idea is, there'll be so many of us over Cologne that Jerry is going to be so busy with some other poor bugger that you'll just slip in sort of unnoticed—"

Extraordinary the difference in this briefing. Another difference, too; there was a new kind of target map, no hospitals, churches and whatever marked, no miss-me symbols. A very different briefing. Laughter kept breaking out and the biggest boffo of the highly entertaining event came after a question by Jake.

"Some of the more apprehensive among you," announced

Twinkletoes, "may be wondering, will there be more collisions tonight with all of a thousand kites cluttering up the sky in so short a time. Well, let me put your minds at rest. The boffins at Bomber Command assure us that only two extra aircraft are expected to collide tonight—"

Jake on his feet. "Yes, sir. But please, sir, which two?"

You could see the fires of Cologne fifty miles ahead and over the city there were kites all around Wanker's Doom (which two?). Butterflies fluttered in stomachs but, God, you couldn't deny, there was comfort in numbers, all those other chaps for flak and fighters to bang away at.

Not that there wasn't an occasional twitch. "Left, left. Steady. Left, left." From Digger in the astrodome, calm as you please, "Stirling a hundred feet above us." Slightly less calm, "He's opening his bomb doors."

Immediately, "Bombs gone. Flash dropped." Never-ending seconds ticking away. "There goes the flash, let's fuck off." Wanker's Doom standing on its wing, splitarse, diving away.

Next afternoon in the Crew Room they put Digger in the Line Book. "Date: 31.5.42. Place: Crew Room, Onley Market. Name: P/O Digger Lindsay, Royal Australian Air Force. Line: 'Don't mind dodging searchlights, flak and fighters but I do draw the line at flying through some other bugger's bombs.' "

Thousand bombers. Made you think.

* * *

They went to Hagen—well, Happy Valley, anyway—that was where Durrel bought it and they went to Bremen, nineteen, twenty, neither was a piece of cake, mind, bags of flak; but flying with this crew was like a rest cure after dicing with Fuller and the other deadbeats, oops, didn't actually mean that; for Sills really was dead and who knew what had happened to the Cheppie and Ramsarse after they'd jumped out of G George into the fires of nearby Krefeld? Eck, anyway, was safe and sound; a letter full of rather exaggerated thanks had also told Tony that he'd been discharged from Ely Hospital "Feeling fine but very disappointed that they gave me a medical and told me I couldn't fly on ops any more." Perhaps he was.

A rest cure because Tony no longer had to carry out the whole op on his tod. Jasper (who'd moved in to share Tony's room—unlucky bed? "Fuck that.") and Jake, Digger and Our Ern were a marvellous team and Tony knew how lucky he was, they were a bunch of professionals compared with most of Bomber Command's crews; not that those poor amateurs got much chance of learning their trade, apprentices going down on their first, second or third op.

New faces, now, more amateurs coming on the squadron, people come, people go. Tony was a veteran, the novices watching him at briefing, nonchalance came easy with a gallery to play to, not that he and his crew put on many airs and graces. For, although Tony's tiger was quieter in its cage, you could never forget that somewhere there might be an 88mm or cannon shell clearly marked "Wanker's Doom". "But the only one that really puts the shits up me," mentioned Digger, "is the one marked To Whom It May Concern."

A quieter tiger, too, because of Wacko, Peek, Big Head, Oswald and Ginger. They looked after Wanker's Doom as if they'd bought it out of their Post Office savings. Clean, bright and slightly oiled was their Wimpey, envy of all the other squadron crews. Never a smudge on the shining perspex to make Jake's or Our Ern's heart leap at the sight of a flyspeck, is it an Me 110? Click stops on Digger's radio always spot on. Nice cushion on Jasper's seat to keep him comfy as he pencilled their way across Germany.

Round the NAAFI van, "What's a click stop, Wacko?"

"Marks a pre-determined frequency for ignorant Australians. OW!" Direct hit from Digger with a rock cake.

Time flies. 1w, 3d, 6h, 9m it had been to Kate's forty-eight-hour pass when Tony had come to in his hospital bed and now not only had 1w 2d gone by but he was due for seven days' leave the day after they climbed wearily out of Wanker's Doom after Bremen. "Nothing bent?" anxiously asked Oswald.

"Piss off from eight a.m. tomorrow," start of Tony's seven days, start of Kate's forty-eight hours, Twinkletoes told the crew at debriefing ("Primary. Good show."). On the dot they were out of camp, Jake's Wolseley heading for a day at Ely Hospital to see Casey, the crew's original, wounded pilot; and Tony's Morris on the way to Worcester, pausing first for black-market petrol at the Good Pull-up.

Kate squeezed the soap in a tightened fist, it curved out and up, first-slip Tony caught it before it hit the water. She asked, "Why did Stripey Trousers want to see you?"

"The hotel manager? Told me he had a son on Manchesters. Said he'd only be charging me for one room, not for the two we booked."

"Modesty pays off."

"Not always," said Tony, leering. They climbed, happily damp, out of the bath, began to dry each other and one thing led to another, right there and then on the bathmat.

"Gorgeous," commented Kate happily, cocooned in towels. "You must have been practising." Guilty thought: what's her name, Helen—

Kate said. "Co-respondent's course. Why," she asked as they went into the adjoining bedroom, "am I wearing all these towels?" and they never had a stitch on again until they went downstairs and found the dining-room closed. But they were invited into the hotel's vast old-fashioned kitchen and, perched on a table, they ravenously scoffed the Spam sandwiches the almost spherical matron of a cook cut for them, sharing an occasional mouthful with a very attentive spaniel. By then it was time for bed.

In fact, it was time for bed during most of Kate's forty-eight. "Just making sure," she said, bouncing, really bouncing, she was starkers, on the mattress, "that it won't go ploi-ing."

Although they did take a couple of walks, if not in autumn woods, in summer woods, pausing among the ferns where the turf was soft and springy; if not buttered toast by a roaring fire, then margarined toast (rationing, you know) in a Ye Olde Tea Shoppe.

Certainly they talked, chat, chat, chat, chat. As Dick ("How is he?" asked Kate. "Nudey with Judy," said Tony) had so wisely remarked, it's what she's like between you-know-whats that really matters.

Chat, chat, chat, entwined in bed: what was it like learning about Intelligence, all right, really, like being back at school, fattest girl you ever saw at the next desk, call her Bessie, after Bessie Bunter; Bessie Bunter? Only know Billy. Haven't lived, have you, she's his sister. Wouldn't a Mars Bar go down a treat?

Talking of Billies, heard anything from dear old Bill Wilberforce?

He'd never told her about Bill wanting to pack it in, bonfire of wooden houses, full of people like my Beryl and kids like Shirley and Norm . . . "But if some women and children," Twinkletoes had said, "have to die so that bastard Adolf and all the shits around him don't end up running the world, all I can say is, tough titty."

Tough titty. Not perhaps an acceptable summing-up for Kate, not if you'd never been there in a Wimpey, didn't know it wasn't peaceful, harmless houses over which you were opening your bomb doors but a concentration of hundreds of guns filling the sky with thousands of shellbursts, searchlights everywhere probing for you, lighting you up all ready to swat and an instant away, tracer from hunting fighters.

So when Tony wrote to Kate he had told her Bill had been posted, that's all. There are some things you just don't talk about. Or think about. A burning doll spinning like a Catherine-wheel, Sills's head rolling behind him . . . best not to brood. Slam the door of the cage.

"Haven't heard from Bill yet," he said. Sometimes a Beaufort comes out the other side—stop brooding. He slid a hand down warm, gloriously silky skin, stroked with his nails just *there*.

"Ooh," murmured Kate, "and about time, too."

* * *

Forty-eight hours he had with Kate—delivering her to the gate of WAAF Quarters at Worcester at two minutes to midnight, precisely. At four minutes to midnight, she sweetened their farewell, telling Tony she'd have a week's leave when her course finished—"1m, 5w, 2d, 8h, 2m . . ."

He missed her dreadfully but it was wonderful to see Mum and Dad again. And Trixie, who insisted on sleeping on his eiderdown after many a thump of her tail and extensive washing that shook the bed.

Lots of social obligations. To the office with Dad, anxious to show off Tony's DFC ribbon; not that Dad made mention of it, of course; but he stood, tall, beaming, grey-moustached, ramrod-straight, as quiet-spoken Mr Lucas, his one-legged clerk, spotted it immediately. To the golf club with Dad, where the Secretary wouldn't let them pay for drinks and that Brigadier's wife, Maisie, more than once bent forward so Tony's eyes could graze the valley of her interesting bosom.

With Mum, delightedly wearing the brooch he'd bought her, RAF wings, to the little terrace house of Mrs Carter, the tiny energetic pensioner who obliged her three mornings a week with broom, mop and duster—"Airyplanes! Wouldn't get *me* up in one of them things!"

Really, parents were awfully easy to please, just let Dad show off the gong and find Mum things to launder, iron, sew and darn. Kate's picture to be shown: "Oh, Tony dear, she's lovely!"

"Your mother," said Dad, "was the prettiest girl in Babbacombe. Glad to see you're keeping up the family tradition." Blush from Mum, but you had to admit she was good-looking, even if she was getting on a bit, forty-three, wasn't she?

They hardly talked about the war, as if by mutual agreement, such a lot not to be spoken. Read *The Times* and the *Daily Telegraph*, naturally, that came through the letter-box, listened to the BBC news, pretended not to notice, if you can ignore Sills's rolling head, ignore that seventeen, twelve, twenty-two of our aircraft have failed to return.

Except once, the last night of his stay.

"Crafty." Dad studied Tony's sneaky snooker. Soft taps of the white against two cushions, clatter as a red went down. Click, plop, of the pink into the pocket. He chalked his cue. "You know, Tony, I'm glad you're on bombers. Like to think of you paying them back for all that stuff they dropped on us." He chuckled. "Not that I've always been that anxious for revenge. I remember, it was ten to eleven on the eleventh of November, nineteen-eighteen. Up comes a despatch-rider, salutes, message from Battalion HQ. German infantry in farm-house, such-and-such a map reference, open fire. Just ten minutes to the Armistice." Blam, down went a red.

"I stood there a moment, then stuffed the damn thing into my breeches' pocket. Oh, let the poor devils live, I thought. Then when you and I and Mum sat there listening to J'aime Berlin bleat our declaration of war, all that was passing through my mind was, I wish I'd blown those bastards to smithereens." Trundle, trundle, the black slowly rolled towards the pocket, wobbled, dropped noiselessly in. "All Sir Garnet," said Tony's father.

Tony lay on what bed Trixie allowed him, in the bedroom that was a cosy, welcome sanctuary, no noise of engines in his ears, no dials staring, even if, with its School cricket and rugger team photos on the walls and its bound copies of *Chums*, it fitted him now no better than the outgrown tweed jacket and flannels that felt like pyjamas after the belted crispness of his uniform.

Biscuit salesman in a pub, ex-Major of Gunners like Dad, they shared something in their feeling about the war, the only good German is a dead German. Odd how, on the squadron, bombing the Germans was only a job to be done. Oh, hell, no point in thinking, only leads to brooding.

* * *

Tony was able to make a detour on his way back to Onley Market and call on Kate's family in beechy Bucks.

("Where are you going for your leave?" the squadron adjutant had asked, gesturing with an amber cigarette-holder, pen poised over Tony's leave-petrol allowance form.

"Prestwick. Staying with an uncle." Cheerful lie, they gave you coupons to where you dared to say you were going.

"I'm inventing you another artificial uncle in John o' Groats, hoots, mon. Should be good for quite a few miles more.")

Mrs Elliot opened the vicarage door, saw Tony, said "Bovril" and went off to the kitchen, finger pointing skywards. The Reverend Mr Elliot puffed away at a pipe even bigger than Bill Wilberforce's, addressing envelopes as everyone told everyone else the news, so glad to hear Kate's well, how does she like it down at Worcester, the dachshund—now spread all over Tony's lap—has had puppies, all gone to good homes, twenty operations you've done, only ten to do, marvellous, more Bovril?

Mrs Elliot brought out the family album. Snapshots: Kate aged ten on a donkey at Frinton, fifteen in school uniform and pigtails, a baby with a toothless grin stretched on a white rug.

Naked. Mrs Elliot caught Tony's eye, they both looked away, both burst out laughing.

He was back at twilight at Onley Market as if he'd never been away. Especially next morning.

* * *

Pilot: P/O Marlowe, DFC. Navigator: P/O Ashby, DFM (Jasper). W/Op: P/O Lindsay (Digger). Front Gunner: F/O Bernstein (Jake). Rear Gunner: Sgt Jackson (Our Ern).

As it happened, six of them, not five, flew Wanker's Doom, where was it supposed to go, Mülheim, that night. There was a Polish crew on the squadron, ex-regulars from the Polish Air Force, they'd escaped from Danzig after the German invasion, heroes all, but who discusses?

"Tony," Twinkletoes asked, "do you mind if Zebbie goes with you tonight?" Flight-Lieutenant Zbrowski was the crew's pilot. "You know what he's like if he's left off the Battle Order. His kite's u/s and he's moping about and making life quite unbearable."

"Dank you," said Zebbie, when Tony said yes, "Dank you very much. I press tit, OK?"

It was an uneventful op, except of course you never knew it was going to be uneventful until you were deep into your debriefing cocoa-and-rum. Flak and searchlights were busy with other customers but you could never be quite certain they weren't going to change their minds. Lot more relaxing with this crew, though, even if an icy hand squeezes your stomach—"Over Happy Valley now," Jasper in the earphones, "can't guarantee it's Mülheim, however."

"Thanks, Jasper. Fires ahead. Could be the target."

Up at the bombsight Zebbie said, "Germans under. Goodnuff."

Down with the big red lever. "Bomb doors open."

"Steady, steady." Bombs dropping away. "Ina, Jola, Krysia, Lise. Bombs gone. Flash gone."

All Zebbie's crew had been waiting for him at debriefing; over cocoa, Tony said to Zebbie's navigator, "Now I know the Polish for one, two, three, four."

"So?"

"Ina, Jola, Krysia, Lise."

"Ina his wife. Jola, Krysia, Lise his daughters. Before Germans came."

Thoughtful sip. Well, quite a few of us take it personally, mused Tony.

* * *

Dick said, "Whisky. Two. Doubles." Baldy reached immediately under the bar for the hidden bottle, scarcely to be wondered at remembering the time Dick had damn near throttled him.

Carrying their glasses shoulder-high, they manoeuvred through a clutch of blue aircrew uniforms to the door of the Wheatsheaf. In the Alvis, whiskies on the lowered windscreen in the Double Daylight Saving Time of a brilliant summer evening. "Look like a lot of kids, don't they?"

"Our age, Dick."

"In years, maybe. Of course, they're not kids, are they? Old men, with a week or two to live. Lose any of your squadron over Cologne?"

"Two crews. Just the usual sprogs. Both on their first op."

"We were lucky. Just one. On their third. Tony, do you know they took crews in training off the OTU's to make up that thousand? And OTU instructors, all flying those battered old kites?"

"Wonderful show, though, wasn't it?"

Sourly, "Made wonderful headlines. Oh, Tony, I'm sorry. I'm like a bear with a sore head these days. Another whisky?" Tony took the hint.

Quiet out here, parked on the grass beside the wood. Like old times. Well, not quite like old times. Seems years, not little more than two months since they'd found Jersey and Hereford chewing their cuds of Smith's Crisps; and now Tony had a medal and Dick the brand-new two-and-a-half rings of a squadron-leader, lot had happened in the fortnight or so since they last met.

Dual congratulations, of course. Good shows both. But shooting up to a flight commander seemed to have made a big change in Dick; not that choking Baldy hadn't been an indication of a change from the former Whitbread-guzzling happy-go-lucky girl-chaser.

"Yes, I seem to be constantly niggly these days, Tony. Doesn't help, you know, sitting with the Wingco and making up the Battle Order, you've got to put the sprogs on, that's what they're there for. Go down like ninepins, don't they, poor devils. Dicey business, ops. Sometimes makes me wonder how wise it is for chaps like us to get really tied up with girls like Judy and Kate."

"How is Judy?" Remembering who's-it, that chap who got married, Proctor, went broody, bingo, got the chop.

"Marvellous." Dick shook himself, like an under-kennelled Newfoundland, in his seat at the Alvis's wheel. "May be leaving the Windmill, new musical opening in London, might be getting a part. Did I tell you," good to hear Dick laughing again, "that I managed to get down to Smoke last week? I collected Judy and we were talking outside the Windmill and up comes a chap in a mackintosh, hot evening it was, too. He just stood there staring at a picture of, well, all right, nudey Judy. Took no notice of the real Judy, just a yard away."

Dick took a sip of his whisky, then a gulp. "Then I thought that's what Pa and all those scrambled-eggers are doing at Bomber Command—looking at pictures in their minds and taking no notice of the real article."

"Could be, though," said Tony, "that they're starting to learn some sense. Not putting up a thousand, I don't mean that, scraping the barrel, sending up anything that can fly without elastic—all that's for newspapers and the BBC and for Winnie to cheer up the Yanks and Uncle Joe. Just that somebody had the bright idea to cram us all over the target at once, get the flak guns in a tizzy. Gleam of hope that we'll be able to get some results, maybe making all this bombing worth while."

Dick sighed. "I suppose this war will be over, some day. God knows when, though. Thousand bombers to Cologne, fine. But it was just a flash in the pan, like Rostock. Thousand went to Essen a couple of days later, what a balls-up that was, did you hear? Makes you wonder if it's going on for ever."

* * *

22, 23, 24, the numbers Tony wrote at the top of his letters to Kate—Kassel, Wesel, Hamm—climbed slowly but surely as if there really was a chance they would reach thirty some incredible day. Can't deny there was tension enough as Wanker's Doom growled and grumbled towards those allotted anonymous latitudes and longitudes on Jasper's charts. But it was necessary tension, the kind that paid off in keeping you alive.

Worthwhile, not the waste of energy that had kept Tony worrying whether Eckersley had got unplugged or Fuller got his sums wrong or Sills had made a cock of a QDM. For the crew was a team, taut, trim, efficient, and if death wanted them, it had to come looking.

For death casually swiped many a Wimpey out of the nighttime sky, the crews too inexperienced or too shagged-out to realise that what you had to do was to make it too much of a bore for the Old Man with a Scythe to come swinging for you.

It was Jake's glimpse of twin tails against the moon that made it too tedious for the Me 110 to stalk them through the sky until it could sit in the blind spot beneath their fuselage and loose off cannon shells to instantaneously turn Wanker's Doom into a flaming cross, a smudge of smoke. Too much fuss to chase them as Tony dived in a splitarse spiral to nip smartly into a handy patch of cloud and then bank through ninety degrees so that the Me 110 wouldn't be waiting for them when they popped out again. Not that the fighter would have bothered overmuch, far too many less troublesome victims were bumbling along; a really ambitious fighter crew could knock off three, four or five bombers in an industrious night's work.

It was Jake who yelled a warning as the blue master searchlight began swinging up so Tony could dive balls-out past the beam and make it all a frightful nuisance for the bods below tinkering with their radar. It was Jasper who juggled with Arcturus and Procyon and Polaris that night when the Met forcast was more than usually to cock; he may have been an awful bore with all that practice, but he bored the Grim Reaper even more.

And it was Digger, when there was cloud above and cloud below, no stars, no pinpoints, where the hell are we, what's the way home, worried Jasper, it was Digger who bullied his piercing Morse through all the frantic radio traffic of Bomber

Command, ruthlessly pounding his key until at last the position fix came in and some of the better-mannered W/Ops were in kites strewn all over England's green and pleasant land.

And always there were Wacko, Ginger, Big Head, Peek and Oswald, all of them fussing over Wanker's Doom, gremlins need not apply.

* * *

A real bastard laid on for tonight, Old Yellowstripe, the Big City itself, Berlin. You could hear more chaps than usual puking in the bogs, not that Tony himself was actually looking forward to it, you understand. Hell of a long way there and back, the red wool that showed you how far you had to fly seemed to go on for bloody ever.

But who you were flying with made all the difference. Like panic, calmness was catching and the churning in Tony's guts gave way to a normal and, in fact, reassuring flutter of butterflies, his stomach signalling that essential adrenalin was fuelling his reflexes. Reassuring to sit here among Jasper, Digger, Jake and Our Ern as the experts droned on from the stage, ending up with a pep talk from the Perambulating Prick.

". . . magnificent chance to strike a really telling blow at the Hun . . ."

"If it's such a magnificent chance," Digger asked in conversational tones, "why isn't the Group Captain coming too?"

Sudden roar of laughter from a hundred-odd aircrew, on the stage Twinkletoes hiding quivering cheeks behind a hand like a ham, the Perambulating Prick gazing open-mouthed. Cockneyish accent. But could be Australian. Not that he knew any of the aircrew's names but that mutinous remark sounded as if it came from that tall wireless-operator.

Discipline demanded a reprimand. But you had to be careful with Australians, put a foot wrong and they were telephoning their High Commissioner, might mean an enquiry. Didn't do your chances of promotion any good, having one's name bandied about—he held out his hand for his cap and gloves, best thing to do, chill them with a dignified exit. In spite of the continuing laughter, getting louder.

It was still daylight as Tony lifted Wanker's Doom off the

runway, with the kite loaded to capacity with petrol, not to mention incendiaries and high-explosive, but Oswald and Wacko and Big Head and Peek and Ginger had done their usual super job and the good old kite got unstuck long before the end of the runway.

Odd how the higher they went the brighter got the daylight as they flew towards Germany, breathing oxygen that tasted like second-hand Wrigley's and leaving the sun setting low behind them, a swarm of Wimpeys clawing for operational height.

In the gathering twilight, stars coming out, with Jasper's muckers Vega and Spica glints above the light-grey horizon. The coastline of Norfolk slipped below, the North Sea stretched ahead and everything had settled down into sharp-eyed routine, all, as Dad was so fond of saying, Sir Garnet.

Sharp-eared, too. Forty minutes out, "Recall!" yelled Digger over the intercom. Relief washed over Tony, thank Christ, but mixed with bugger it, all that preparation and briefing for fuck-all. Almost instantly, "Navigator to pilot, course to Base 325."

Swing Wanker's Doom around, stick the nose down, open the taps. No coddling the kite tonight—first home, first down. No danger of wasting time stooging around the airfield, waiting one's turn, aircraft milling around in the dark, could be a dicey do. So home they went, as Digger said, like shit through a goose and less than an hour after touching down they were on their way in Jake's Wolseley, "What's the course for Pam's Snug?"

Methodical crew, this. Jasper had marked all the pubs within five miles of Onley Market on an inch-to-the-mile Ordnance Survey and map-read them round the twisting lanes of Lincolnshire from one possibility to another. Some promising hostelries had been turned down, mainly by Jake, who insisted on Bass. But then they'd found the Marquis of Salisbury beside a bridge over a mill stream. It didn't have Bass but it did have Pam's Snug.

Pam, a round-faced, round-eyed, round-tittied pixie, peered lingeringly at Jake beneath a fringe that reminded one of Manet's girl at the Bar at the Folies-Bergère, no more thought of Bass. Last night had been their first visit and Pam had endeared herself to all. A wingless wonder of a squadron-leader had stared noticeably at Our Ern's sergeant's stripes and cleared his throat once or twice.

"I thought," he finally said, "that this was a bar for officers only."

"It's for officers and gentlemen." Pam smiled sweetly. "So you can piss off."

Bloody marvellous to stretch out, pint pewter mug in hand, sniffing a whiff of woodsmoke, chilly for June, in the cosy little room and not having to be shot at. Love to bring Kate here.

Long after the other bars of the Marquis closed, they sat in Pam's Snug, nattering; then they spent a rather long time in the Wolseley, playing cribbage by torchlight with the cards and board that lived in the glove compartment.

Jake, gallant fellow, had volunteered to help Pam lock up. "Sorry," he said, "took longer than I thought." Digger had something unacceptable to say about keyholes.

★ ★ ★

Bound for Mönchengladbach, wherever or whatever that might be, Tony shifted the cheeks of his aching arse for the thousandth time, that's bett—"FIGHTER, FIGHTER," yelled Our Ern. "Me 110, coming up, fast!"

Cold clammy fear came and went, wham the throttles through the gate, "Icy calm, chaps, icy calm. Good show, Our Ern. Where is this fighter?"

"Climbing up from starboard."

Check how clearly Our Ern was thinking. "Starboard of the aircraft, rear gunner?" Only too easy to panic, to confuse starboard with your own right when you were facing backwards.

"Bet your arse it's fucking starboard." Good old Ern.

"What's his position?"

"Four o'clock low."

"How far away?"

"Three hundred yards . . . two fifty."

"Good show. Let me know when to take evasive—"

"Corkscrew starboard—GO!"

Shove the nose down, heave Wanker's Doom to starboard, right foot hard against the rudder, the blackish-and-black horizon tilting crazily, speed building up, engines screaming, howling now as the stick comes back hard into the stomach, Our Ern's guns yammering non-stop, must be hosepiping all over the sky, the fighter's shooting, brilliant blobs of orange flashing to port, only just to port—there he is, dense black shadow, bloody close, Our Ern's stopped firing, he's overshot, climbing just in front, twin engines, twin tails, can even see the spiky radar aerials, hasn't hit us, not yet, the bastard's going to roll off the top, cross over, come round from behind for another go, zooming into his climb.

From the front turret Jake fired once, twice, three times. Murderous short rattling bursts. The Me 110 flicked past overhead, a red glow spread along the black shadow of the fuselage.

Guns again from the rear turret, vivid white flash reflected on the Wimpey's wing, Our Ern shouting, "Got 'im! Got 'im! Blew the sod to bits!"

Babble of cheering voices, Tony, shouting now, "Stay off the intercom!" incisive, commanding. In the hush, "Eyes peeled, everyone. Might be another of the bastards about."

And by Christ there was, another black two-tailed shadow, there one instant, passing below, gone the next.

Digger said, "That joker didn't fancy us a bit, did he?"

Two flashlights made a high crossover, pointed to the ground, went out. Exhausted, Tony slumped forward and clicked off the engine switches. The flight home had been quieter than usual, the combat and the second sighting had left the crew flat, exhausted, used up.

Jake was coming through from the front turret. Tony squeezed his nose, blew, his ears clicked. "Fantastic bloody show that, Jake." Really was. Pop-gun .303s versus explosive cannon shells. "Means a gong for you."

"Not for me, Tony. For Our Ern."

"But it was you who hit him. I saw your tracers chew—"

"Our Ern thinks he got that Me 110. Let's leave it that way."

"But Jake, you—"

"What's Our Ern had out of life? Big doings at the Hammersmith Palley, snog in a doorway, back home to Mum and Dad, four rooms over a fish-and-chip shop. Hell, Tony, I had two years at King's—Our Ern gets the gong, OK?"

Tony said, "OK, Jake."

* * *

Our Ern, sure enough, next day sported a DFM beneath his air gunner's wing—he had the ribbon up hardly an hour after Twinkletoes gave him the good news, thanks to Jasper's unpicking his own ribbon, won when he'd been a sergeant, off his best blue.

Gala day for Our Ern, not only the Crew Room to swank around in, but also the gang to show off to around Wanker's Doom, Big Head and the boys looking as pleased as if they'd put up the ribbon themselves.

On top of all this, Midge, the Waaf in the Tailoring Section who'd kindly sewn on Our Ern's gong, had said yes, she'd love to come to his celebration that evening at Pam's Snug. So off they all drove in Jake's Wolseley, Midge, knee-high to a small grasshopper, with her legs stretched across everyone's knees. Comrades, comrades, they sang, Sharing each others' troubles, Sharing each others' joys.

There was beer drunk. There was horseplay. There was a christening, the hero soup this time basically Guinness, the other ingredient soil spooned by Pam out of the pot in the corner of the Snug that held a large ominous leafy plant, known to her as the Spider Eater.

Midge rubbed a tiny thumb and Our Ern's ribbon became an earthy smudge. "That's The BDM," said Digger. "Our Ern got it for surviving the Black Death."

"As we said at the time," Jake reminisced over close to six centuries, "there's a lot of it about."

Pam had put a notice on the door of the Snug, CLOSED, when she'd heard they'd come for a christening. She moved round to their side of the bar to share a cramped armchair with Jake; less cramped, because smaller, were Our Ern and Midge in another.

Tony, wishing Kate were here—less than three weeks before her end-of-course leave began, but not to count chickens—sat on the twangy sofa beside Jasper, who had his feet up on one of the crates of Bass, recently and specially acquired for Jake, which filled what carpet wasn't taken up by several horizontal yards of Digger, stretched out like the Forth Bridge.

More than friendliness in this room. Love was the word, thought Tony, shying away from it. But it was love that kept them sane, or was it from being sane, kept them from fatal brooding, through Mannheim, Cologne, Hagen, Bremen, Mülheim, Kassel, Wesel, Hamm and Mönchengladbach or reasonable facsimiles thereof.

Just as it had been Judy's love (a secret loving kindness never to be told to Kate or Dick—but did Dick know? Look after each other, he'd said) that had saved Tony from cracking up, going broody, after Duisburg, Mannheim, Essen, Hanover, Münster, Wilhelmshaven, Osnabruck, Homberg, Oberhausen, Bochum, Rostock, Cologne, Emden, Milan, Hanover, or thereabouts.

Good people to fly with, this marvellous crew. It's the cunt-happy, pissy-arsed fuckers who get through ops, Tubby had said. Not perhaps delicately put but, in general, true. Chalkey White had finished his tour and you wouldn't think it to look at him, but his prowess among the girls of Onley Market village made Casanova look like a eunuch with pimples.

As for Doc Watson, his navigator, a very strong rumour maintained that he'd even had it off with Mrs Prick, a brow-beaten, stringy, but defiantly dyed brunette, one night when the Group Captain had been called to a conference at High Wycombe.

And yet, and yet. Jasper was boringly faithful to, if not exactly the Girl Next Door Back Home, certainly the Girl Around the Corner. Tony, he told himself smugly, didn't exactly screw around. (Nor did Dick, all that much, now he'd found Judy.) Jake was, at least locally, almost domestic with Pam and, judging from the nuzzling going on over there, Our Ern was about to settle down with Midge, pretty as a sexy dormouse.

Digger. He, now on his sixth Bass, was as always an enigma. He was missing from occasional evenings. Popsie tucked away? No one knew. But one stand-down afternoon he'd been seen in the back seat of a chauffeur-driven Daimler, no less, heading through Onley Market for the races, with a delectable sheila in a hat like a hyacinth.

"Who was she, Digger?"

"Never thought to ask her name. But she bangs like a shithouse door in a storm."

Jasper stretched out his legs and heaved a long, long sigh. "This is why I'm fighting this war," he said. "So I can sit very still with a mug of Bass and do bugger-all else for the rest of an extraordinarily lengthy life."

" 'Ear, 'ear," said Our Ern, from somewhere amongst Midge. His voice became excruciatingly BBC as he held out an imaginary microphone at Jake. "And now we ask another hero of the skies—what are your war aims, you brave airman?"

"To Make," said Jake, in capital letters, "The World Safe For Democracy."

Digger said, "Bollocks."

Midge said, "Ooh."

"Bollocks I said and bollocks I mean. Look at us, two cars in our crew. How many other cars on the squadron among twenty-five crews? Four? No, three, since What's-his-name got the chop. Want to democratically share your car, Jake? Want to *walk* back most nights after you've finished locking up?"

"That's not democracy, that's communism."

"Same thing in the end. Start giving people what they want and they end up taking all they can get."

"You know, Digger," said Jake thoughtfully, "sometimes you think you're talking cock and yet it somehow comes out pukka gen. But anyway," he added, to confuse the issue, "hardly anyone on the squadron can drive."

Pam had startled eyebrows, they shot up under her Manet fringe. "Really? Not even the pilots?"

"Especially the pilots," said Jasper. "Most of them can't even drive aeroplanes."

"Oh, all right." Tonight Jake was everyone's chum. "Bollocks to democracy. I'll make Wacko call me sir next time we polish perspex together."

"Bollocks to democracy," agreed Tony. "I wanted to vote for a nice big Air Force back when I was in the Upper Fourth, any nit could see what Adolf was up to, But nobody asked me to put an X."

"Felt the same meself," said Our Ern, "back when I started in the shop. But no-one was interested in letting me vote. Nor any of us, I bet. Anybody 'ere old enough to have voted?"

Pam coughed, delicately, behind a polite hand. "Change the subject," said Jake.

Midge chipped in. "None of you had to be aircrew. You're all volunteers. You all democratically voted to fly."

A pause. Jake yelped with laughter. "Good for you, Midge."

"Just what I said," last-word Digger, "bollocks to democracy."

"Now come on," Pam insisted. "Jake—why are you fighting this war?"

Jake yawned cavernously. "To get the bloody thing over with."

Put it in a nutshell, thought Tony. To get the war over with, no more wandering about Germany for blood-thirsty Air Marshals and staff officers who played with trains, dropping bombs on families you've never even been introduced to. What would they say, Jasper, Jake, Digger, Our Ern, Tony wondered, if he suddenly asked: how do you feel about burning women and children? Did they hide a hatred for the job they had to do as they hid their fear?

Oh, bollocks. Bollocks to Allardyce. Bollocks to Air Marshal Butch Harris. Bollocks To Adolf. Bollocks to searchlights. Bollocks to flak. Bollocks to Me 110s.

He finished his fifth Bass. More than friends: a bollocking good crew.

* * *

The next day was a stand-down and for once Tony was separated from his crew, this was a day when the others went to Ely to visit Casey, who'd stopped a sliver of flak over Düsseldorf after which Jasper got his medal for something he'd done to help the wounded Casey get their kite home, not that anyone ever told Tony about it, a job's a job.

So Jasper, Jake, Digger and Our Ern Wolseleyed off to catch the early train from Lincoln—bit of a rush to Ely and back the same day. Tony waved them off with unusual time to spend on his tod. He left the airfield right after breakfast, no bullet-hole in his perspex.

He had hoped that Dick might have been on stand-down, too. Nothing, however, but the engaged signal. Ops at Flaxfield tonight.

Somehow Tony filled in a lonely day, missing his crew. He drove over to Flaxfield, Pop. 4,614; early closing Wed., Market day 2nd Fri. in month; 15c oriel window 14c church, St Botolph's; 18c inn, mentioned Chas. Dickens. (What Chas wrote was: "A mean, despicable barn-sized hovel, the landlord surly to his wayfarer customers and forever snarling at starveling potboys.") He parked the Morris and explored the little town, seeing it for the first time in daylight, taking all of twelve minutes. Then he set off along the flat lanes of Lincolnshire for a really health-giving walk.

He realised, as his shoes got dustier and dustier, what little time you got in Bomber Command to consider what was going on around you. Reason was, most of the time all that was going on was too much to grasp.

Twenty-five ops flown since the second of April and today was the twenty-seventh of June. Not bad going. Incredible, too, that he'd known Kate so short a time—less than three months. So much happening so soon.

He sat on a white five-barred gate, thinking. Able to think a bit more now that he was flying with Jasper and the crew, with Wacko and the boys tending Wanker's Doom. The tiger was still there in its cage but the knowledge of the skills that ministered to and flew Wanker's Doom kept it much quieter although admittedly the bars did rattle now and then. He'd got the freedom of mind now to ponder without the worry of brooding, to open his shut mind. How was Bill Wilberforce? What had finally happened to Fuller and Ramsarse? But even so, almost all that was in his thoughts was Kate.

In nineteen days she would finish her course and start her leave. Cross fingers, might happen just after he flew his thirtieth. Five more to do on this sodding tour, chancing his life, Jake's, Jasper's, Digger's, Our Ern's, all for fuck-all. If their bombs didn't fall in fields, they killed women and children. He didn't want to ponder any more, see where it led?

* * *

Kate darling,

I miss you so much. It feels like forever since we were last together, so much more than 3w 1d 5h 26m. Thank you so much for your letters, for a while you seem so close, as if you really were sitting beside me. I'm sorry I don't write so often to you. It sounds odd to say there's so little to write about, what with me being on ops. But life is always so much the same.

I spend almost all my time with Jasper, Digger, Jake and Our Ern. We're either climbing in and out of Wanker's Doom or swanning off to Pam's Snug. How I wish you could meet them, the crew and Pam and Oswald, Big Head, Peek, Ginger and Wacko.

The crew and I, as I've said, spend all our time together, do everything together, we're all the friends we've got. Of course we swop jokes with the other chaps on the squadron, sink a pint or two of wallop with them now and then but we do keep a fence around ourselves.

That's why I'm writing you a very different letter from the one you usually get, all about thrashes in the Mess and people shooting lines and someone you've never heard of getting paralytic. It's about half-past five in the morning. Jasper's in the other bed, absolutely flat out, we're all just back from, more or less, Wiesbaden, you'll hear all the usual lies about it on the BBC news.

But I know I won't sleep unless I do something about the fence between you and me. There are too many secrets between us and I can't go on like this any more. I don't mean girls, I'll never forget my whining confession about Helen and the way you laughed.

What's brought this on is someone again you've never met, a bod called Chalkey White. He was one of the chaps we all looked up to on the squadron, not that he seemed to do much more than just get on with the job but he was an example to everyone and when he finished his thirty it encouraged a lot of chaps to keep on.

Chalkey had been at an OTU, he wrote to me and said how cheesed off he was. Somehow or other he managed to fiddle himself and his crew back on the squadron before his OTU stint was up and this morning, yesterday morning it is now, all of a sudden there he was in the Crew Room in a brand-new officer's uniform badgering Twinkletoes to put them on the first possible op.

So they flew on tonight's trip to Wiesbaden and got a dose of flak. They got back as far as Manston, the big emergency airfield on the coast by Margate, on one engine. That's when the other engine caught fire. Chalkey managed to keep the kite in the air long enough for his crew to bale out and then it was too late for him to get out and he turned the Wimpey out to sea so it wouldn't crash on the town and Doc Watson, his navigator, was almost hysterical when he phoned to Onley Market, he'd parachuted on to the runway at Manston and stood and watched as Chalkey hit the sea and the Wimpey exploded.

That's why me and Jasper and the rest keep that fence around ourselves, if you stop from getting to know people it doesn't twist you inside when someone goes down. But it breaks your heart when a marvellous chap like Chalkey goes for a burton and it starts you thinking, which is a thing you mustn't do on an ops squadron.

But that's what I've been doing since we heard about Chalkey. Thinking. Thinking about all the chaps like Chalkey who are sent out to die for sweet damn-all. For we're all just going through the motions, Kate, we almost never find the targets we're supposed to bomb. I suppose like everyone else you believe we wipe out war factories and docks and marshalling yards. Nobody seems to know what the truth is, that the only damage we do to the Germans is to kill them and their families in their homes.

I've never told you why Bill Wilberforce left the squadron, just let you believe that he was posted, not that he refused to bomb women and children any more, didn't mind what they would do to him, just said no. I expect you're wondering how I could go on doing it.

I don't know if you will accept this as an explanation but it's true as far as I can express it. Thinking while you're on ops kills you, it's as simple as that, I've seen it happen so often. For the first thought you have is that you're going to die, it's just about certain, nothing you can do about it.

Start thinking about that and you give up, you don't try any more. You let yourself get tired and give way to fatigue, don't keep your eyes peeled, don't keep yourself on the top line all the time you're flying and a searchlight catches you before you can dodge, or a night-fighter sneaks up without you seeing.

Worse than thinking you're going to die is the thought that you're going to die for nothing, just for lies in the newspapers and on the BBC. Worst of all is to think what you're actually doing, killing people in their homes.

We didn't realise that's what we had to do until we'd done it. The RAF let us believe that we were going to hit military targets, we had to find out for ourselves what our job really was and once we'd done it we knew we couldn't think about it, on ops there's nothing to think about except staying alive.

When I wasn't able to keep what we were really doing out of my mind I've always reminded myself of a couple of things my Dad said to me almost three years ago.

"You're nearly seventeen," he said. "Time you and I got drunk together. Today's the anniversary of the Battle of the Somme, the day I always get drunk and I'm not drinking alone tonight." First of July, 1916, the battle began, that day both my uncles were killed. He didn't talk often about the war but he did that night before I had to go upstairs and throw up my four pints. He told me a lot and two things I always remember when I think about our bombs going down on houses.

One was how, when he was in the infantry before he was commissioned into the Gunners, he was on a firing squad, to shoot a deserter. "Twelve of us," he said, "and twelve rifles, one of them loaded with blank. So you can never be sure." I'm never sure; so many of our bombs could land in fields or even hit factories, never sure that they hit houses with people in them.

The other was when he was a Gunner. "You've got to do terrible things in war. We used to fire what's called a creeping barrage, the shells dropped in front of our soldiers as they went across No Man's Land to attack the enemy trenches, moving in front of them as they walked forward through the barbed wire. But the shells weren't always reliable, many would drop short, we'd kill one in ten of our own soldiers before they reached the Germans." I tried to tell myself that if Dad had to kill our own soldiers to win a war, then I could kill German civilians. And I tried to convince myself that if I had to kill ten German children so ten British soldiers could live when the time came to invade Germany, that was a fair exchange.

The way I think now is that I've got my duty to do, four more ops to fly on this tour, and I'll do it like Chalkey.

I love you, darling Kate.

Tony

When he woke five hours later, he tore up the letter. Only one thing worse to do on ops than think and that was to think out loud.

* * *

"Getting out of strange beds in the middle of the night," was Digger's diagnosis; probably right at that, because Jake's ferocious cold began after an evening at Pam's Snug when the pegs went round the Johnny Orner many more times than usual and watches were markedly consulted by the cribbage foursome when Jake finally got back to the Wolseley. This morning he was wheezing, coughing and sneezing like a performing seal.

In the Crew Room his predicament was met with the usual sympathy and understanding. "Stay away from me, you infectious sod!" In the end he accepted kindly advice ("Bugger off and take your bloody microbes with you!") to pay a visit to Station Sick Quarters. Tony drove him over in the Morris; the MO lifted his glasses, took one look at Jake and pointed him out of his office like a Methodist minister greeting an unmarried daughter at the door with a squealing baby.

"Pit!" he ordered. Then he turned to Tony and in full hearing of a line of waiting patients enquired kindly, "How's the pox, old chap—"

Seems a lot of fuss to make over a mere cold but the point was, if Jake were bleeding to death he'd be expected to keep firing his guns but with this cold of his he wasn't allowed to fly; at operational height he'd be incapacitated by agonizing pains at ears, jaw and cheekbones.

What one thereupon hoped wouldn't happen promptly did. The Tannoy amp-amp-amped. Up went the Battle Order. "Sorry," said Twinkletoes, "had to put you on. Maximum effort."

Front gunner: Sgt Stevens.

"Who the hell's Sergeant Stevens?"

"I am, sir." Tony was completely floored, fancy being called "sir" by an aircrew bod. Revealed what a sprog this slightly-built, curly-haired gunner was. Also indicated that Tony's twenty-six ops were showing.

Well, Steve-oh wasn't Jake, of course, but he turned out to be a likeable sort of chap, if shy. First op. The crew rather took to him.

The way to cage his tiger was to keep him busy, so they kept Steve-oh on the hop. Made him check his electric hat, oxygen mask, dinghy, all his equipment. Our Ern squeezed up beside him in the front, Jake's, turret of Wanker's Doom in the hangar and went over all the gun stoppages with him, what to do if. Digger instructed him in parachute drill. "Main thing to remember," advised Digger, "is to keep out of my bloody way as I go through the hatch."

So what with discovering, coincidence, as he climbed down from Wanker's Doom, that he'd been at school with Ginger, Steve-oh was in good nick when take-off time approached. Which is more than could be said of Tony, Jasper, Digger and Our Ern.

For somehow or other Jake had learnt that they were on ops tonight and there he was, sick-bed abandoned, in My Brother Sylvest's ('Don't you dare spray me with your germs!") van, whooping and splashing like a hippopotamus having it off.

Perfect pest, getting in everyone's way, Jake was trying to help where no help was needed, handing up parachutes into the kite and blocking the little red ladder, dropping Digger's signals logbook on to the muddy grass and generally carrying on so much like a wet wheezing hen that it was a relief to turf him out and taxi away for take-off.

They were all very charming to Sprog Steve-oh, pointing out all the sights—the blue radar-controlled master searchlights, the night-fighter visual beacons lighting up one by one beneath them, the too-symmetrical fires of the dummy target. Quite a few kites were getting the chop, rather spectacular explosions starting quite soon after they crossed the enemy coast.

But they cheered up the sprog by telling him that the Jerries pooped up special scarecrow shells which went off for all the world like bombers going for a burton. Good for his future morale and might even be true.

Steve-oh was a bit shocked when Digger shouted "Good on

yer! Bonzo!" when Tony announced that a Wimpey had just been nicely coned before they began their bombing run over what might possibly have been Wuppertal, but he did see the point of going in when the searchlights and flak were otherwise engaged.

Not wanting to keep Jake waiting, Tony upped the speed on the way home. As soon as Wanker's Doom landed and Tony clicked off the switches, here was Jake again, ashoo, handing round Thermoses full of too-hot coffee, trying to help carry out parachutes and dinghies and Jasper's navigational satchel, "Mind my sodding sextant!" and what with one thing and another making a complete bloody nuisance of himself.

Steve-oh thanked them very politely for the trip and said how useful it had been. Not, as it happened, that it did him all that much good, he got the chop with his regular crew a couple of nights later. Ginger was very cut up.

And, wouldn't you know, two days after that, Warrant Officer Wilkins's front gunner went arse over tit on his Aerial Red Hunter and sprained his wrist. Twinkletoes made up Wilkins's crew with an aspirin-and-Johnny-Walker-cured Jake, ars longa est. Talk about panic. Anxious discussions with Peek and Big Head.

"Flying in L London? Not a *bad* kite. Not a patch on Wanker's Doom, though—"

In Jake's Wolseley on the way to the hardstanding they usually chattered like a flight of starlings, singing the occasional chorus—never, by Tony's request, The Good Ship Venus—and generally behaving like a school outing. But that was with an ordinary op in prospect. Tonight, in Tony's Morris, everyone packed tightly in, there were only bitter remarks.

"Careful with his parachute, clot!"

"Don't tread on his helmet, you clueless sod!"

They watched L London lurch out into the twilight to join the Wimpey queue. "Ham-fisted fucker, that Wilkins!" They bunched, scowling, in a corner of the saloon bar of the Grumble until it shut, then they all went back to the Officers' Mess, Our Ern somewhere inside Tony's spare battledress, and worriedly emptied a chipped enamel jug or two.

In the July dawn they drove out to the dispersal and found Wacko and the others already there with L London's ground crew. In silence they listened for returning Wimpeys and when L London rolled sedately up from wherever it had been, they had the hatch open almost before the props stopped spinning.

Tony was first inside. "Flying Officer Bernstein," called Wilkins, "Nanny's here!"

"So now," said Big Head, "you know how we feel."

* * *

After the 28 Tony wrote at the top of his letter to Kate (Frankfurt-am-Main) the squadron began to take an intense interest in the return of Wanker's Doom. Watch the crews as they came into debriefing, dirty, dishevelled, dead-tired, as they glanced swiftly round till they saw Tony, Jasper, Jake, Digger and Our Ern, all safely at their table swigging cocoa and rum.

For, as everybody knew, sprogs come and sprogs go, if you're lucky you might get an extra operational egg; but when a veteran crew goes missing, it makes you think, will anybody—and that means you—finish his tour? The twenty-ninth was Bochum, again; bags of kites going down, many an anxious eye searching for Tony and the crew as the rest of the squadron came slouching and stumbling in.

He tried to tell himself it was routine, that the thirtieth, the final op of the tour, was routine, just like any other op. Nonchalance. Once he'd been a sprog looking out of the corner of his eye at Chalkey White, now the sprogs took their cue from Tony.

Nonchalance. He was reading that morning's *Daily Express*, he'd tucked it under his arm when he left the Mess and now as the Tannoy amp-amp-amped he didn't look up, just went on casually reading 'ing the possibility that the German aircraft industry may' 'ing the possibility that the German aircraft industry may'.

Many a long moment after Twinkletoes had thumbed up the Battle Order Tony ambled casually over to take a casual look. He was so prepared to be casual when he saw his name that when he didn't he almost revealed that he was taken aback. He strolled across the Crew Room to where Digger, Our Ern, Jake and Jasper were casually playing nap.

He waited while they finished the hand, pretending not to

notice that Jake trumped a diamond even though he held the Curse of Scotland. "Night off," said Tony. None of them glanced up and a gunner booked for his first op looked suitably impressed.

Click, buzz. "Pilot Officer Marlowe please report to the Squadron Adjutant."

"Wotcher, Tony. Someone rang you on the blower just before they closed the switchboard." The Adj pushed paper across with his cigarette-holder, black this time.

"Message for P/O Marlowe. Need looking after. Eastleigh Hotel, Flaxfield. Gale."

"Compassionate day off? Or passionate?" Twinkletoes enquired sternly; but aircrew with only one op left to do were privileged. A scribbled pass, unconfining him to camp, a stamp rolled to and fro on an almost inkless pad, thump, signature. Passed across Twinkletoes' desk with a mysterious, "Show this to the dog at the river."

The Eastleigh Hotel was opposite one of Flaxfield airfield's dispersals, where a Wimpey was being loaded from a very long line of bomb trolleys. Up whitened steps and into the lounge, lined with masks of long-ago hunt trophies and equally inanimate skull-faced residents, refugees all hiding from the prospect of city bombs and the stringencies of city rationing and staring indignantly into a World Sadly Changed By This Boring War, can't get a wink of sleep with all those aircraft flying all times of the night.

He saw her immediately coming towards him, green dress, yellow scarf, not a word until they were inside the Morris.

"I could hear the Tannoy from our room and I knew it meant ops. Dick told me before he left that he would put himself on first chance he got, so he'll be flying tonight." She turned in her seat.

"It's the last op," she said. "The thirtieth. Thank you for coming, Tony. I couldn't sweat it out alone."

"It's routine, nothing special, I saw them loading a kite. Heavy bomb-load. Means less petrol for the tanks. Means Dick hasn't far to fly."

She said, "Happy Valley."

Damn it, she knew too much. He tried again.

"I saw our squadron's Battle Order. Our Wingco isn't on, he

always flies an op if it's a tough one." But she just nodded.

It was strange being with her that day, through the rest of the morning, the afternoon, the early evening. He made her walk with him across fields, through woods, along the river-bank. She hardly spoke, nodding in reply to anything he said until he, too, fell silent.

Only time she took notice was when the Wimpeys circled the airfield on the Night Flying Tests: "Dick's on Y Yorker." But the bombers were too high to pick out their letters.

"Judy—that might be Dick." Off came her scarf to stream in the breeze. But the Wimpey turned out to be X X-Ray and, anyway, you'd be lucky to catch anyone's eye at that height with a square yard of yellow.

He drove her round dusty roads, using up time, in search of a hitherto unvisited pub for lunch and, eventually, decided on an inn with a pleasant garden, mellow in the July sun. She didn't tell him until after the flat beer, gristly meat pies and flabby apple crumble at a wobbly rustic table that she'd lunched here as badly before, with Dick.

No matter how long they tarried over lunch, how slowly he drove—lovely hot day, he opened up the sunshine roof—how far they walked, the afternoon seemed never-ending, the attempts to start a conversation always met with nods, the remarks sometimes unheard. Even when he asked her, "Did you get that part in the new musical show, Dick said you might?" all he got was a dull, uninterested, "Yes." Judy was somewhere else, with Dick on Y Yorker's air-test, with Dick at briefing, with Dick as he, too, waited.

They were back, during this endless day, at the Eastleigh Hotel, masks and the skulls of refugees still staring into space, too early for dinner. They sat for a while looking at ancient copies of *Country Life* and were first into the dining-room, Brown Windsor, mutton and undercooked potatoes and, once again, inferior apple crumble.

Bit of a worry now. The Eastleigh was obviously a hotel which disapproved of what it thought might be goings-on, how was Tony to join Judy in the bedroom? She left the table and her almost-untouched dinner, Tony stayed for dishwater coffee. He left an unearned tip for the bowed, shambling waiter, chose a moment when the manager was defending himself from a complaining skull and, unseen, hurried surreptitiously upstairs. An elderly couple were tottering along the landing, he nipped into a room marked Bath. The loo was an original Crapper, there was his name on the pan; Tony admired it as the two hotel inmates shambled past, quarrelling about marmalade.

Feeling like a disastrously inexperienced spy, he tapped at Judy's door. She was tying the belt of an over-large blue silk dressing-gown. "Dick's," she explained. "Nothing much to read, I'm afraid. Just yesterday's and today's *Daily Telegraph*."

He read every single word, carefully, at slow speed, including an interesting recipe. "Making Your Meat Ration Go Further." (You used mashed parsnips.) As Judy lay silent on the bed, he examined the water-colours on the wall, the pattern of the carpet, the wallpaper itself. Then, thank God, he found Judy had a pencil and he settled down to the two crosswords.

It was almost eleven before the sound of engines warming up began, first a spit of noise as a propeller spun, then another and another and now one continuous rumble.

"Late take-off," Tony said. "Told you so. Short trip. Routine."

From the bed, "Uh-huh."

Each take-off was a bellowing roar, twenty of them, each Wimpey seemed to howl right over the hotel roof, aspirins for the residents. When the last crescendo had died away, Judy said,

"If you don't mind, I'll go to bed. Tony—"

"Yes, Judy?"

"I've asked the switchboard to leave me an outside line. Answer the phone when it rings, would you, please?" She slipped out of Dick's dressing-gown and climbed between the sheets, Tony could see her nakedness through the transparent nightdress and knew that for her, tonight he was no more than a presence, someone here against her fear and loneliness.

Later after a severe tussle with 12 Across, he dozed off in the armchair, woke to hear her calling him.

"Come in here with me, Tony."

He took off tunic, shoes, slacks, unloosened his tie. He got into the bed, the side by the bedside table with the telephone, with his back to her. She moved herself against him, two spoons in a drawer, he felt her softness and warmth, not a stir, not a twitch of desire. He thought she was asleep when she said, "Dick's not afraid to die."

"I know."

"But he's afraid every time he goes up. Afraid of killing innocent people. Burning homes with old men and women in them. Blowing up mothers and children. The night before I came to Onley Market for that ENSA show, he was in that chair you were sitting in. He was crying. Dick crying—like a child himself, couldn't stop. I couldn't do anything for him, Tony. And then he told me he wanted to finish with ops, didn't mind what they did to him, court-martial him, strip his wings off. But he had to go on, you see. Because of his father."

"I can see that, Judy. I was going to go and say I couldn't fly any more and my first thought was of my Dad. But I wasn't like Dick, I was just scared. Then. But now I feel like Dick, I'd come off if I could, I hate what Bomber Command makes us do. But the thought of Dad being ashamed of me—and it's worse, too, for Dick, his father an Air Commodore, holding him up to contempt in the RAF. And now I've just got one more op to do . . ."

"Tony—"

"Yes, Judy?"

"Promise me you won't tell Dick we talked."

"Cross my heart and hope—no, Judy, I won't tell him. That was why, wasn't it, when I came to you, you asked me if I wanted to—"

"Yes. Tony—Dick will come back, won't he?"

"Of course."

He woke, the bedroom light still on, to the first rumble of the homecoming Wimpeys, she was awake beside him, muscles taut. 0335 by his watch. "Told you. Short trip." He tried to count the Wimpeys, three, four, five, as they roared overhead, then couldn't distinguish the sound of the new arrivals from the others circling the airfield and coming in to land.

0415. Silence.

A long, long silence, when the phone rang, he snatched it from its cradle. "Hello?"

"A moment, please." Oh Christ, a woman's voice, a Waaf's? Not Dick's.

Now a man's voice, thought he recognised it, "Miss Judy

Gale?" That awful father of his, she'd called him.

"Yes," he said stupidly. "No. I'm Tony Marlowe."

Unsurprised, "Hello, Tony. It's just come through on the teleprinter." Tonight he wasn't a clueless staff officer but a man who loved his son. Thankfully, "Tell Judy that Y Yorker landed fifteen minutes ago, Dick's probably swilling rum right now."

He turned to Judy, she saw his face, he didn't have to speak.

"Oh, my God, my God, thank God," and he felt the pain in his shoulder where her fingers had gripped. The phone rang again, he handed it to her, "Dick! Oh, Dick darling . . ."

He climbed out of bed, not listening to what she was saying, got fully dressed, turned back, she was still on the phone. She grabbed his hand, kissed it, he smiled goodnight and tiptoed down the stairs past the snoozing porter and out into the chilly freshness of the night.

* * *

Dick had done his thirty, thank God; but, for Tony, a good or bad omen? Odds were heavy enough against one of them making it, but two? Well, not to brood.

Three days had already gone by since that strange, tense day and night with Judy. He hadn't written to Kate since Bochum. (Although there was always one letter waiting, a little crumpled now, addressed to her, like the one to Dad and Mum, that he always left stamped on his pillow before every op.) He wasn't going to put that number 29 above "Kate darling," to tell her there was only one more op for him to fly, not after the hell he'd seen Judy go through. Not that Tony was having all that easy a time of it himself.

For now it was half-past two in the morning, his thoughts were churning, he couldn't sleep. Twenty-nine done. One to do. He realised what was unsettling him: for the first time since Hickey and Tinker and Geordie and—he was horrified for a moment, couldn't remember the name—and Phil had died over Cologne, he wasn't certain he was going to be killed.

Killed. He didn't expect to be wounded or taken prisoner. A pilot badly wounded was usually a dead pilot, couldn't fly his plane, kerr-umph, straight in. True his crew's first pilot, Casey, had been wounded but not so badly that he couldn't fly his Wimpey home, with Jasper's help. But Tony didn't expect the unusual.

Taken prisoner? The pilot had to stay with his burning kite, fighting to keep it straight and level for the rest of the crew to bale out. Then if it didn't explode, he'd have to try and fight his way out against the G force thrusting against him, pinning him to his seat as he let go the control column and the aircraft spun in a fatal spiral.

All right, now and again a pilot got out, if he didn't tumble into the flames of what might be the target, he spent the rest of the war, safe if miserable, in a prison camp; but it was certainly something you couldn't count on. Best to accept, with the half of your mind you couldn't deceive, that you were going to die, put those thoughts to rest. But that half of your mind was the tiger's cage, keep the door slammed shut.

Yet he'd looked into the cage earlier that day; at last he'd had a letter from Bill Wilberforce. Bill also, had one more op to do. He'd flown two of his three. Sometimes a Beaufort comes out the other side.

"We fly sweeps over the North Sea, Tony, searching over a square. Most often we never see a German convoy. When we do we go in with our torpedoes at sea-level, through the ring of flak ships straight at the cargo ships. Everybody bangs away at us, including the freighters and as you used to say, it's a bit dicey. We lost three out of five to flak on our first sighting and again three out of five on the second, although a fourth kite, our Wingco's, Twinkletoes' brother, hit a mast and pranged.

"It's a bit of a bind, really, as we go out a couple of times a week, never knowing whether we'll see a target or not. At least in a Wimpey one knew there was a city waiting, even if I didn't often find it. But I'm glad I made the choice and I'm grateful to Twinkletoes for offering it to me. And I'll always be grateful, Tony, for the way you stood by me . . ."

Now the cage was opened, now Tony was thinking with that undeceivable half of his mind, he knew why Dick had been so interested in Bill's rejection of the duty of bombing homes, and killing women and children. A duty that had torn Dick's heart—crying like a child, Judy had said. And Tony now knew why, in frustration and fury Dick had nearly strangled that barman. Well, Dick had done his thirty.

One more for Tony to do. With the hitherto unthinkable prospect of not being killed, just the ordinary ending of Bill's letter had opened previously forbidden lines of thought. "The kiddies are doing wonderfully well and Beryl is fine. She sends her love."

Thirty done, he could think of marrying. He'd never dared imagine Kate as his wife, their being together without pretending each time might not be the last. Survive one more op—he slammed the cage on the thought that he would, even then, have another tour to do, that was six months ahead—no, face facts, survive this thirtieth and those ops of a second tour and there'd be decades ahead of living together. Children. A boy to bring up, to teach how to drive a ball to the off, to whip a ball away from the scrum. A girl to watch growing up more and more like Kate.

But it was too early now for such hopes, with his thirtieth still to do. 0340. He got out of bed, pulled on battledress slacks over his pyjamas, crammed bare feet into his shoes and slipped into his blue uniform trench-coat.

The latch of the door clacked quietly as he let himself out of the hut and began to try to walk off his restlessness in the summer night. He met no-one as he marched along the muddy path out of Site Four and stepped past the silent huts, past the darkened Mess, heading nowhere.

The airfield seemed empty, not a sound; he paused by the staring windows of the deserted Crew Room. Deserted by so many: Hickey, Tinker, Geordie and Phil; Tich Cattermole; Sills, Fuller, Ramsbottom; Woodham, Griffin, Blake, Proctor, McCall, Wilder, Rowe, Crichton, Durrel, McAllister, Overton, Stevens, dear old Chalkey White; so many others—almost always one, often two, occasionally three, once four, Wimpeys missing when the squadron flew, you wiped the names out of your mind, fatal to brood. Not that there was always time to get to know their names, the one-, two- and three-op sprogs.

But there were voices coming from Number Two Hangar. He let himself in and was immediately dazzled by the glare of the lights. As his vision came back he saw the row of spotlights brilliantly illuminating Wanker's Doom and busy around and inside were Oswald, Peek, Wacko, Big Head and Ginger.

Peek saw him first. " 'Ullo! It's the birdman!"

They were clustering round him. "Come to have a look at the kite?"

Tony said, "You're working late."

"We had a major inspection to finish," explained Big Head. "Got it done about midni—just a while ago, so we thought we'd sort of look Wanker's Doom over."

"For your thirtieth," said Oswald. "Come and have a dekko."

They'd checked every bleedin' rivet on Wanker's Doom, they boasted as they crammed themselves inside with Tony. Drybollix, instruments, controls, electrics, anmunition feeds, bomb doors—Ginger said, "It's ready for you." Wanker's Doom shone inside and out like an exhibit in the Ideal Wimpey Exhibition.

Tony admired everything, shining dials, well-swept floor, gleaming perspex, his newly-oiled seat and then, "We've got Late Meal Passes," Oswald, Peek, Wacko, Big Head and Ginger carted him off to the Airmen's Mess.

Long empty early-morning tables, wet smell of newly-scrubbed wood, a cook behind the kitchen counter in dirty white overalls. "Rustle up a bit of gash grub, Cookie?" asked Ginger. "Someone extra's turned up."

The cook stopped slicing a long loaf with a knife that banged on the breadboard with every slash and looked with mild interest at Tony's officer's trench-coat. "Special sort of bod, is he, then?" Oswald said, "He's our pilot," and the way he said it made Tony turn away his head to hide the glisten in his eyes.

Stuffed with doorstep Spam sandwiches and seconds of stewed rhubarb, to a chorus of Goodnights he walked tall back to Site Four. Doubts resolved. Whatever dreadful, despicable things he was doing to the Germans in their homes, he was privileged to put his life on the line to do what he could to win a war for Big Head, Oswald, Peek, Ginger and Wacko. He owed it to them.

He understood now, too, why he hadn't asked Twinkletoes if he might go on Beauforts with Bill Wilberforce. In that tiger's cage hidden in his mind he'd always known that he owed it to those layabouts, the crew of the Deadbeat Express, Ramsarse,

Sills and the surprisingly redeemed Eckersley, to stay flying with them. They hadn't been much, but like B Bastard, they were what he'd been given, entrusted with, to do his best with; that much he owed them.

And how much more he owed to Jake and Jasper and Digger and Our Ern; he'd die for them, if he had to; they'd die for him. Simple as that.

"Comrades, comrades,
Sharing each other's troubles,
Sharing each other's joys,"

He was surprised to find himself singing, as they so often sang in Jake's Wolseley; but tonight the sentimental music-hall ballad had a new, true meaning.

Jasper turned over as Tony climbed back into bed. "Where the fuck have you been?"

Tony prevaricated. "Out for a leak."

"Noisy bugger."

Tony woke, oddly refreshed after less than three hours' sleep, and lay with his hands clasped behind his head in the shortly-to-be-disturbed stillness of the Nissen hut on Site Four.

Soon Jasper's secret (using forbidden electricity) radio would come on, loud and clear. Soon the hut door would shut behind Digger and Jake from the next-door cubicle (they'd moved in after Overton and his navigator bought it—Bremen) as they went slopping over to the ablutions, shoes untied, macs over their pyjamas.

But first the hut would echo from the next-door room with Digger's early-morning hymn and Jake's noisy keep-fit exercises. Be it ever so humble, this Nissen hut with its flimsy pasteboard partitions was home, sweet home, a house of friends.

"Eternal Father, strong to save,
Whose arm doth bind the restless wave . . ."

". . . next on the Forces programme . . ."

"Twenty-three, shit. Twenty-four, shit. Twenty-five, thank God."

"Oh, hear us when we cry to Thee,
For those in peril on the sea."

Comrades, comrades.

* * *

Late that afternoon, "Hell's bells, I'm bored," lied Tony, churned up by waiting through too many clicks of the Tannoy, his mind a tumble of frustration, no ops tonight, mixed with guilty relief, thank Christ for that.

Jasper stretched. "Can't stop yawning." The whole Crew Room was one big yawn after the day's edgy touch-and-go weather, ops unlikely one minute with the sky all Harry Clampers, likely the next as the sun peeped teasingly through dirty-laundry clouds. Lethargic was the mood, as Twinkletoes remarked as he came ambling in.

"Wakey-wakey, rise and shine! Right, you dozy shower, sesh in the Mess tonight! England expects—" appalling imitation of Horatio, sleeve in tunic, hand over one eye, "—that every officer will be pissed as a fart."

"Stuff that," said Jake to Our Ern. "Can't leave you on your tod."

Our Ern hummed and hawed. "Well, you see—"

"Midge?" asked Tony.

"Well, I did tell her if—"

"Sex-mad, these Arse End Charlies," said Digger.

Try and guess the Wingco's age, you'd have said forty. But tonight he looked nearer his true twenty-six as he led his aircrew around the Mess obstacle course—stagger along the back of a sofa, hop to the top of an armchair, wobble, giant step to the mantelpiece, crash, Jasper's pranged—and Twinkletoes looked even younger, conducting with a half-empty mug and spattering beer all over his leather-lunged choir as Ackroyd, the sprog from Vancouver, thumped away at the joanna, loud pedal down, tune of "Waltzing Matilda":

"Ops in a Wimpey, ops in a Wimpey,
Who'll come on ops in a Wimpey with me?
And now a stupid pilot flew her over Germany,
Up came the flak like a Christmas tree,
And the rear gunner sang
As he reached out for his parachute,
'Who'll come on ops in a Wimpey with me?' "

Slash of tiger. Open turret, flick of lighter, a flame falling away, darkness. Tony looked up, found Twinkletoes' eyes on him.

"Ops in a Wimpey," baritoned Tony, fortissimo, "ops in a

Wimpey—" Wink from Twinkletoes.

Everyone was still rather fuzzy at breakfast next morning, just toast for me, thanks; tinkle of broken glass from the anteroom as Low Forties swept up, muttering. In the Crew Room Our Ern was ready with a merry greeting.

"Talk about death warmed up!"

Confessions were made. Mouths like zoo-keepers' boots and Japanese wrestlers' jockstraps.

"Serves you bleedin' right!" All grin and giggle was Our Ern this morning.

"Stop being so sodding cheerful," said Jake. "Let a chap enjoy his headache."

"Yes, pack it in, you're getting on my Royal Australian wick. Hey, wait a minute! Know what? Midge, last night—Our Ern got stuck in!"

Scarlet flush. Always a man to respect a fellow's secret, "First fuck for Our Ern," yelled Digger to the Crew Room. Claps, cheers, cries of "Not before time!"

Tony's turn this morning to pick up the mail; on the way to the Mess birds made a fuss about the glorious summer day that promised, threatened, ops tonight. Good omen, mused Tony, Our Ern breaking his duck, as he collected a bill from Jake's box, a letter from the Girl Around the Corner for Jasper, another for Digger, scrawled SWALK, Sealed With A Loving Kiss.

For Tony, a picture of the Imperial Hotel, Torquay. "Our room's the one with curtains drawn. D and J." From Kate, a birthday card, squirrel with a nut in its paws. "Many happy returns, darling. 3d 9h 14m." His birthday was tomorrow, actually; he hadn't forgotten, just that on ops one tended not to count the days ahead—he drew in his breath with a shiver of desire, happy return tonight and then he and Kate would be together, please God, please God. "Stand by for broadcast," squawked the Mess Tannoy, "amp-amp-amp," hiccuped the echoes, waiting's over, Tony told himself he was glad.

Pandemonium in the Crew Room, except for Jasper, Jake, Digger and Our Ern, sitting quietly at a game of nap. Wasn't till after Tony handed over the letters that Jasper looked up to say, "We're on tonight," casually, as he laid the Queen of Hearts on the King and scooped up the trick.

Now routine took over to slow down heartbeats and speed up the day. Wasn't quite routine, all the same, at the NFT for Number Thirty. Big Head, Ginger, Wacko, Peek and Oswald were more than usually solicitous and the crew quieter than usual, no jokes, as Chiefy Woods spun a finger and Tony, in a cockpit aromatic with Duraglit, started engines. Off the deck unusual courtesy reigned aboard Wanker's Doom, would you please, oh, thanks a lot, as Jasper at the bombsight checked drifts with Our Ern in the rear turret and Digger, for once with never an unkind word, consulted Wacko about click stops and loop aerial.

Trust Digger, though, to break the spell when they'd landed, as they stood aside for each other at the Wolseley, "After you," "No, after you."

"Why are we all being so bloody polite? It's just another fucking op!"

Just another op, yet shades of Chalkey White and his tap, tap, tap. Tony was alarmed, bad omen, he'd stepped into Station Headquarters right foot first instead of left. Had to let Digger, Jake and Our Ern go ahead to the Briefing Room, "Catch you up, shoelace undone."

Not that left-footing it necessarily paid off. At the scarred table was Jasper, busily sharpening a Royal Sovereign HB with his Boy Scout penknife. He murmured,

"Yellowstripe."

Oh, shit. Berlin. Bomber Command's toughest target, how unutterably bloody *unfair*. Watch it, be casual, everybody's got their eyes on the Number Thirty crew. Doesn't have to be a bad omen. After all, it was an ice-cream op that clobbered Stuffy McAllister and his crew on the squadron's last thirtieth. Pull yourself together, Marlowe. Just another op.

Same old Tubby, flying tonight with Twinkletoes, up there on the stage. Same old signet-ring as his pinkie traced the map's far-stretched red wool, hell of a way to go tonight, over a thousand miles there and, hope to God, back.

"Right, chaps. Daylight take-off but don't get into a twitter, it'll get lovely and dark over the North Sea. Off we go from Onley Market and scarper across the oggin to Alkmaar, that's here, in Holland. Now we craftily turn northeast so the home team will think we're going to prang Hamburg, so they'll keep their night-fighters waiting there with their thumbs up their bums. But we'll turn away southeast here over the River Weser and then it's balls-out for Yellowstripe. Press the tit, no hanging about, belt straight for Den Helder here on the Dutch coast. Then it's Bob's your uncle, hot cup of coffee across the North Sea, cross the coast just south of Skegness and home for your operational egg. OK? Fair enough? Any questions?"

Lots to do, the day had whizzed past compared with snail's-pace yesterday, but now in the Mess time wasn't moving fast enough in the roughest patch so far, between Meal 2000 and Take-Off 2220. Tony was perched on the arm of Ackroyd's chair—first op, tonight, poor sod, with his crew of S Sugar—trying to control the beat of his heart, thirtieth, it thumped, thirtieth. Devilishly crowded here. Aircrew pretending unconcern in serge battledress; admin wallahs bored—such a bind having to stay in the Mess just because there's an op on—in best blue. Off-duty Officers had to change for the evening, Prick was most particular.

How do they feel, these brass-buttoned bureaucrats, wondered Tony, knowing that by their night's fifth gin-and-tonic, many of those battledresses may be fire-blackened shrouds? Odd how one got used to everything. Even the thought that tonight he'd be flying to Berlin and before dawn his thirtieth op and his first tour would be over. One way or the other.

At last, at last, they were driving out to Wanker's Doom, the Wolseley's windows down in the warmth of the late evening and that was when Tony had to face up to the worst of all possible omens. A van passed them, full of S Sugar's crew singing,

"It was the Good Ship Venus,

By God, you should have seen us—"

Shook him rigid, Tony had to admit. Almost as much as when Digger, uncoiling out of the Wolseley, said to nobody in particular,

"Wonder who we'll kill tonight?"

Although Digger was immediately himself again. "Straight line, get fell in! Pre-op piss—who pees the furthest? Cocks out! Ready! Fire!" On the hardstanding, puddles were inspected. "Our Ern by a foot," judged Digger, crossly. "And Midge wasn't even aiming." Toot-tiddley-toot-toot, congratulated My Brother Sylvest, driving slowly by.

Just like cricket and the way your heart stopped banging when you got out to the wicket; once you'd clicked your parachute buckles and fastened your Sutton harness, only essential butterflies fluttered. Bit of a pang, though, to glance out of the side window and see Chiefy surreptitiously crossing himself and it was a sharp reminder of how far they had to go when the bowsers came to top up the tanks of the waiting Wimpeys, replacing petrol used to run up engines and taxi to the runway.

From the Tower, dash dot dash dot blinked green, surprisingly bright in the daylight. C Crumpet, Twinkletoes' kite, lurched round to point down the runway. Thunder of engines, C Crumpet trundled forward, fuselage rising and sagging on the hydraulics of the undercarriage legs, beginning to pick up speed, faster, faster, lifting off, turning away from the setting sun towards the east and Yellowstripe.

Dash dash dash, Tony fed in port throttle, the airfield slid across the windscreen, the waiting runway stretched straight ahead.

"Right, chaps, here we go." Here we go, Kate. Throttles hard forward, engines clamouring a shrieking crescendo, Wanker's Doom ponderously starting to roll, just another op.

* * *

Oh, God, do we have to fly into that, Yellowstripe, the huge black smear of the city below reaching far to the night's horizon, the sky ahead a glittering canopy of shellbursts, nothing to do but to stooge so slowly on towards the seething, sparkling layer of flak, no need for the gunners to aim, just load and fire, load and fire, they know our height, they know where we're going. Fly on and on because those aren't houses, churches, hospitals or cathedrals down there, whatever that quim thought who dropped that photoflash, they're camouflage over Berlin's lakes. Flak crackling all around and we're only just over the outskirts, three kites on fire flying straight and level, on they go like riderless horses in a race, two more kites coned in searchlights.

Nothing to do but sit tight and take it, flak dead ahead, kettledrums, Wanker's Doom trying to leap and plunge, sting of cordite. "Oh, fuck, no, two Wimpeys just collided, going down mashed together—"

"Never mind the scenery, Our Ern, stay off the intercom."

"Bomb doors open," swivel of a searchlight blindingly past the windscreen, night vision gone, reach for the invisible lever, "Bomb doors down, Jasper," night vision coming back.

"Left, left. Ste-ady. Ste-ady." Hurry it up, Jasper, press that tit. "Left, left. Ste-ady," Come on, come on, "Ste-ady," Wanker's Doom rearing up, have they hit us, no, that's the bombload going down, wonder who we'll kill tonight, "Bombs away. Flash gone." Smoke in the cockpit, we're on fire, don't panic, it's what's left over from that Wimpey that was coned, thousand and one, thousand and two, five seconds gone, seven, diciest time of all, sitting target, nine, eleven, another kite coned to port, tracer, there he goes, some hungry bastard in an Me 110 dived down through his own flak, seventeen, nineteen, there's the flash.

Instant splitarse, haul around Wanker's Doom, throttles hard forward, full boost, get the hell out, swim through this sea of flak, one, two, three parachutes drifting down a searchlight beam, kettledrums, fighter flares lighting the sky, Stirling below on his way in, welcome to the party, flak dying off, half a fiery, smoking Wimpey twisting slowly down.

Flak again, like a storm of bursting stars.

Stopping suddenly. Sky's clear. We're out of Berlin.

Exhausted, swamped with relief, all you want is to put your feet up and have a nice cup of tea; leave the target, the tension goes, you feel you're already safely home and that's when some bastard sneaks up and kills you.

So, curt, businesslike.

"Everybody okay? Jake? Jasper? Digger? Our Ern?" Yesses snapped back, everybody on the top line.

"Good show. Twenty-nine and a half ops done, but there's half a bugger still to do. Keep it up, chaps."

An hour and twenty-eight minutes to the coast and Den Helder. P4 on Jasper's 286, gyro on 286, ASI, altimeter, artificial horizon, automatic sweep of the row of dials, automatic scan of the windscreen, port to starboard, starboard to port, up, down, up, down.

All quiet aboard Wanker's Doom, everyone too shagged for chat, but always the front and rear turrets swinging their arcs,

Jake and Our Ern with their eyes peeled, and down below Germany moving slowly behind.

"You awake back there, Our Ern?"

"Oh, ha-ha. Up you, Jake."

"We're just going over a pranged kite, decent little bonfire. Can you take a drift on it for Jasper?"

Navigation by ghosts; no umbrage, help yourself, they'd say. No luck for them, fucked by the fickle finger of fate. Christ, we were lucky to get away from Yellowstripe. Times like now when you're really shagged you feel so bloody helpless, feel that luck and luck alone is all that can get you home—same kind of helplessness you feel about having to drop bombs on children.

No.

Takes more than luck to stay alive for thirty ops. A bang-on kite, damn good ground crew, shit-hot navigator, super chaps flying with you, that's what makes the life-or-death difference. Together with a pilot who gets on with his job, pull your finger out, Marlowe. P4 288, gyro 286, adjust, gyro on 288, slight nudge to Wanker's Doom, P4 286, gyro 286.

0108. Fifty-seven minutes to the enemy coast and Den Helder, less than an hour, thank God, but don't count chickens, not yet. Hardly more than an hour, unbelievably, since Tony at midnight had heard the click of a switch on the intercom, breathing, what the—Jasper,

"All together now, ah-one, ah-two, ah-three—"

"Happy birthday to you,
Happy birthday to you,
Happy birthday, dear To-ny,
Happy birthday to you!"

"Shut up, you clots," he'd said, laughing, as a kite bought it over Münster.

0110. 0113. The sky, port to starboard, starboard to port, nothing but black emptiness. No flak, no searchlights; every op had peaceful intervals like this, bus trip to Wumpton, but the hard-to-remember truth was that any tenth of a second you'd care to mention an Me 110 or a Ju 88 could be putting you just so in his gunsight, thumb on button, cannon shells up your arse. 0115. Fifty minutes to the coast, three thousand seconds, thirty thousand tenths of seconds.

Sparkle in the sky. "Flak ahead, Jasper."

From Our Ern, "Flak at six o'clock."
"Oh, good," said Jasper. "Looks as though we're nicely on track."

Really thought we were going to buy it over Yellowstripe. Sodding awful target. Yellowstripe, Happy Valley, such chummy names we give to things we're frightened of, got the chop, went for a burton, written off. Just as well. Suppose Tubby at briefing hadn't chummied it up.

"Right, chaps. Berlin tonight. Worst target there is. Such a bloody long way to go, so much hate to fly through, nothing much to tell you where you are and it's so fatally easy to wander off track and end up where the searchlights and guns want you. And if you get as far as Berlin, you'll have to fly in and out of an enormous great tunnel of flak. Then after you've killed a family or two for all the good that'll do towards winning the war, do your best to get home with all the night-fighters in Europe looking for you, easy meat for their cannons. Best of Royal Air Force luck, chaps, you'll need it. Can't say how many of you crews will go down. Could be as few as three out of twenty-five. Pity about you sprogs in S Sugar, doubt if you'll be back for the operational egg. OK? Fair enough? Any questions?"

Gyro 286, ASI, altimeter, artificial horizon. 0120.

Any questions? Try to stop brooding. Can't, too tired. Any questions?

Yes, Digger's: wonder who we'll kill tonight? Tough, don't-give-a-damn, nothing-personal Digger, of all people. The agony that had wrenched those words out of him, the loathing he must have for the murderous uselessness of the job that Bomber Command had tricked us into—was it also shared by Jake, Jasper, Our Ern? Did they, too, hide the same horror that had made Bill Wilberforce willing to go LMF with the prospect of cleaning out shithouses for the rest of the war? Did all of us have another tiger to be caged, like the tiger of fear that chewed everyone's guts on ops and during the Gethsemanes between, the tiger of guilt?

Stop it, Marlowe. Concentrate. From one tenth of a second to the next, all the time you've got to react to the clutch of a searchlight, a cluster of flak, a glimpse of a fighter. Concentrate. Because flying home you're so emotionally and physically whacked that your sense of reality leaks away, you keep 286 lined up in the gyro window only because the dial demands, not because your life depends on it.

Never mind the scenery, he'd said to Our Ern. What you saw through the windscreen really did become nothing more than scenery, only mildly interesting as tracer stitched the sky and a beetle-sized Stirling flamed and vanished in that drearily familiar white flash. Only scenery, too, as Wanker's Doom rumbled on, engines soporific, dials hypnotic as, far to port, a lost homeward-bound Wimpey crept along, centred in the crossed stalks of searchlights, sparkles all around, twinkle, twinkle, little Wimpey. So true that the tiredness of ops drains away all reality, maybe that's why we're able to drop bombs on people like Mum and Dad and Dick and Judy, too far to see their faces looking up, too high to hear the screams.

0124. 0127. 0131. Gyro 286, ASI, altimeter, artificial horizon. 0135. Half an hour to Den Helder. Beginning to hope that this thirtieth op and this first tour might possibly end, fingers crossed, with cocoa and rum. Wanker's Doom droning on and on over the featureless ground below, 0139, 0144, 0150, 0157; after an eternity of dry-throated waiting, a lacy white ribbon—

"Coastline ahead, Jasper."

At once. "Don't get too happy, chaps. That's only the Zuyder Zee. Eight more minutes to Den Helder."

"Cold-blooded lot, you Pommy bastards. I'm giving a cheer when we get there, almost rather see it than Bondi Beach."

Seven minutes, six, five, four and then Jake was saying, "Get ready, Digger," and a wave of thankfulness swept over Tony, "Holland to port, gentlemen, Texel Island to starboard, fantastic navigation, Jasper. Coming up to Den Helder—here it comes—over Den Helder *now*!"

Deep breath from Digger, "HIP! HIP!" from above and to starboard the tracer streaked in two converging lines to slash into Wanker's Doom, the clatter of bullets striking home instantly drowned in the bellow of engines, full throttle, full boost, as Tony flung Wanker's Doom up on its starboard wingtip, engines screaming in the curving shit-or-bust dive, tracer following, falling behind, an Me 110 climbing up the windscreen, growing bigger, bigger yet, we're going to collide, considered Tony calmly, even bigger, white-lined black cross on a wing, gone, "FIGHTER! FIGHTER!" yes, Digger, I noticed, he saw the tracer and joined in the fun, what's that bloody fighter doing, oh, that's what he's doing, done, white flash from behind, Our Ern, "Me 110, six hundred yards, four o'clock, he's turning away, eight hundred yards, six o'clock, there he goes." Urgently, Tony demanded, "Everybody check in. Anybody hit?"

Nobody, thank Christ. "That was a fucking Wimpey firing at us," Wanker's Doom coming straight and level, yes, Jake, I saw his turret, no offence taken, thought we were a Ju 88, got his squirt in first.

"I saw the squadron letters when it caught fire," said Digger. "One of our Wimpeys. S Sugar."

S for Sprogs, poor bastards. "Course for home, please, Jasper. Any damage, anyone?"

"Got some holes in my turret, they just missed my goolies. Bloody draughty in here," complained Jake.

Zero on the ASI. Zero on the altimeter. Oh, Jesus.

But we're still alive and still in the air. Other dials okay? Good. Check the hydraulics.

"Course for base 291 Compass."

"Roger, 291, Jasper." Still be thankful. Gyro 291. Even if we can't lower flaps or undercarriage.

Tony cleared his throat, clicked his microphone.

"Listen, everyone. We've been hit in the hydraulic lines and our pitot head's been shot away—"

"Oh, Christ," said someone.

"—but it could have been a hell of a lot worse. Jake's still got his balls, nobody's hurt and the kite's still flying. Nothing to worry about until we get to Onley Market." Tony took a deep breath. "You know as well as I do that there's not a hope in hell of landing the kite with nothing to tell us speed or height, let alone having no flaps or undercarriage. So when we reach base I'll ask them to light up the field and then it's parachutes on and out we go."

Long silence, Then,

"Well don't just sit there," said Digger. "My egg is waiting."

"And my hot cocoa," said Jasper.

"With rum," said Our Ern.

"And remember my poor feet," said Jake. "They're freezing."

After which, quiet; they'd all shown, pretended, that they couldn't care less, ready for anything; ready, specifically, to bale out of Wanker's Doom. Not that the prospect didn't give Tony a bit of a twitch, couldn't be all that cheerful about having to step out into fuck-all if you'd never done it before but far better than than being a red smear all along the runway.

Shame about having to let Wanker's Doom prang on its lonesome, super kite, such a lot of work Wacko and the gang had put into it. Bloody shame. But there it was. Just have to fly Wanker's Doom straight and level over lit-up Onley Market airfield; nice and flat below for easy, harmless parachute drops, no panic as the crew jumps, as Tony jumps, goodbye, Wanker's Doom.

Silence all the long uneventful stooge across the North Sea, everybody reminding themselves, knees bent, arms before your face as out you go, count ten, pull the handle, roll when your feet hit the ground; taught by the classroom lecture the RAF gave you, one quick lesson, didn't want you to brood.

"Crossing coast now. Skegness five miles to starboard." On track, fantastic navigation by Jasper. Not much longer. Stooge on, the tiny aircraft of the artificial horizon below the line, time to descend.

"Onley Market beacon ahead flashing Victor King." Jake sounded glad the waiting was over.

Here we go, then. "Marvellous show, Jasper. Looks as if we're first back. Right, everybody, you all know what you've got to do—"

He hesitated in mid-sentence, realising that the decision had been unknowingly taken as soon as he'd seen the dead needles on the ASI and the altimeter.

He wasn't going to jump.

Wonder who we've killed tonight? Wonder who I've helped to kill, pressing on regardless, dropping sixty tons of bombs on thirty ops, all those Emils and Franzes and Karls, Friedas, Evas and Heidis . . . well, tonight, he'd kill nobody else.

Jump out of Wanker's Doom and the kite would fly on but sooner or later it would fall out of the sky. Maybe on to empty farmland. Maybe on to a street full of houses and that was a chance he couldn't take. There was only one way he could go on living with himself.

Tonight as a slight apology to the anonymous dead he'd make sure that unknown others would live. He'd bale out the crew and take the odds on landing Wanker's Doom, a thousand to fuck-all against.

Right.

"You all know what you've got to do," he said again, and never before had he felt so at peace with himself. "I'll call Onley Market, tell them to light up the field and then out you drop when I give the order to jump. Right. Parachutes on."

But Digger at least had sensed what his hesitation meant.

"Bullshit," said Digger.

In a moment, Jake, "Are you thinking of landing this kite alone?"

Our Ern said, "Fuck that."

"We've come this far together," said Jasper. "We'll bloody well stay together."

You don't have to die, too, that's no part of the bargain, sweat poured down Tony's forehead, he waited until his hands on the control column stopped shaking.

"I'm in command of this aircraft. I've given an order and I expect it to be obeyed. Parachutes on."

"Oh, come off it, Tony," said Jasper. "We're not jumping."

Jake said, "We're staying with you."

"All of us," said Our Ern.

"Too right. Take your choice, sport. Jump with us or land with us."

Oh, God, it had seemed so simple a moment ago, such an easy, inevitable decision. He couldn't think, his mind a turmoil of deep, humble gratitude and full of the shuddering thought of the crew burning with him as he pranged Wanker's Doom—

"—request landing instructions," someone was saying in his earphones. Dotted lights suddenly below, Onley Market runway.

"C Crumpet from Boomerang, you are clear to land."

Jesus God Almighty. It was a prayer of thanksgiving.

Tony's mind was clearing, now there was a shadow of a chance that he and the crew might walk away from what was going to be left of Wanker's Doom down there on the runway.

He pulled his Sutton harness stranglingly tight. "Crash positions, everyone." Press transmit button.

"C Crumpet from O Orange, are you receiving me?"

Hiss, crackle of static. "O Orange from C Crumpet, loud and clear," Twinkletoes. "What can I do for you, Tony?"

"C Crumpet, we have lost our ASI and altimeter. Have also lost hydraulics. Require assistance for landing. Request you lead us into flarepath for no-flaps, wheels-up landing."

Almost, Twinkletoes kept the anxiety out of his voice. "Roger, Tony. Glad to help."

"Thank you, C Crumpet. Please flash landing light."

Brilliant light on, off. "There he is, two o'clock."

"Thank you, Jake, I see him." Transmit. "C Crumpet, we're behind you and below. Climbing up to formate on you to your starboard." Red and green wingtip lights up ahead, coming nearer, green bead to port, black loom in the darkness resolving into the shape of a Wimpey, rear turret and part of the tail shot away, Twinkletoes hadn't mentioned that. In formation now, three wingspans apart.

"Nice work, Tony. We see you."

Runway lights below paralleling their flight along the up-wind leg, Onley Market Tower telling some kite to stay out of the circuit, green-beaded wingtip sloping gradually skyward as Twinkletoes starts the turn to port, rudder, bank, Rate One turn, one-eighty degrees, lining up again with the runway, leaving it behind, far behind, turning one-eighty again for a long low approach to the airfield, losing height slowly, tiny adjustments of throttle and control column to stay at C Crumpet's wingtip, crossing over the boundary lights at the unguessable correct speed, correct height, the runway lights beginning, "She's all yours, Tony, good luck," Twinkletoes zooming away in a banking climb, no sense in being close if Wanker's Doom goes up in flames.

Runway going past at a hell of a speed, hold off, edge the throttles back, hold off, hold off, throttles back, further, further—oh, God, we should have touched down by now, I've fucked it up, we're going to prang in arse over tit, sorry, chaps, sorry, no, touching down NOW, head snapping back as Wanker's Doom slams in with a hell of a crunch, bounce, crunch again, continuous ripping tearing shriek, propellers instantly back at right angles, something breaking loose, rattling behind, dials leaping, jerking, in an up-and-down shimmer, being flung to and fro, side to side against the bruising straps of the Sutton harness, Wanker's Doom slowing, slewing, skidding, stopping, there goes Jasper, there goes Digger, after them, out, out through the hatch, stars, sweet smell of earth and grass, run.

Fifty yards away the wreck of Wanker's Doom sprawled, its tail fin a slanting tombstone, at the end of the long grave it had furrowed as it swerved off the runway. Panting, Tony and the crew turned to watch as the first flame licked and at once Wanker's Doom was a blazing inferno crimsoning the smoke-clouded sky as the vans came racing up and here were Chiefy and Wacko and Big Head and Peek and Oswald and Ginger laughing and thumping their shoulders and pummelling them, hard, ouch; kisses! from My Brother Sylvest.

As the nineteen other surviving crews came in one by one to debriefing, shagged rotten, their eyes searched the room until they saw them at their table, Tony, Jake, Jasper, Digger and Our Ern, swigging their cocoa and rum, and each crew raised a cheer—they'd done their thirty, they'd made it, so could we.

Made it.

Made it, Kate.